Also by Miriam Wenger-Landis

Girl in Motion

Miriam Wenger-Landis

BREAKING POINTE

A Ballet Novel

Copyright © 2012 by Miriam Wenger-Landis

Front cover photo © Bob Mooney
Dancer: Miriam Wenger-Landis

ISBN 978-1-46814-431-4

For dancers everywhere

Prologue

"Fifteen minutes. Fifteen minutes, please," called
the stage manager over the intercom. He interrupted the
familiar sound of the orchestra tuning up and the hum of the
audience as they settled into their seats.

Dancers checked hair, touched up lipstick, and
dusted powder over their faces in the dressing room. The
dressers hooked ballerinas into their costumes. Men
readjusted their dance belts and women tucked in the satin
ribbons on their pointe shoes.

On stage, two women reviewed choreography
together near the red velvet curtain. A shirtless principal in
tights jogged in a wide circle around the stage, his body
already glistening. Near the backdrop, the ballet mistress
gave instructions to the principal ballerina, who nodded as
she ran her hands over her jewel-encrusted purple tutu. The
conductor walked out from the wing to discuss tempo with
them. In the opposite wing, the artistic director checked out
the scene, a beer in his hand.

"Ten minutes. Ten minutes, please," called the stage
manager.

Ballerinas in costume gathered around the rosin box
to rub their shoes in the sticky powder. The cast for the first
ballet on the program started to assemble onstage. A girl
fired off jumping jacks to keep warm, another performed

karate kicks, and another moved her arms in brisk wide circles.

"Five minutes. Five minutes, please. This is your five minute call."

There was one girl downstairs in the dressing room, brushing her damp brown hair back into a ponytail. Me. Eventually I pulled and shaped my hair into a French twist, flat against my scalp.

That was what I did every day. The routine, the people, the excitement, and the beauty of dancers were the story of my life.

I bent over to rummage in my theater case, and then sat up and caught my blue eyes in the mirror. My gaze burned into my reflection, glowing with intensity. I worked hard to be there.

Before every show I reminded myself that my job wasn't about me at all. My body was there to be an instrument in an orchestra of dancers. Despite that, I didn't believe that the ballet world wasn't personal. It was my heart, body, and soul that gave everything when I went onstage to dance.

One

When I started my job as an apprentice with Los Angeles Ballet Theatre, I was still in shock I had been hired. William Mason, the artistic director, was in the audience when Hilary Marshall ran onstage and finished my part in the School of Ballet New York's annual workshop performance. Sick with a high fever, I had insisted on dancing and fainted mid-performance in the wings.

It didn't matter. William offered me a job that same day, a week before I graduated from high school. He also hired two of my classmates: my good friend, Faye, and my worst rival, Hilary.

I'd been dreaming of a ballet career my whole life. I was born and raised in Rock Island, Illinois and finished high school in Manhattan as a student at the most prestigious ballet school in America. I always dreamed I'd join the school-affiliated company. To my great disappointment, I never grew past five foot three, and everyone in the corps de ballet of Ballet New York is at least five foot five. So when I got a job with the renowned Los Angeles Ballet Theatre instead, I jumped at the opportunity.

The day after we flew in from New York, Mom and I walked from our hotel in Santa Monica to investigate the company studios on the Third Street

Promenade. The huge palm trees were a drastic change from the skyscrapers I was accustomed to in New York. A cool breeze blew in from the ocean and the air smelled fresh and clean. I hoped the sun would burn off the fog before lunch.

A banner across the black awning pronounced Los Angeles Ballet Theatre in elegant cream letters. A home furnishing store on one side and a bookstore on the other emphasized that LABT rehearsed smack in the middle of a mall. Shoppers and tourists strolled along the sidewalk. I hoped we'd see a celebrity and wondered if the thrill of that could possibly be any better than the excitement of seeing members of my new company. I knew I would recognize some of their faces from the photos in an old program I found in the SBNY library, and it would be inspiring to see the dancers in the flesh, talking with each other, stretching, and rehearsing the ballets.

A crowd peered into the window under the awning. "Wow. There's nowhere to hide," Mom said. Faye wasn't kidding when she told me on the phone that everyone looks right in at the dancers. The window stretched from floor to ceiling.

I could only imagine what my best friend from ballet school, Jen would say if she were here. "You could have been in Ballet New York if you were taller," she would tell me, reassuring as ever. "You were good enough. LABT shouldn't intimidate you."

Jen might say that, but she's in the other top company in New York, National Ballet Theatre, and she was intimidated when she first started there. Neither of us got into BNY, Jen because of her weight and me because of my height, and that left us both feeling insecure even though were at the top in terms of talent and technique.

I tried to relax and appreciate the possibilities in front of me. There was no rush. I could worry about all the challenges and expectations later. In the moment, I did my best to allow myself to be excited that I was there at all, about to start my professional ballet career.

Inside the studio, two lines of six girls performed synchronized movements in front of the mirror. Before I looked at their technique, I examined their bodies. How would I fit in? The height seemed more varied than the company in New York, but all the girls were thin. They looked older than me and their muscles were more fully developed. These dancers were no longer girls. They were women. As they rehearsed, I could hear the wooden boxes inside their satin toe shoes clacking on the floor.

"Is that the ballet mistress?" Mom peered in the window. She pointed at the woman with a notepad at the front of the room, who looked as good as the retired dancers that haunted the Upper West Side in New York. Her posture was commanding and her narrow head gave her a bird-like look. She wore black cat-eye glasses and cut her dark hair short, just below her ears. My mother, meanwhile, was anything but commanding or elegant. She was an ordinary housewife from Illinois who always wore her hair in a ponytail. Mom saw no reason to bother with makeup or fashion. The women my mom socialized with back home didn't look anything like the woman running the rehearsal.

"Probably. Don't point." I recognized the ballet mistress as Lila Jebroy, a former soloist with Ballet San

Francisco. Lila had a reputation as one of the most demanding bosses in the country. I had heard stories about her even though she was never famous as a dancer. She kicked dancers out of class just for yawning.

Mom put her hand up to the glass. "She looks good. Fifties, maybe?"

"No idea." I pulled her back from the window. It was so much easier for me to go home and enter my parents' world than to have them come into mine. When we were apart we talked about once a week, and their side of the conversation was always predictable. Mom would tell me that she ran into so-and-so at the grocery store and found out her daughter had received a National Merit Scholarship. Dad would report back on mowing the lawn and repairing the furnace. What I wanted to tell them, on the other hand, seemed too far removed from their life. So instead of saying, "The new principal dancer in Ballet New York taught our class today and Hilary messed up right in front of her," I used to say things like, "It's snowing in New York. I should get a new pair of gloves." After those kinds of conversations, my mom wasn't fully prepared to witness my life up close. She was nervous and overly enthusiastic. All I wanted was to be able to pick up a remote control that worked on her and hit the mute button.

"Let's go around back," I suggested, and she followed me around the building. I was tired of my self-consciousness already.

Two male dancers in sweatpants and tank tops sat on a bench by the back door. I couldn't remember who they were from the program but knew they looked vaguely familiar. They were both smoking cigarettes and gave me the once-over as I walked up to them. I was nervous but also excited to be face-to-face with real live company members. "Is this the entrance to the studios?"

"Who are you?" asked the smaller guy. His tone was so matter-of-fact that I wasn't sure if he meant to be nice or rude. His thick brown hair hung like a mop over his eyes, but I could still see they were heavy-lidded and green and conveyed a mix of boredom and exhaustion. His body was wider than his friend, and he had a nice-looking, friendly face and the build of a gymnast. The defined muscles in his calves caught my eye.

The bigger and grumpier-looking guy took a long drag on his cigarette. He wore his reddish hair cropped short and his ruddy face seemed older to me, but maybe it was the dark stubble.

"Anna," I said, offering my hand. "I'm one of the new apprentices."

"I'm Susan Linado," Mom said, stepping forward. "Anna's mom. It's *so* nice to meet you both." Her expression was one of exuberance. I wondered if she was intentionally trying to embarrass me.

"I'm Mikey," said the mop-haired one, shaking my hand.

"Ian," said the redhead after he blew smoke out of the side of his mouth. "When do you start?"

"My first official day is Monday," I said.

"What are you doing here?" Ian asked in a mocking tone. He breathed loudly and cleared his throat. I could practically hear his lungs rotting. "You have three more days of freedom."

Immediately I felt a rush of anxiety and wondered if I seemed too eager, or if he was going to ask why I brought my mom. "I thought I'd look at the schedule," I said, trying to play it cool. "You know. Look around."

"She's another SBNY bunhead," Ian said to Mikey, rolling his eyes. "They're the same way every year." Ian leaned forward and grabbed my arm. "Don't worry, darling, you'll get over the excitement soon enough."

"Don't let Ian's bitterness infect you," Mikey said to me, clearly for the benefit of my mom. Ian smacked Mikey's arm.

"Oh, I hope she'll be okay!" Mom chirped. "This is a big change for her, you know."

I laughed it off, embarrassed, and did a mental countdown of how many minutes I had left until she went home to Rock Island. "See you guys later," I said. I pulled the door open and Mom followed me into the front hallway, a threadbare entrance with green linoleum and a company poster on the wall. The air was hot and oppressive. I wondered if there would be any guys as nice as Tyler, my boyfriend and dance partner back in New York. Things had been left open-ended between us. We only got together at the very end of the school year and were mostly just friends. I couldn't imagine whatever our relationship was would continue with him permanently in New York and me in LA, but it was hard to imagine thinking about anyone else. I wished we had ended up in the same company. Tyler was the most talented guy the school had trained in years and being with him gave me confidence. Ballet New York would never have passed him over like they did with me because of my height. He was tall and handsome. Plus, he was a *boy*.

A rehearsal ended and the door at the end of the hall flew open. Girls poured out of the studio, trailing snippets of conversation like, "Did you know blueberries are a power food?" and "These pointe shoes are *so* dead." They were covered in sweat and their leotards stuck to their bodies in patches. The temperature around me turned warmer from body heat.

Their colorful outfits were a far cry from the black leotards and pink tights we wore in ballet school. One girl passed me in a floral bathing suit and yoga pants, followed by another wearing a brown halter leotard with zebra legwarmers. How could they look in the mirror and see what their muscles were doing under all those crazy clothes?

"Hey. I know your face from SBNY," said a pretty girl with brown hair, dark eyes, and full lips. I recognized her from my first year in New York and remembered she had amazing extension. William promoted her from apprentice to the corps de ballet after one year. I was happy to see she was almost exactly my height.

"Hey, Rebecca," I said. "How are you?" I remembered her from school as the second in command to the queen bee in the older popular group. She was the one who copied outfits and hairstyles and, despite her beauty, always had an air of neediness. I liked her because she didn't look down on people and she spent her time trying to please others. Usually the people Rebecca followed around were the stuck-up kids who could never be pleased, but hey, she meant well.

"Good," Rebecca said. "Anna, right? Welcome to the company. Glad you're here." She squeezed my arm before moving on, making me feel welcome and relieved that I knew *someone*.

Lila Jebroy came walking down the hall towards my mom and me. She looked straight through us and I wondered if she knew who I was. Her walk was entirely unapologetic and almost aggressive, as if she were running a race.

My mom didn't miss a beat. She stepped right in Lila's path and put out her hand. "I'm Susan Linado, Anna's mother," she said. "We're glad to meet you."

"Oh!" she exclaimed. "I'm the ballet mistress, Lila." She extended her hand in a business-like manner to my mom. She had on black leggings, a black t-shirt with "Los Angeles Ballet Theatre" written in red across the front, and salmon-colored teaching shoes. "You must be Anne, then," she said, turning to me. "Well, aren't you a little sprite?"

"Yes, I'm Anna," I said, stepping forward to shake her hand. Nice to meet you." I wonder if I should call her Lila or Ms. Jebroy.

"Call me Lila," she said, answering the question as if she could read my thoughts. "We're glad you're here. William was pleased you accepted the apprenticeship."

"Oh, thank you!" I said, a little too loud. "I'm grateful for the opportunity."

Lila nodded and shoved a pen behind her ear. "We have a lot of ballets to teach you. Rehearsals will be crazy next week. I have to run now, unfortunately, but feel free to peek in at any of the rehearsals." She looked me over shrewdly. "I hope you're not out of shape."

"Oh," I said, frightened because she'd voiced my insecurity. ""I've only been off a few days." My mom looked from Lila to me, worried. I tried to smile convincingly.

"Good," Lila pronounced. "See you later." She gave us a dismissive look and barreled away down the hall.

"I'm so happy she's going to be a part of this, thank you!" Mom called after her.

"Well, that was interesting," said Mom. I nodded, concerned by Lila's initial reaction to me. Was she always like that?

I walked down the hall and around the corner in the same direction as Lila, hoping to find a rehearsal schedule. Mom trailed behind. We entered a central lounge connected to all the studios. Dancers crowded the room. I sat Mom down on a bench and told her to play with her smartphone while I looked at the bulletin board. Surprisingly, she agreed. I walked over to where two girls chatted and drank sodas in front of the schedule. One of them was tall with dark brown skin, a long neck, and even longer legs. She had one bare foot up on the bench in front of the bulletin board and her toes looked completely misshapen. The second girl was shorter than the first and taller than me. She had blonde hair, a statuesque nose, and high cheekbones. Her legs looked short next to the first girl and not nearly as well proportioned.

"Excuse me." I stepped up next to them at the board and accidentally brushed against someone else sitting on the bench on my other side. "Oh, sorry," I whispered to a third girl sitting on the lap of a muscular guy with dirty blonde hair. She had ebony hair and skin so pale it was almost translucent. She shrugged and smiled, her perfectly straight teeth startling me with their whiteness.

I turned back to the first two girls. "Is this the schedule for Monday?"

"Yeah," said the first bronze and leggy girl with mangled feet, sipping her soda from a straw. She wore a red racer-back leotard and black sweat pants. "Seriously," she said, turning back to the second blonde with the striking features. "Can you believe this? Lila wants to put all of *Frontiers* together on Monday. That rehearsal will be a nightmare."

"No kidding," the blonde says. "I'm not going to let it get to me. I'm still going out with Lorenzo this weekend. I refuse to spend every weekend studying performance videos."

I enjoyed their easy banter and the general atmosphere. I could hear the familiar music of *Violins* coming from behind a closed door and assumed another rehearsal was in progress. Everything felt so new and yet comfortable. I had been around dancers since I was a little girl, so this world felt like home.

"Are you one of the new apprentices starting next week?" asked the taller girl.

"Yes," I said, "I'm Anna."

"Stephanie," she said. "You should go to all of these complete rehearsals." She pointed at the schedule. "Lila taught everyone's parts in *Frontiers* during the last two weeks and Monday will be the first time we run the whole ballet with everyone together. That rehearsal on Monday afternoon is probably to catch you up."

"Have I missed a lot?" Nerves threatened my enthusiasm.

"Don't worry," said the blonde. "My name's Carolyn, by the way. You'll see *Frontiers* almost every day this summer. In two weeks, you'll know it backwards." Carolyn offered a kind smile. "You should come to *Georgia On My Mind* too," she added, bending her right leg at the knee and grabbing the arch of her foot, pulling it towards her back to stretch her quad. "It's inevitable that somebody will get injured."

"It just better not be me," said the third dark-haired girl on my right, who had been silent up until then. She climbed off the guy's lap and stretched her arms over her head. Her body was one long thin line, mostly legs. She was as beautiful as any model on the cover of a magazine, one of the lucky ones whose physical presence takes men's breath away.

The guy stood up too. "I'm off, ladies," he said, running a hand through his unkempt hair. When he smiled, I noticed his dimples and sparkling eyes. He was handsome and confident, dangerous qualities in a straight ballet guy. I told myself right then and there not to develop a crush. There was no question most of the other girls in the company probably liked him. He was just that kind of guy, and there are never enough of them to go around in ballet. "Elizabeth, see you later?" he asked, winking at her.

"No, I'm hanging out with Teddy tonight. Sorry, babe," said the dark-haired girl. I remembered Teddy was the friendly guy I met outside on the bench. Elizabeth tossed her bag over her shoulder and opened the door to one of the studios, slipping in quietly.

"Nice try, Ryan," Stephanie said when Elizabeth was gone. "Rebecca would have felt *great* seeing that. What was the point? Elizabeth is hopelessly hung up on Teddy."

Ryan shrugged, clearly trying to play it cool. He must have been irritated, but he didn't let it show. "Yeah, whatever. Rebecca and I aren't serious, and neither are Elizabeth and Teddy. You girls are ridiculous. I'm going. Bye." His back muscles rippled under his t-shirt as he walked away. I decided to be grateful there was at least one straight guy in the company *and* he was cute. I hadn't dared to hope. Even if I was never going to date him, it made life more fun to have some prospects around.

"So where are you living, Anna?" Carolyn asked, deftly changing the subject.

"Downtown, actually, just south of the Pier, on Main Street. We wanted something within walking distance. I'm rooming with Faye, the other new apprentice."

"Oh, that super-skinny girl," Stephanie says. "We saw Faye on Wednesday." Stephanie bent backwards and her spine let out a loud crack. I wondered what they thought of Faye. Faye was a little bit taller than me with large-muscled legs and narrow hips. She was a clean and polished dancer, with good turns. We were in the same class in New York and friendly without being super close. She grew up in Washington D.C., so while I was far away from Rock Island, my hometown in Illinois, she was *really* far from home. We decided when we got our contracts that we would room together. I liked our new furnished two-bedroom one-bathroom apartment. It wasn't that big and it was strange to have someone else's furniture, but it was close to the studios and the big windows let in plenty of sunlight. We signed a one-year lease. It wasn't worth committing to furniture or anything else too permanent until we knew if things were going to work out with the company.

"Do we really dance eight hours a day? Is there a lunch break?" The schedule looked intense.

"About eight hours. Lunch is at two," Carolyn said, pointing at the schedule to show me. "They rehearse the principals during our break."

I knew this was what company life would be like, but eight hours a day in pointe shoes sounded excessive. At SBNY I only had to wear them about three to five hours. It had been years since I'd danced in soft ballet slippers because SBNY expected the upper level girls to wear pointe shoes in every class. If I were really in pain, would Lila understand if I had to take them off? I feared everyone would think I was weak or lazy. Taking my shoes off wasn't going to be a realistic option. If I wanted to fit in, I'd just have to get used to it. Besides, it felt different to dance a ballet on *pointe* than in technique shoes. I'd been taught to rehearse the same way I was going to perform.

"You'll get used to it," Stephanie said, registering the fear on my face. She looked amused as she picked up her bag. "I have to go."

"Me, too," Carolyn said. "See you on Monday, Anna." She gave me a wave goodbye.

I watched them walk down the hall. Stephanie had a noticeably taller build than Carolyn, who was at least two inches taller than me. Carolyn was probably about one hundred and ten pounds. I weighed a whopping ninety-six. If William and Lila liked Carolyn and Stephanie, there was one reason I was sure they would like me. I was thinner.

My mom walked up next to me. "I peeked in on a rehearsal," she confessed. "How you all do this, I have no idea. The human body isn't designed to work to this extreme."

"We practice, I guess." It was hard to know how to respond when there was no obvious answer. "Can we get some lunch?"

"Of course," she said, putting her arm around my shoulder. The gesture embarrassed me so I quickly pulled away. I was emotionally exhausted by all the new information. The girls that made it to SBNY were unusually gifted, but the professionals were the best of the best. I could tell the stakes would be even higher in a real company. It wasn't enough anymore that I was an exceptional dancer. I needed to develop superhuman endurance.

Two

On the first day of work, Faye and I arrived at the studio half an hour before class began. The building was nearly deserted, offering the impression that not all professional dancers warmed up before class as much as ballet students did. I looked around for Hilary. She was bound to be there early and I was edgy about the first run-in. We hadn't seen each other since school in New York, where she was always one of my major competitors. She was also one of the meanest girls I knew. Faye had heard that Hilary rented her own apartment, but we hadn't seen her at all around the neighborhood.

Dancers crowded the locker room and stood around in various stages of undress. I averted my eyes and followed Faye over to a bench in the corner. We were like high school freshmen in a comedy film, decked out in frizzy hair and braces and smiling pathetically at the cool seniors. I discreetly changed into my dark blue leotard, pink tights, purple leg warmers, and a black skirt. I still looked like a student and felt painfully nerdy. Class would be a chance for William to notice me, and this was what he'd see? I had heard he taught company class almost every day and based many of his casting decisions on what he observed there.

Across the room, I noticed a strawberry-blonde dancer with pencil-thin legs, sharp hipbones, and no chest. Her body looked emaciated and her nose and chin reminded me of a horse. She eyed Faye opening a locker.

"The lockers are for the principals," she said condescendingly. Her voice had the rasping sound of a heavy smoker.

"Oh. I didn't know," said Faye, closing the locker. She looked embarrassed and I felt her shame as if it were my own.

"That's why I'm telling you," raspy voice said, heaving a floral bag exploding with pointe shoes over her shoulder. Her face looked like she'd done some hard living, but what did I know? She seemed much older than us. A few other girls glanced over with mild curiosity.

"I'm Faye," said Faye, trying hard to be friendly.

"Allison," she replied, without so much as a smile or a handshake. She turned and let the door slam as she left the dressing room.

"Whoa," Faye whispered. We exchanged a look and silently agreed that Allison seemed mean.

I tied my skirt and squeezed past some other girls to check my reflection. Stephanie, the tall girl I met the first day, arrived as I smoothed out my tightly pulled-back hair and examined my makeup. She stopped by the sink and tossed a pair of tights from her bag into the trash.

"I'm done with pink tights," Stephanie grumbled as she put her bag down on a bench next to Elizabeth, the gorgeous dark-haired girl. "They make me look fat. Hey Elizabeth, how's your knee?"

Elizabeth pulled black tights on over her brown leotard and said, "Feeling better, thanks. The swelling went down. I should be fine for *Frontiers* today." The smell of vanilla body splash wafted over as Elizabeth sprayed it across her neck and chest.

"You should get some physical therapy anyway. Are you going to see Carla?" Stephanie asked. I assumed Carla was the company's therapist.

"I don't think so," Elizabeth said. "It'll go away on its own. If I see Carla and she says I need physical therapy, Lila and William will hear about it. I'd rather not concern them."

Her comment wasn't surprising. At ballet school, plenty of people danced on injuries. The teachers acted like if we got hurt, it was our fault. As a professional, there would be more pressure to hide problems because the company paid us to rehearse and perform. Dancers who sat out too much of the time looked lazy even if they were genuinely hurt, and then roles slipped away. Those who danced with chronic problems, like tendonitis, garnered respect. I was eighteen and knew I was lucky to have stayed mostly injury-free. As we aged, our body's ability to rebound would decline. We all lived in fear of aging. When my body hurt, my policy was to ignore it and keep dancing. The pain had always gone away eventually.

I wondered how old Elizabeth was. Maybe she was twenty-five or so? The age range in a company was usually between seventeen and forty-two. The upper end of that range was the exception, not the rule. Injuries, burnout, and babies tended to get in the way.

When I walked into the main studio, I found myself standing on the other side of the storefront window with nowhere to hide. Random people stared in from the Third Street Promenade. The visibility was a brilliant business tactic. Access to "ballet behind-the-scenes" garnered attention and encouraged people to buy tickets to our performances. I needed time to get used to it and, especially that first day, the people in the window made me uncomfortable. Many of them looked like they had never seen a girl in a leotard and tights before. Some of the people seemed genuinely curious, some admiring, and a few were downright creepy. I did my best to ignore them, and part of me worried that the setup was a recipe for creating ballerina stalkers.

I spotted Hilary at a portable *barre* in the front of the studio by the mirror. She was sitting with her hips in the frog position, the bottoms of her feet touching each other and her knees on the ground. Her leotard was obviously new; a fancy green velvet with a low back and silver trim. She looked a little too eager, I decided.

Faye left me and found a spot in the back corner by the window. Hilary saw her and hurried over to say hi. I waited in the doorway and looked for a *barre* spot as far away from the window as possible. Carolyn, the blonde with strong features, was stretching by a portable *barre* near the wall. I caught her eye. "Carolyn, is there a good place for me to stand?" I inched closer to her. "I don't want to take anyone's spot."

"You mean like her?" Carolyn smirked, nodding towards Hilary. "Elizabeth is not going to like seeing her standing there. You can stand behind me, here," she said. "Adam usually stands there, but he's out already with a back injury." Carolyn pushed herself deeper into an already-perfect middle split and glanced at her reflection.

"Okay. Thanks." I put my bag down. "Who's Adam?"

"One of the principals," Carolyn said, still watching herself in the mirror. "He's almost forty, and this is probably his last season. William already took Adam out of some of his regular roles last year, but I don't think he wants to go. They had fireworks last year over casting."

"That sounds terrible," I said. What could be more humiliating than forced retirement?

I sat down, stretched forward over my extended legs, and grabbed my ankles. Taking a deep breath, I buried my nose in my knees. My body felt stiff as I pulled my legs up into a frog position. It had been over a week since I took class, and I had to gently coax my muscles into cooperation. From the frog, I flipped on my stomach and bent my right leg behind me over to my left shoulder. My back cracked, letting my spine open up and lengthen out, and I sighed.

"Hi Anna," Hilary said, breaking my concentration. Her shadow loomed over my head.

I groaned inwardly. "Hi Hilary." So she was going to pretend we were friends. She'd done it before. In fact, she'd fooled me into thinking she was my friend the first few months at SBNY. I could play her game, but I was no fool. She'd stabbed me in the back more than once and I knew she wouldn't hesitate to do it again.

Hilary sat down on the floor next to me and scooted closer than I would have liked. Carolyn glanced over, already suspicious of Hilary. Carolyn was a sharp one.

"Do you know anything about William's class?" Hilary whispered. "I've heard he doesn't correct much and his combinations are confusing."

"Not really, no."

"I've been doing two hours of Pilates every morning, can you tell? My thighs are ripped." She extends her leg in front of my face and points her foot. I raise my eyebrows and say nothing, so she goes on. "Did you stay in shape? Faye obviously didn't. Have you looked at her? She looks like a farm animal."

"That's rude," I say. Carolyn snorted. I finished tying the ribbons on my pointe shoes and stood to point and flex my feet.

Hilary stood up too. "Well, it's the truth," she said.

"Whatever, Hilary."

"Well, I'll let you warm up. Good luck." She turned around and that's when we both noticed that Elizabeth was at Hilary's spot. Elizabeth watched Hilary approach with an amused smile.

"I usually stand here," Elizabeth said with narrowed eyes, standing possessively close to the *barre*.

"Oh," Hilary said. "I didn't know. I'll just stand next to you."

"This *barre* is actually always full," said Elizabeth. "You can stand over there." She pointed to a spot way in the back corner.

Hilary chewed on her lip. "In the back?"

"Yep, in the back."

Elizabeth turned away from Hilary and began warming up. Hilary stood there for a minute, unsure what to do, before she picked up her bag and headed to the other spot. She wasn't used to anyone talking to her that way, even though she was just an apprentice. I didn't revel in the moment because I was worried Hilary's behavior would reflect on Faye and me. I didn't want Elizabeth or anyone else to think we were as presumptuous as Hilary. She didn't even seem to understand why Elizabeth had talked to her that way. Instead, she just seemed irritated about having to stand in back.

I did my best to put Hilary out of my mind. The better part of my brain knew that whatever she did shouldn't matter to me. I placed my hand on the *barre* and stood with my heels touching. My toes pointed flat to each side at a hundred and eighty degree angle. Out of the corner of my eye, I checked myself in the mirror and pulled every muscle in my legs, butt, and stomach up against gravity. My reflection lengthened along with my muscles, and from the side I looked like one long linear line. I pushed my shoulders towards the ground and lengthened my neck. To test out my latest pair of shoes, I slowly rolled up onto *pointe* and then down to a deep *plié*, my knees bending while my heels remained on the floor.

Mikey, the nice guy from outside the first day, took the spot across from me at the portable *barre*. His hair was a mess and he looked half-asleep. "Ten o'clock. Ugh," Mikey said. He didn't bother to warm up and just sat there looking tired. I wondered how he could function that way.

The room filled up with beautiful people during the ten minutes before class. Dancers stretched and greeted each other, buzzing with energy.

At ten o'clock on the dot, William strode into the studio. It was the first time I had seen William since he offered me a job, and he seemed different in the context of LABT with forty-five dancers clamoring for his attention. He looked invigorated. Dressed in a t-shirt, khaki trousers, and jazz shoes, William seemed much younger than sixty, even though he had recently celebrated that milestone birthday. His broad football shoulders were still muscular. The only give-away that he was aging was his full head of silver hair.

LABT was obviously William's pride and joy. He was a man who respected discipline and tradition, and as an artistic director, he was following in the footsteps of an elite few whose names were nearly synonymous with ballet.

The rotund Russian pianist, Olga, shook William's hand and they nodded congenially, comfortable in each other's presence. She sat down at the piano, ready to start class, and the chatter died down. I put my left hand on the *barre* and faced Carolyn's back, assuming the company did the same *plié* combination every day since William hadn't demonstrated anything. Some of the dancers had been taking William's ballet class for years. I followed Carolyn's lead. With a great flourish and a bang on the keys, Olga began to play a slow and steady 4/4 march.

As we danced, William walked around the room, quietly observing each dancer. Everyone tried a little harder as he passed by. Although William had a reputation as a laid-back and popular guy among his dance cronies and the members of the board, to us he was an artistic visionary like his mentor and the founder of Ballet New York, Nicholas Roizman. Although he downplayed it outside the studio, William was a serious man. To those of us a generation behind him, it was obvious that despite his success and fame, William thought he had something to prove, be it that straight men exist in ballet, or that ballet was a serious art form, or just that he was *the best* artistic director in the country, maybe the world. That aspect of his personality had driven him to the top of his profession as a dancer and we admired him for it. He was a man determined to have his own way and certain of his opinions. Being that it was my first day, I was prepared to take his congenial laugh and friendly manner at face value, especially because he'd done me the great kindness of making my dream of becoming a professional ballerina come true. Whatever complexities lay beneath the surface of his personality, I wasn't ready to know about them yet.

Beyond his role in the dance world, I also knew that William's wife had died recently after a long battle with ovarian cancer. They had no children. It had been a long and drawn out illness, and he had maintained a high degree of privacy over the matter. I had heard that he barely missed work and that only a few dancers and staff members attended the funeral.

At the end of the third combination, William held up his hand at the front of the room. "I forgot," he announced to the entire company. "Let's give a warm welcome to our new apprentices, Faye, Hilary, and Anna." The room exploded in a mix of applause, whistles, and catcalls. I felt my face turn red. He smiled kindly at each of us.

When the noise calmed down, William demonstrated the next combination. "Ready," he said. We snapped back into position. Olga played the introduction. William clapped out the rhythm and counted along with the music. "And one. And two. Three and four. Five and six and seven and eight. And one. And two. Three and four. Five and six and seven and eight." The way that William syncopated the music intrigued me. He focused on what was happening in our heads rather than how our bodies looked, and that was new to me. At SBNY, they always corrected us on how we held our arm, or the way we presented our foot. At LABT, the concern was our thought process and how we moved to the music. William's prodding was both intellectually challenging and physically demanding. The mirror didn't have the answers anymore, and I struggled to achieve the precise timing he wanted.

Forty minutes later we cleared the *barres* away to come to the center. Faye and I huddled together in the back corner as the dancers took their places around the room. "How's it going?" Faye asked.

"Okay, I guess," I said. "I can't get the syncopations right. It's getting embarrassing being off the music."

"I'm having the same problem," Faye said sympathetically. We grimaced at each other.

I tried the *adagio* and ended up dancing squished against the back wall. There were too many people around to find space. The *pirouette* combination was no better. Why was I doing something completely different than everyone else?

William indicated a small jump. The dancers executed the step, traveling forward from the back in groups of eight. Adrienne Castle, one of LABT's most famous principals, stood front center. She was impossible to miss. *Dance Magazine* had recently run an article about Adrienne, and I was happy to see the story didn't exaggerate her talent. Every muscle in her body was perfectly defined. Adrienne's legs were long and her extension was so high that when she lifted her leg to the side her knee almost touched her ear. Her feet were beautifully arched and when she moved her body seems to roll out the music with liquid-like movements. She was admirable for her for her natural talent and energy, but today was the first day I saw the hard work that went into looking as good as she did. Despite the intensity of her efforts, Adrienne gave the appearance of being relaxed and cheerful.

Adrienne's husband, Zif, was tall and wiry with kind brown eyes. They had met in the company as corps members. William had nurtured both their careers, and eight years and a wedding later, they were major icons of the company, appearing on billboards, program covers, and radio interviews. Zif seemed as down-to-earth in person as he did in the media, and it was obvious his whole life revolved around Adrienne. Of all the people that worshipped her, Zif was her biggest fan.

All the principals—Adrienne, Zif, Elizabeth, Natasha, Lorenzo, Adam, and Jeff—were noticeably talented and stood out in class. Adrienne, however, was my favorite from that first day on. She didn't have Elizabeth's glamour; instead she seemed like the girl next door, someone everyone would want as a friend.

"Is everything okay?" a deep male voice said behind me.

Startled, I turned and looked up into William's eyes. "Yes," I said. "Thank you."

"It's the first day, don't stress," he said. "It takes time to get used to this." The comment made me worry that he had noticed how I was struggling with the class, and even though I knew he was trying to be kind, I didn't want his sympathy. I wanted his respect.

As much as I wanted to believe that by choosing me for his company, William thought I was an amazing dancer, but when I saw myself through his eyes I knew he hadn't judged me on par with other students; he had judged me against his world of the company. William had probably decided I was adequate for his purpose of filling out the corps de ballet, and that's why I received an apprenticeship. My goal at LABT became clear: to win this man's admiration.

I nodded and managed an awkward smile, hoping to show my appreciation for his attention. He smiled back and walked on around the room, clapping his hands and carefully inspecting feet and legs. I knew William had seen generations of dancers performing ballets he originated and many first days for new company members. The years and people must have blurred together for him. I swallowed my frustration and tried not to be too hard on myself.

William's class was so different than any ballet class I had taken before. It wasn't just that all the dancers were professionals, or that they all loved to dance, or that everyone was very, very good. What was markedly different is that we all were dancing for the sake of one person: William. Even the best dancers, who were confident enough to portray the image of being above it all, had William in mind to some extent when they danced. He was the reason we were all there.

"That's the end, Olga," William said, raising his hand to the pianist. "Thanks, guys." The room broke out in scattered applause and the dancers dispersed. I sat down and took a long swig from my water bottle, resting for a minute before the first rehearsal began.

"Anna," a voice called in a loud stage whisper. "Anna Linado?" There was a short Chinese man in the doorway, gesturing at me to come over. Hilary and Faye were already standing next to him and I scrambled to my feet and walked over.

"Tong here," he said, giving me a little bow. "I run the wardrobe and shoe department. Come with me. We will get you the perfect pointe shoes. You will look fabulous!"

We followed him down the hall as eager as puppies. Free shoes! We had waited our whole lives for the privilege.

"Never think I am hard to find, girls," said Tong, chattering a mile a minute as we walked. "If you see a needle and thread, a smiling ballerinas, or a particularly spectacular hairdo, I have been there. I love my dancers. I just love them."

Tong charmed Faye and me. Hilary was not amused, but even she relaxed when we saw the wardrobe and shoe room, spacious and filled with treasures. Everything from bejeweled tutus to rows of hanging leotards to handsome tunics filled the comfortably cluttered space. I fingered the sparkly bodice of a pink tutu and imagined wearing it.

Tong pulled out his measuring tape and examined each of us one at a time, writing down the dimensions of our bodies and our shoe specifications. "So beautiful," he muttered as he measured the circumference of my head. "Look at that long neck and what full lips! Oh, Anna, you are lovely!" He went on and on, lavishing each of us with compliments and promising to order the shoes we needed immediately. I noticed that the more Hilary snubbed him the less he fawned over her. How stupid of her, I thought. Tong was the last person she should offend, unless she wanted the wrong size shoes and the itchiest costume.

When he gave us some stock shoes to get us through the first two weeks, Hilary responded with, "I hope our real shoes come as soon as possible, Tong. It would have been nice to have our special order shoes here when we arrived."

"Oh," Tong said, stung. Faye and I exchanged an embarrassed look. He glossed over the moment and moved on. "Here are your theater cases. You will need these for tour and whenever we are performing. I am sorry but I only have two new trunks, so one of you must take a used one. You can write your names on them and decorate as you see fit." He pulled out three black trunk-like suitcases that look like they came off the truck from a Broadway show.

"I'll take a new one," Hilary said, grabbing the nicest case.

"I'll take the used one, unless Faye wants it," I said. "I like the idea of having a theater case with history."

"It's yours, by all means," Faye said.

"Good then, and welcome to the company," Tong said. "Now get back to rehearsal so I don't get in trouble for keeping you. Shoo, butterflies."

Hilary beat it out the door. Faye and I gave Tong a hug before we hurried off to stash our precious loot in the dressing room.

By the second Friday of work, I sighed with relief that I didn't have to come back to the studio for two days. My body hurt almost as much as my self-esteem. It was a miracle that my feet hadn't fallen off. Even after years of pointe classes, eight hours a day in pointe shoes was much more than I could tolerate. In addition to the physical pain, there was so much choreography to remember that I felt like my brain might implode.

I was so tired and sore that I could barely get myself to move in the dressing room. "Let's go home," Faye urged me for the third time. She looked equally exhausted.

"I'm coming, I'm coming," I said, zipping up my backpack.

My mind was busy mulling over the day. It had been hard to practice in the back of the room and I was second cast for everything. When they put Faye and me in with the full cast, I wasn't sure I knew what to do and where to go and nearly knocked people over. At that point, I didn't feel like I knew the steps or the spacing for any of the ballets we'd learned. Eventually, I would have to dance my parts without the mirror. I could get by with checking everyone in the reflection, but I knew I would need to develop a sixth sense or a third eye in the back of my head to be aware of where everyone positioned themselves on the stage.

To add to the demoralization of being new and clueless, I'd also had an embarrassing incident that morning with one of the male principals, Jeff. He was shorter than the other male stars—Lorenzo, Zif, and Adam—and the only gay one. Lorenzo was warm and outgoing, Zif was reserved, Adam was parental, and Jeff was sour, cold, and elitist. Allison and Whitney were the only corps members Jeff spoke to outside of class and rehearsal, and he came off as overly narcissistic in class, always staring at himself in the mirror. I'd overheard Jeff berating Ian for getting in his way and had been afraid of Jeff ever since. "Are you always this stupid or are you making a special effort today?" Jeff had said. "Calling you a moron would be an insult to the half-wits out there." Ian laughed it off but I could tell he was hurt.

My run-in with Jeff was even worse than Ian's. I'd walked around a corner with a cup of coffee and ran into him, spilling hot coffee all down the front of his shirt. "Crap!" Jeff bellowed, frantically wiping at his shirt. I felt awful. Jeff gave up on the mess and pulled his shirt off, revealing a pale and skinny torso. He muttered obscenities while he used his shirt to clean himself up. I stood there useless, unsure how to remedy the situation. *Why him, of all people?* I berated myself.

"I'm so sorry, Jeff, it was an accident," I had said helplessly.

"This would be a good time for you to become a missing person, apprentice," he snapped. I backed away, apologizing. Later in rehearsal, I saw him talking to one of the other principals, Natasha, and he gestured in my direction. It was obvious he was telling her the story. She glanced over at me and patted his arm sympathetically. Ian told me not to worry about it, but the accident hung over my head like a dark cloud.

It bothered me that Jeff had complained to Natasha, of all people. She seemed to have a lot of political power within the company. I first noticed it when she stood in the back of class with William, whispering and laughing. As far as I could tell, he didn't talk to any of the other dancers in such a familiar way.

My first impression of Natasha was in the dressing room. She'd been arguing with Lila over her interpretation of a role and had aired her grievances to everyone. "How dare she try to tone down my style?" Natasha demanded, practically yelling at Adrienne. "I have a bigger personality than all of you! That's what makes me special. William loves my expressiveness. Who does Lila think she is?" Natasha glanced around the room, looking for agreement, and soon several girls chimed in with words of support. She gave an impressive performance even behind the scenes.

Natasha was from Moscow and used to dance with the Bolshoi. There were no other Russian dancers in the company, and even though she'd only been in the corps before she came to LABT, she carried herself like an international star. Which is not to say that she danced like one. Although she alternated with Adrienne and Elizabeth in all the plum lead roles, she was the sloppiest dancer of the three. Her classical training shined when it came to her arms and carriage of the neck, but she had never learned how to move her feet quickly and that showed in a lot of the neoclassical Roizman choreography. Many of the soloists and corps dancers could have performed her parts with better technical precision. Natasha's ego was what carried her and although people socialized and laughed with her all day long, I could tell she didn't have the respect the other principals possessed. There was no need for Elizabeth or Adrienne to chat up William or flit around the studio, kissing everyone along the way. They didn't need the attention the way Natasha did. She talked to everyone, and if she didn't like me, that meant plenty of people would receive an earful of her opinion.

Pulling myself up off the bench at last, I followed Faye out of the building and blinked at the brightness outside. The late day sun felt good on my shoulders. We waved at the smokers sitting on the bench.

"Bye, guys," I said. "Have a good weekend." There was too much of a scene in progress for anyone to notice us. Sasha and Rebecca were chatting animatedly with Ryan, Rebecca's hand resting possessively on Ryan's knee. Lorenzo was telling Jeff how he and Ryan charmed some female donors at a benefit. Jeff looked skeptical. Allison looked as grouchy as ever, shooting an annoyed glare at Ian, who was complaining to Mikey about hurting his foot in rehearsal. Stephanie listened to Ian and Mikey's conversation while she flipped her lighter and held it up to a new cigarette.

Faye and I passed them and headed home. With our pinned up hair, turned out walk, and net bags filled with pointe shoes, we were conspicuous in the pedestrian crowd.

"Linado. Sheridan. Wait up," we heard Mikey call behind us. We stopped and waited for him. "Are you coming to my party tomorrow? It's BYOB. Oh wait. You aren't old enough to buy the appropriate beverages."

"Thanks for the reminder, " Faye said.

"I don't know…we have a lot of ballet tapes to watch," I said, teasing.

Mikey rolled his eyes. "Oh please," he said. Before he disappeared in the crowd, he looked back over his shoulder and said, "Be there. I'll text you with the address."

It was not a request. If we were truly going to be part of the company, our participation had to extend beyond the studio.

That night, I closed my bedroom door to called my parents while Faye spent the evening glued to a video of *Frontiers*. Because of the time difference, it was late enough that my dad was home from work and picked up the phone. "Hello?" he said.

"Dad!" I said, happy to hear his gentle voice. "I miss you." Dad had always been mystified by my obsession with ballet, and while he supported me unconditionally, he wasn't particularly in favor of my career choice. He always knew it wasn't practical in the long run. If anything, his resistance pushed me even more towards dance. Eventually, I imagined I might grow out of my self-righteousness and understand the wisdom in his perspective, but for now, all I wanted was to prove to him that I was on the right path. While my mom had always believed in me, I never knew if my dad did, and it was his approval that I craved.

"Anna! I miss you too," he said. "Although admit it, if you were home, you'd be bored a minute after you saw the dog."

I knew he liked to tease me, but I felt misunderstood. "I'm serious," I said. "I'm homesick."

Mom came on the line. "Sweetheart! Why the sad voice?" she said. "You're in one of the best ballet companies in the United States. When I was your age I would have killed for a life like yours. Living in LA in my own apartment, surrounded by beautiful people, fulfilling my life's dream…"

I allowed myself a moment of self-pity. There was no one outside the company that I knew in LA, and the people I thought of as my best friends were far away. I hadn't spoken to my old SBNY roommate, Jen, since she was so busy at National Ballet Theater, and the time change made it impossible to call New York at a reasonable hour. My other ballet school friend, Marie, who had to quit ballet because of an injury, was home in France with her family for the summer. Even Rachel, my best friend from growing up in Rock Island, was unreachable, working as a counselor at a summer camp in Wisconsin.

"I know what you need," Dad said. "A car. You'll want it in the fall when you go to the theater in LA, or when the company performs in Palm Springs and San Diego."

"I guess so. It's weird that kids my age are at college and I've already started my career." I even had a modest but real retirement fund. George, the company manager, helped me set up my health plan, 401K, and direct deposit my first week in LA. I didn't feel like an adult and retirement funds seemed like such a grown-up thing. I was only eighteen years old. My normal friends were on their way to college. Rachel would be at Northwestern and Marie would be back from France and at Columbia in the fall. Both would be living the campus life while I was practically on another planet.

"In four years, the kids in college now will be doing the same thing you are," said Mom. "Everyone starts a career eventually, you just started sooner."

"You can always change your mind and go to college instead," Dad said lightly.

"I know," I said. "That doesn't make it easier right now, but thanks. Anyway, I better go; I just wanted to say hi. I love you."

"We love you too," they said.

"Hang in there," Dad added.

"I'm okay."

"It's not you I'm worried about," he said. "It's that world."

My room was a mess, so when we hung up I started cleaning. After I folded my clean laundry and put it away, I opened up the theater case and piled my pointe shoes and extra warm-ups inside. There was a stray pair of shoes under the bed and I pulled them out and tossed them across the room into the open case. One shoe hit the back and fell down into the trunk. At the same time, the inside of the lid dropped, exposing a hidden compartment.

I sat down in front of the case and performed a closer examination. Apparently, the lid had a false cover. The hidden compartment was empty except for one pink silk pocket on the upper left side. I reached inside and pulled out what looked like a journal.

The dramatic music from Faye's video seeped through the door and heightened the moment. It crossed my mind to call out to her and show her what I found, but I hesitated and the moment passed. I liked having a secret. My fingers traced the embossed gold design on the cover before I flipped it open. The journal was handwritten and dense, with page after page filled with scribbled writing in blue pen. I flipped through it, looking for a name. There wasn't one, so I turned to the beginning and started to read.

How could this happen to me? I broke my leg in the third movement of Fire *rehearsal. Lila kept pushing me to jump more and lift my leg higher (it was a jump where I kicked my left leg out to the side and pushed off the right standing leg). I was trying so hard to do the step the way she wanted and then I don't even know what happened, but bam, I landed at the wrong angle and my leg slipped and I fell hard on my left side. Everyone heard my leg snap. It was sticking out at a unnatural angle. I screamed so loud. They called an ambulance and the rest is a blur. I'm scared I might never be able to dance the same again.*

I stopped. Was she a former company member? Her accident sounded like my worst nightmare and I assumed that must have been the end of her career. An injury like that is where every dancer I knew draws a blank. We couldn't even imagine what came next.

I wondered how the diary ended up in my theater case. I decided I would ask around and see who knew anything about the girl who broke her leg. The older dancers probably knew her.

Three

Faye and I spent an hour getting ready before we walked over to Teddy's party. We made ourselves up and put on bright tank tops and skirts. Once we got out the door, I changed my mind and ran back to switch to jeans and a t-shirt. Faye stuck to the original plan and waited patiently while I put on the new outfit. I felt like I had been trying too hard.

I barely recognized Ian when he greeted us at the door in a blonde wig, pink dress, stilettos, and a feather boa. He had shaved the dark stubble on his chin, stuffed his bra, lined his eyes with black liner, and applied heavy false eyelashes. I had never seen a real man in drag.

Ian was a surprisingly beautiful woman, feminine down to the sensitive tears that stained his cheeks. "My goldfish died today," he lamented, relishing the dramatic opportunity. He pressed the back of his hand to his forehead. "Come, mourn with me over a drink. Welcome to Teddy's apartment. I live in the building too so this is practically my other home."

We followed Ian into the kitchen past a cluster of people in the living room. He swung his hips in a ridiculously exaggerated way and held his arms daintily in front of his chest like they were paws. We found it hard not to laugh. He *wanted* us to laugh and make him the center of attention. In the ballet studio, Ian was a an ordinary member of the corps de ballet, but as the only drag queen at the party, he commanded attention in a way he never would when we were all at work.

The counter was set up as a full-service bar. Ian fixed both of us a vodka and cranberry. "Lorenzo is here," Ian whispered. "Just for the record, I am in love with him. I keep hoping he'll dump Carolyn."

Ian had good taste. Lorenzo was gorgeous, although to be fair, Ian could have said the same thing about any of the soloist or principals and I would have understood. The higher someone's rank and the better their dance ability, the more desirable they were.

"I suspect Lorenzo has a waiting list," Faye said.

"So true," Ian agreed. He fluffed Faye's brown hair. "Honey, we should get you some highlights."

"Really?" asked Faye. "I've never colored my hair before."

At that point, I zoned out on their conversation and surveyed the scene. I had never been comfortable at parties and preferred to spend time with a small group of close friends. When Ian took away Faye's attention, I pushed myself to walk over to where Rebecca, the girl I knew from SBNY, and Sasha, one of the older corps dancers, lounged against the wall. Unless I got to know other people besides Faye, people would lump us together forever.

Rebecca had on a white halter-top, a short mauve skirt, and tan heels, and Sasha wore wedge sandals and a funky dress that looked like a pink lava lamp. I had already picked up on the fact that Sasha was the coolest girl at work. Rebecca followed her the same way she followed the popular girls in New York. Sasha had a belly-button ring, layered blonde hair, and a perfect nose job. She followed the indie music scene and I'd heard her tell Rebecca after a rehearsal that she was wanted to get a group together to camp at a music festival next May. Rebecca immediately offered to take care of the tickets. I heard them mention a bunch of guy names I didn't recognize, so I assumed they had a group of friends outside the company.

"Hey, Anna," Rebecca said. I clinked glasses with her and she smiled warmly at me. "How are you?"

"Good, thanks," I said. "Nice to see you. Hi Sasha."

"Hey," Sasha said and flashed a smile, the most conversation I'd ever had with her.

"Thanks again for going over the counts for *Fire* with me the other day," I said to Rebecca. There were only eight corps girls in *Fire* and I was in the second cast. Considering the fact that there were twenty-two girls in the corps of LABT, it was a huge deal that I was going to be in it at all. Dancing *Fire* in a professional company was a huge privilege. Besides, it was my favorite ballet.

"It's no problem," Rebecca said. "*Fire* is tricky to count, isn't it? The Stravinsky ballets are a challenge."

"Yes," I admitted. "Your help is very much appreciated. I'm just excited to learn it." I flashed back to my last experience with *Fire* in New York. Eight months earlier, the teachers at SBNY cast me as the lead for the school's annual spring workshop. Hilary, another girl named Nicole, and I were supposed to share the role and each dance one performance. I was so excited about it for a few reasons: I loved the ballet, the guy I liked, Tyler, was my partner, and Stacy Lester, the original dancer the role was choreographed for, taught us the role. She was one of my idols and the first to suggest that William might pick me for LABT. Stacy was a short dancer with beautiful feet and a lot of energy and attack, qualities that I knew shined in my own dancing.

After months of rehearsal, the school changed their mind and took me out of the ballet right before the actual show. They told me it was because I was too short to get into Ballet New York. I was devastated. Later, I heard that Hilary's parents had made a huge donation to the school on the condition that she dance multiple performances of the role. Losing my part the first time made me want to dance *Fire* even more.

I'd seen Adrienne and her husband Zif rehearsed the *Fire pas de deux*. Adrienne was perfect in the part and it made me happy to see a dancer I liked dancing my favorite steps rather than someone like Hilary. In general, I longed for justice whenever it came to casting. I always wanted to see good people in the good parts.

"I have a question for you," I said to Rebecca.

"Okay," she said. I noticed I had Sasha's attention too.

"Do either of you know if there was a dancer in the company who broke her leg a few years ago?"

"Oh, of course," said Sasha in arrogant way, as if she knew everything there was to know about the company. "Karina Huntington. I think she left about five years ago. She was here for a long time and came up the ranks."

"Oh, right, Karina," Rebecca said. "Sasha is right. That was before I was here. Karina was gorgeous. Didn't she break her leg right after she became a principal?"

"Yes," Sasha said. "She was out for a year and tried to come back, but she could never dance as well again and left a few months after they tried to put her back onstage. I think she and William both agreed her career was over. It was very sad."

"Wow," I said, curious about the girl who fit with the diary. She was real.

"Why do you ask?" inquired Sasha.

"Oh," I said casually, "My theater case is used and Tong said the person who had it before me had a broken leg. I was just wondering." I was glad I was able to keep the secret. Who knew what kind of dirt Karina had written in her journal?

Someone turned the music up. Marcus, one of the guys in the corps, walked over and put his arm up on the wall next to Rebecca. When Marcus danced he looked like he was trying so hard he might pop a vein. He had a whiny voice and either addressed people with complaints or talked exclusively about his problems. Even though he had a tall build, Marcus seemed smaller because he walked with a slouch. He had small eyes and a pointy noise that reminded me of a weasel.

"The two hottest girls in the company," Marcus said to Rebecca and Sasha, blatantly ignoring me. "What a pleasure to see you all dressed up with your hair down." Grateful not to be his target, I stepped back and took note of the yellow sweat stains under the arms of his white tank top.

Sasha leaned around Rebecca to look at him. "Oh, Marcus," Sasha said. "You're too much."

He took her attention as encouragement and dropped his arm, scooting his way in to stand in between Rebecca and Sasha. He draped an arm over each of their shoulders. "What do you mean?" he said. "I'm giving you a compliment."

"Oh honey," Sasha said. "It just gets to be a little much after awhile." Rebecca laughed.

"You're just so cute," he said. "I can't help it. I'll stop." He took his arms off their shoulders and crossed them awkwardly across his chest. "Let's change the subject. What can I tell you about my week? William has been really positive about my dancing since we started back. This should be a big year for me. They're just working me *to death* already and I have a ridiculous amount of roles to learn. I have been *so* exhausted by the end of the day."

There was an awkward silence while Rebecca stared into her cup, Sasha inspected her cuticles, and I watched his face for some sign of self-awareness. There was none. He took a deep breath and got ready to launch into another monologue about himself.

"Okay," Sasha said loudly before he could launch into another monologue. "Come on, Rebecca. We need to talk to Ryan about helping me build those bookshelves. See you later, guys!" She threaded her arm through Rebecca's and they walked off together.

"Geez," Marcus muttered. I stood rooted to the floor, feeling abandoned and unsure of how to make a graceful exit. Thankfully, Ian paraded over to us. He gave the feather boa a toss over his shoulder and cupped Marcus's chin in his hands.

"Poor Marcus," Ian said. He looked at me to explain. "He just wants a nice ballerina girl."

Marcus gave Ian a dirty look and said, "I don't date apprentices."

I shrugged. Ian cackled and pinched Marcus's cheek, long and hard. Marcus swatted Ian's hand away and stomped off.

"Don't take it personally," Ian said.

"I would never be interested in Marcus anyway," I said. Even though it was true, I felt demeaned. "I'm going to talk to Carolyn and Faye. I see them out on the balcony."

"Have fun," Ian said, strutting off to talk to Allison and Whitney. Whitney was the only black member of the company. I'd never really spoken with her. She seemed friendly enough with Allison because they were both senior corps members, but in general she kept to herself. She seemed bored most of the time. I had tried to ask Whitney a question about a step once and she didn't even let me finish, she just said, "I don't know, ask someone else."

I walked through the kitchen and bumped hard into the table. The alcohol had kicked in and made me feel warm and slightly dizzy. Mikey's counters were covered in paper cups and bottles, except for one corner piled high with tins of cat food. The cat was nowhere in sight.

"There you are," Faye said as soon as I opened the screen door and stepped outside. She sat comfortably in a plastic chair next to Carolyn and Lorenzo. They seemed relaxed and happy to enjoy the fresh night air.

Carolyn's appearance was a contrast to the same focused and perfectly groomed girl I stood next to at the *barre* everyday. Dressed in jeans and a t-shirt, her face scrubbed free of makeup, Carolyn seemed much more comfortable with herself than Rebecca or Sasha. She didn't have Sasha's cool appeal or Rebecca's needy loveliness; instead, she gave off a down-to-earth no-nonsense vibe. I could see how Carolyn and Faye clicked. Faye was down-to-earth too, but she had more innocence and naïve affection for people. Carolyn was warier.

Lorenzo sat next to Carolyn with one bare foot hooked over the opposite knee. He tipped back on the rear legs of his plastic chair and looked me over. A robust and broad-chested guy, Lorenzo's white smile displayed perfect teeth. His hands, I noticed, were huge and manicured. He gave off a whiff of power that only William could match, and I imagined that the other guys in the company must have felt emasculated just by being around him. I felt terribly self-conscious under Lorenzo's scrutiny. As much as I liked Carolyn, I found it surprising that he was with her. She seemed too, well, ordinary for a god like him. He was so out of my league that it didn't even occur to me to have a crush on him. Lorenzo was so intimidating. I could merely admire from afar.

"Hi. How are you?" I said, pulling over another plastic chair next to Faye. "Sorry, I was talking to Sasha and Rebecca. I didn't mean to leave you."

"No problem," Faye said. "Carolyn and Lorenzo have been telling me about a salsa club they like."

"Oh," I said, "That sounds fun. We could stand to do some other kinds of dancing."

"I'm glad you're wearing jeans too," Carolyn said, leaning over to pat my knee. "I don't get fancy for these parties. Who cares? It's not like everyone here doesn't see us sweaty and disheveled on a daily basis."

"Thanks," I said. "I debated."

"Yeah," Faye adds, "I had to wait fifteen minutes while Anna ran back and changed."

"Women," Lorenzo muttered, watching us with amusement.

"So how are things going?" Carolyn asked. "Ignore him." She smacked Lorenzo's knee. "Faye filled me in on her first few weeks. Tell me about yours."

"Oh, you know, things are pretty good," I said. "I'm still struggling with that last section you taught me in *Georgia On My Mind*."

"The style is tricky if you haven't had a lot of jazz training," Carolyn agreed. "That's Lorenzo's favorite ballet though, isn't it, babe? It's fun to watch from the audience."

"I like *Georgia* a lot more now than when I first danced it," Lorenzo said. "When I was first cast, I didn't think; I just floated through the choreography. Then I would get sloppy and the critics complained. I think about it more now. You don't want to become comfortable. Some of those steps are difficult and look terrible if they aren't done right. That's probably why I've grown to love it, because of the challenge. I've learned that if it doesn't feel difficult, then I think perhaps you're not doing all you need to do. We should all be a little uncomfortable from time to time, and William knows that. He likes to see us put in the extra effort. *Georgia* is a ballet that pushes us. It's good to struggle."

"I agree," I said, grateful to hear that even Lorenzo battled with his parts sometimes. His thoughtfulness surprised me.

"Then you'll do fine here," he said and winked.

"Where's Stephanie tonight?" Faye asked.

"I wondered," I said. "I haven't seen her either."

"She was here earlier," Carolyn said. "Today's her twenty-first birthday."

"It is?" I ask. Faye and I exchanged a look. We were both thinking the same thing: twenty-one was *so old*.

"She's probably passed out somewhere by now," Lorenzo said. "Props to that girl for partying hard at night and dancing well during the day."

"How does she get away with it?" Faye asked.

"Who knows," Carolyn said. "Some people can just do that. William likes her. She's been rehearsing the principal in *Tidal Moods*. They don't seem concerned when she misses class and gets sick half the time. I could never get away with that."

When there were dozens of dancers just waiting for an opportunity like Stephanie's, it was hard to understand why they didn't move on to someone more eager, willing, and able if she wasn't taking her position seriously enough. "Why her?" we all wondered, whether it was about Stephanie or some other chosen one.

"She's good," Lorenzo said. "Stephanie is going places." He was oblivious to the deflated look on Carolyn's face.

The door to the kitchen opened. "Where are your drinks?" demanded Ian.

"We drank them," Faye said.

"Well, time for a refill," Ian announced. "Lorenzo, handsome, what can I bring you? Carolyn?"

"Not me," Carolyn said. "I think we're about ready to crash." She stood up and stretched her arms over her head.

"I'm good, thanks," Lorenzo said. He picked Carolyn's straw purse up off the ground and handed it to her. "Guess we're calling it a night. Let's go thank Mikey, Carolyn."

"Okay," she said. "Bye guys." Lorenzo took Carolyn's hand and led her back inside.

Ian watched them leave. He picked up his skirt and sat down daintily in Carolyn's chair.

"William loved Carolyn when she first came," he said quietly. "She did several big roles. Then last year, William told Carolyn he wouldn't promote her unless she lost weight."

"Oh?" asked Faye. I scooted my chair closer to Ian. I hadn't heard that Carolyn used to be one of William's favorites. She didn't seem like a favorite now. I hadn't seen her cast for much of anything and she always stood in back during rehearsals.

"She didn't lose the weight," Ian said, crossing his legs and folding his hands over his knees. "William put Carolyn onstage for a short while in soloist roles. He thought it would motivate her to slim down, but when she didn't drop the pounds he pulled her out of almost everything."

"I haven't seen her rehearse any of the ballets," Faye said. "She always helps us learn the counts and stuff in the back, but she's never in first cast. She has more seniority than Sasha and a lot of the other girls though. What's going on with that?"

"She's a fabulous dancer," Ian said. "But they won't cast her until she loses the weight, even though she's better than most of the girls in the corps. They're playing a mind game. It's ridiculous."

"That's so wrong," I said. I stood behind Carolyn at *barre* every day and knew her technique was impeccable.

Ian shook his finger at us. "Let that be a lesson to you. William doesn't like dancers he can't control. If you want to move up, stay as skinny as you can and do whatever he says."

"That's jacked," said Faye.

"What about Carolyn's career?" I asked.

"That's the way it works," Ian said. "Ballet is so much more than a career. Everything is personal. This is about our bodies and the way we look. William may have been in our shoes years ago, but he isn't now. The artistic staff doesn't care about us. Even the principals are expendable."

How had Ian become so cynical? No wonder he laughed at me in all my eagerness on the first day. I hoped I never became that bitter. What would be the point if all I could see were the negatives?

Ryan, the other cute straight guy besides Lorenzo, walked into the kitchen wearing a black tank top and jeans, his hair wet from either the shower or surfing. At first glance, he looked relaxed and happy. When I looked a little closer I noticed his eyes were bloodshot. A short bleached-blonde guy in baggy shorts and a ratty old t-shirt walked up in the doorway behind Ryan. I didn't recognize him.

"Hey," Ryan said. "Getting the new apprentices drunk, Ian?"

"Hey," Ian said. "Somebody has to break them in."

Faye gave Ian a surprised look.

"Ladies!" Ryan said. "This is my buddy Ari. He's a professional surfer." Ari smiled a crooked smile at us. He was probably in his mid-twenties. Ryan's muscles were a lot leaner than Ari's, and even though he didn't have a ballet body, Ari was toned and very tan. Faye had been admiring guys just like him at the beach all summer.

"A pro surfer, huh?" Faye said to Ari.

"Yeah, I try," said Ari, appraising her. "The key is to keep focused. When you're dealing with the ocean it is so easy to make mistakes. I try to learn from them instead of banging my head against the wall. Hanging out with you guys reminds me to make the effort to stay in better shape. I can feel a huge difference with my confidence level when I work out so Ryan and I do the gym together. Then I go out there feeling like I deserve to win."

"We've cleaned up our diet too," Ryan said. "Just getting rid of the junk food improves our energy level."

"Big time," said Ari. "I'm stoked about our progress. My surfing gets better every day."

"Wow," Faye said. "Do you travel a lot? What's the trajectory of that career?" She put her elbows on the center island and leaned towards him, smiling.

Ari seemed to enjoy her attention. "It's a lot of travel. I love Australia and spend quite a bit of time there. I'm based here though. This year I'm after some good results in the 4-6 star contests. Then hopefully next year I'll be able to surf the prime events and get myself up in the world rankings."

"That's so cool," said Faye.

"Let's get a beer, man," Ryan said, punching Ari in the shoulder.

"They're in the cooler in the hallway," Ian said.

"We'll be right back," Ari said. As they left we heard them talking. "Damn," Ari said to Ryan from out in the hall. "I love these ballet parties. These girls know how to look amazing, no matter what they do."

"It's their job," Ryan said. "Ballerinas look good in every position. And I do mean—every position." They laughed.

"Let's go in the living room," Ian beckoned. We followed him.

Before long, Ari and Faye were flirting in a corner and Ryan wandered over to Rebecca and Sasha. Ian and I sat down on the couch.

"Ryan is going to talk Rebecca into staying over," Ian said. "They're on and off all the time. She's going to go home with him and think they're back in a relationship. He won't realize until after a few weeks that she's emotionally involved again and then he'll blow her off. It's painful to watch."

"Oh," I said. "He doesn't want a relationship?"

"Doesn't seem like it," Ian said. "Ryan obviously has a crush on Elizabeth so maybe he's trying to stay available. What an idiot. He has no chance with her. Rebecca is oblivious that Ryan isn't serious about her and Elizabeth is totally hung up on Teddy, even though Teddy constantly strings her along."

"That's unfortunate." I let out a sigh. "You're a fountain of information, Ian, but I'm tired. Time to collect Faye and go home." I propelled myself off the couch and walked over to interrupt Faye and Ari's conversation.

"Is it time?" Faye asked.

"Yes, please."

"Hope to see you around, Faye," Ari said, winking at her. "Bye, Anna. Nice to meet you both."

"For sure," Faye said. She linked arms with me. We waved thanks to Teddy and headed out the door. The festive noise from the party followed us out into the street.

Four

I've been injured for a few months now. Every day I go to physical therapy, and sometimes I watch class or rehearsals, but sometimes I just can't take it. There's so much empty time. I'm on worker's comp and they assure me my job will be waiting when I can come back. I don't know if I believe them. Every week means I lose ground. Other dancers are coming up and taking my parts. I would go home to see my mother in Minnesota but I don't think I can take the cold, and my therapy is here anyway. I haven't heard from my dad in years, and sometimes I wonder about tracking him down. I don't think he'd want to hear from me now though. He left when I was five.

I don't want to leave the company. This is my home. If I keep working hard and focus on coming back somehow it'll work out. Watching class and rehearsals kills me but it's how they'll remember I'm still alive, so I know I need to show my face.

I've always wanted to write about my experience, and while I'm recovering is the perfect time to do it. I asked William about starting a book and he seemed skeptical, although I think he appreciates that I'm trying as hard as I can. He agreed to a brief chat about his role in the company. I would like to have a better record of LABT. The thing about dance is it's basically over the minute the curtain falls. There has to be a way to hang onto what we do. The public has no idea who we are as people. I want them to know us. I want to be able to look back on my time in the company and remember who we were. My plan is to interview people and record their perspectives here.

William: "*My run at LABT has been very controversial, and I'd be the first one to say that I fail regularly in many respects. And, you know, sometimes I wonder if I'll just end up leaving the company in frustration. But, it continues to be a great experience for me. Great experience. You know, I learn a lot every day. I really do. It's hard, because I want to create something new and dynamic, a company that can do lots of different styles and perform the classical ballets on a higher level. I'm one of the few left who can uphold the Roizman tradition, and I take great pride in that. But we need to keep moving forward too.*

When I first took over the company, it was unusual to have modern choreographers doing pieces for classical companies. Then people asked, what the hell is he doing, what's next? Now it's common, but then everyone from the folks on the street to the critics thought I was crazy. I knew what I was doing, it was a time for new work, new ideas in the theater, and a lot of newer choreographers had very fresh and interesting point of view towards classical companies.

I wanted to try to choreograph too. I did that the first few years but my pieces never really had the impact I'd hoped. The other choreographers I brought in were people who I used to work with. We're a different generation. The company looks at me like they'd like to get some part of this old man's ideas. They're looking to understand the complexity of aging, because they don't have many opportunities to work with "old" people. So I like to bring in older retired dancers with life experience to make new ballets. It's a different vocabulary, a different accumulation of experiences that young people do not have.

I also knew LABT needed a school. We had no breeding ground of our own for younger dancers, and I have no choice but to hire away from other programs. As an institution, we will never be of the highest caliber until we train our own dancers. So we got that started a few years after I lost interest in choreographing. Some things I succeed at. Some I fail. Either way I have to keep trying, keep persisting. That's how this company has become what it is today.

Working with dancers is a delicate and difficult thing. They are emotional creatures, and they are children. All they know is dance and ballet is their whole world. They take it very seriously, as I do. I have learned not to tell somebody to just lose weight. But you do need to address it and it does require some professional help. It may be something as simple as a kid not understanding what to eat. And I say it the same way I would say that if you have chronic tendonitis, "You have to go to the physical therapist and take care of this," and equate it on that level. If there's a problem that's getting in the way of their dancing, they need to fix it no matter what it is. We give them the name of a doctor and send them off. I want them to succeed, I really do. But not everyone can. This is a very hard life. Survival of the fittest and all that, you know.

I'm very close with the dancers. I really love and admire them. I do. I can't dance anymore so I dance through them. We have the most beautiful dancers in the world. People come to see us just to marvel at the beauty of our ballerinas. I'm very proud of them."

Karina's diary lingered in my thoughts. I read bits and pieces when I had time. I could never read too much at once because it made my head spin—it was like going back in time and then every morning I had to go in and work with many of the same people she wrote about. I knew things about them they didn't know I knew. I read a section and then tucked it away for weeks at a time. Her journal was the best secret I'd ever had.

Almost every night after work, I sewed ribbons and elastic onto a new pair of pointe shoes to keep them on my feet when I danced. Pointe shoes only came as a simple slip-on, so I had a whole routine with each new pair before I felt comfortable wearing them to class or rehearsal. Once I attached the elastic and ribbons so they would wrap around my ankles, I cut the satin off the toe to prevent slipping, bent the shank so the bottom of the shoe was flexible enough to make my feet look pointed when I went up on toe, and gently closed the crack of the door on the shoes so they weren't too loud when I jumped. I went through them faster than I ever did at ballet school. Money was tight for company operations, so as generous as Tong was, we still received a limited supply. Restricted or not, I still considered it a gift that my pointe shoes were finally free. I could have gone through more than LABT's three allotted pairs a week if the company had been able to afford it. My shoe disposal rate depended on the ballets I danced. Sometimes, soft, broken-in shoes were more comfortable for rehearsal. But dancing ballets with a lot of pointe work in dead shoes felt like jamming my toes into the sharp tip of a knife.

For the few hours when we weren't wearing the shoes, Faye and I went to the beach or the movies.

Dad helped me buy an unremarkable used sedan when he came to visit, and I switched my driver's license to California so I'd be all ready when touring season began. It felt weird to drive again. I had had my license for a few months before I moved to New York, but I didn't drive for very long. It had been a few years, and I was nervous in LA traffic.

"Don't be scared, just press on the gas," Dad commanded when we first bought the car. "It's like living. You have to do it and let whatever will happen, happen."

With the time change and our busy schedules, it was difficult to keep in touch with my best friends. When we were in New York at SBNY, Jen and I used to talk several times a day, and even though we talked far less after I moved away, I felt like no time has passed when she called to catch up.

"How's LA?" Jen said. "Tell me everything. I miss you!"

"It's okay," I said, wishing I could pour my heart out to her the way I used to, when we reviewed the details of every day. I remembered back when Jen and I were roommates and she confessed to me that she'd been cutting herself. The school always gave her a hard time about her weight and that was her coping mechanism. I had never had a friend be so vulnerable with me and we'd been uniquely bonded ever since. The rivalry that affected friendships in ballet never applied to us. I had many friends because we had dance in common, but with Jen, our friendship wasn't about our shared love of ballet. It was about our values, our humor, and our resilient attitudes. Neither of us had good things handed to us without a fight and we understood each other because of that.

"I've only danced in the back of class and rehearsals so far," I confessed. "We leave on tour in a week. Will you be around when we're on the east coast? How's National Ballet Theatre?"

"When are you coming on tour?" she asked.

"We leave for North Carolina on October second. After that Philadelphia, Pittsburgh, and New Jersey. I think we're in New Jersey by October fourteenth."

"The fourteenth?" echoed Jen. She sighed. "Shoot. We'll be in Japan."

"Oh no," I said, disappointed.

"Maybe I can come out during layoff, if I have the money," she said. We both were silent a moment, knowing that it was unlikely on a dancer's salary.

"That would be great."

"On another subject, I got my corps contract last month," Jen said. "And, I met someone."

"Congrats! That's great news," I said, happy to hear. "Tell me more." I knew that when Jen liked someone, the problems that seemed so big and all consuming, like her weight, faded into white noise. When she was anxious or worried, she focused on the anticipation and excitement of seeing someone who she knew thought positively of her, and that made a huge difference when she had to confront the extraordinary criticism that was part of our daily life. I would do the same if I liked someone, and since I didn't have a crush of my own, it was fun to experience the excitement vicariously. I knew romance wasn't a cure-all, but I longed for it all the same.

"Well," she said. "I met him at the gym. We'd been checking each other out for a few weeks and one day he offered to buy me a smoothie. He's an investment banker from Vermont. You'd like him. "

I was lukewarm about the idea of an investment banker, but there was no need to infect her with my negativity. How would someone who focused so much on money understand why we worked so hard for such meager salaries? I swallowed my skepticism. "He sounds good so far. I love that he's not a dancer. Text me a picture, will you? And seriously, when do you have time and energy to go to the gym?"

"Oh," she said, "well, actually, right before I got my corps contract the ballet mistress suggested I drop a few more pounds. So I had to make the time."

"Oh no. Not that stuff again." SBNY told Jen she wouldn't get into Ballet New York because of her weight, and that's why she accepted the contract with National Ballet Theatre in the first place. I hoped that would be the end of her weight problem, much like she hoped joining LABT would make my height a non-issue. As far as I knew, NBT had never said anything to her about dieting. I was so disappointed to hear the weight thing had come up again. They were telling someone who in the normal world would be considered stick thin that she could lose a few, and that was just crazy. Jen was thinner than a celebrity on a magazine cover. I wished I could be there to help her laugh it off. Guy or no guy, I realized she couldn't possibly be as happy as she wanted me to believe. The only reason she would spend regular time at the gym, in addition to all the studio hours, was because she was under pressure and trying to lose weight.

"Don't worry, Anna, I'm trying to be healthy about it," she said, sensing my anxiety.

"Ugh. I hope so. Keep me posted on things," I said. "I miss you."

"I miss you too," she said sadly.

When Faye and I didn't walk home together because of different schedules, I liked to walk the long way through the residential neighborhoods. I loved to admire the beautiful houses on the quiet tree-lined streets. Someday I wanted to have a house and family, it just seemed so far away.

I was on one of my favorite blocks when I stopped to get my sunglasses out of my bag. Suddenly I felt a crushing pain on my head and fell to the ground sideways, hitting the sidewalk. My pointe shoes went flying onto the grass. I closed my eyes and gritted my teeth, wincing from the pain. There was a thump as someone jumped out of a tree.

"I'm so sorry! I didn't see you at all. Are you ok?" a male voice asked.

I opened my eyes and saw a man with a lean and well-muscled build studying me with watchful blue eyes. He had a giant electric saw in one hand. He couldn't have been much older than me. Despite the pain, my heart beat a little faster.

"What happened?" I asked, my eyes filling with tears. "And why are you brandishing that at me?" I touched my head gingerly. "Ow, it hurts."

"I was up in the branches pruning the tree," he said, "and I guess I didn't see you below. A branch fell on your head. I am so sorry. What can I do? Can I get you some ice?"

"Yes, please," I managed, feeling very sorry for myself.

"I'll be right back." He jogged confidently into the house and I tried to get my bearings. There was a lump forming on top of my head. My hair was still pinned up from work, and I took out the clip, letting it fall around my shoulders. I supposed I was lucky I didn't black out.

As I took in the house I started to feel silly. Did he live here? It must be his parents' house, I thought. The airy Mediterranean-style home had a cheery front porch and meticulously landscaped front yard. It portrayed a sense of comfort and stability I could only dream about. I wondered what it was like inside.

He reappeared on the front porch with a bag of ice. "Do you want to come sit up here or is it hard to move?" he asked, patting the patio furniture. When I didn't react he walked back over to me.

"I can get up," I said, but I wasn't sure. We regarded each other. He took my arm and gently helped me to my feet. With great care, he placed the ice pack where I clutched my head and moved my hand to hold the bag in place.

"Thank you." I felt a heightened self-awareness that wasn't uncomfortable exactly, just unnerving. If I hadn't been in so much pain I would have laughed. I had never seen such a handsome guy, and in my normal life, I would never have met someone like him.

"You're welcome," he said rather pitifully. "Again, I'm terribly sorry. I feel like such a jerk."

"It's okay."

"I'm Ethan," he offered.

"Anna."

He picked up my bag and scattered shoes and guided me up to his front porch, where I sat in a comfortable chair while he brought out sodas. I guessed he must be in his late twenties. There was dirt from the garden all over his clothes and face and he smelled like freshly cut grass.

"Do you need me to call someone for you? Are you on your way somewhere?" he asked.

"Oh, it's okay, I was just walking home from work. I have an apartment a few blocks that way," I said, pointing down the street. "I work over on the Promenade. Is it okay if I just sit for a minute until my head stops throbbing?"

"Of course." He sat down next to me, kicked off his shoes, and put his legs up casually on the rail. "Are you one of the ballerinas? Shoot, if I hurt you I'm in serious trouble now."

"I am, but don't worry, I'm going to live. I guess the pointe shoes gave me away."

He shrugged. "I've seen the ballet a few times. My mom was involved in the board and the early fundraising for the company when it first got off the ground. My buddies and I always liked looking in at the pretty girls in the window."

"Oh really?" I could feel my walls going up. He wasn't just being nice out of guilt anymore. He was flirting because he knew I was a ballerina. "Is she still on the board?"

"No," he said and looked away.

"What happened?" I asked.

"Oh nothing," he said. "She just passed away last year, that's all."

I couldn't think of the right thing to say.

"It's okay," he said. "That's actually why I'm here. This was her house and it's been sitting empty while my older brother and I figure out what to do with it. I want to keep it in the family. The house was left to both of us and I'm hoping to buy him out. I've been living here while I fix it up." He took a sip of his drink and wiped the excess off his mouth. His lips were very distracting.

"I see," I said. "Where did you live before?"

"I was doing a master's in architectural engineering up at Stanford," he said. "Mom got sick right around the time I finished, so I took a consulting job in LA to be around for her."

"Wow," I said, impressed. Intimidated, actually, and moved.

"Yeah," he said. "And you? Are you from around here?"

"No," I said. "I grew up in Rock Island, Illinois, and moved to Manhattan for my last two years of high school to attend the School of Ballet New York. When I graduated last June I got a job at the ballet here."

"Wow," he said. "So you just graduated high school? You're not even close to twenty-one."

"I'm almost twenty. How old are you?"

"Older than you," he said. I think I see a shade of a smile in his expression, but it's hard to be sure.

"Fair enough."

"I'm twenty-five," he admitted. "Probably too old to take you out on a date."

I felt a rush of excitement that I quickly tried to squash. There was no way he was serious. And yet, I wanted the moment to go on and on. We sat there brimming with potential.

"Are you suggesting you want to take me out on a date?" I blurted out.

"Maybe," he said. "It depends if there's another guy in the picture. I know you ballerinas have lines of admirers."

I shrugged, caught off-guard by his boldness. I resolved to play it cool.

"Well, you know, there are a lot of guys who admire us from the windows. Besides, you probably are too old to take me out." As soon as I said it I regretted discouraging him. We stared at each other awkwardly, as if we both wanted to take back the implication. I did my best to change the subject. "So, are you really into gardening?"

"Yes," he said, "except when I'm dropping branches on pretty girl's heads."

I flushed. "Ah yes, that's not good."

"Well, I like to work with my hands. Do you garden?"

"Not really," I said. "I used to garden with my mom when I was growing up, but I haven't had much opportunity living in a dorm and an apartment the past few years. And I moved away from home when I was sixteen to go to ballet school in New York."

"Oh. That would get in the way."

Our eyes met and the tension hung between us. I needed to get away and think. His life seemed to be about caring for everyone but himself: his mother, the garden, and the house. I found myself wanting to offer to help out with his projects. He so clearly needed someone to take care of *him*. The offer was totally inappropriate, and with my schedule and constant exhaustion it wasn't even possible, and yet I was intrigued and wanted the chance to get to know him.

"I better get going," I said, to bring myself back to reality. "Thanks for the ice and the drink."

"Oh, of course. Again, I'm so sorry for dropping that branch on your head. It was nice to meet you."

"You too," I said, hurrying down his front path before he could recognize the extent of my vulnerability.

On the morning we left for our first tour of the season, George, our company manager, passed out the airplane tickets at the studio. He was a former dancer and very type-A. The poor man always looked frazzled. I felt bad for him because there were so many logistics involved in the trip.

We met in the parking lot at work and a huge bus drove us all to the airport together. I already loved the experience of going on the road. There were so many little things that added to my excitement, like packing my makeup in my theater case, picking out the pointe shoes I would need for performances, and watching the company members show up with their bags packed.

The airport was crowded and our group made the security line painfully long. George breathed a sigh of relief as we all gathered at the gate headed for Charlotte, North Carolina. When we boarded the plane, the pilot announced us over the intercom. "It's our great pleasure to be the preferred airlines of William Mason and the dancers of the Los Angeles Ballet Theatre. We'd like to extend a special welcome to them on this flight." The older dancers hardly noticed the announcement but Faye and I grinned at each other. I caught Hilary smiling too as she took her seat, despite how cool she tried to appear on the bus. She had dressed up in a short skirt, heels, and big sunglasses. Most of us were in company-logo sweats.

William and Lila settled into their seats in first class as the rest of us filed into coach. Sasha, Rebecca, and Ryan were already seated when I passed by. The girls had their gossip magazines out and Ryan was already snoring with his hand on Rebecca's knee. All the couples—Adrienne and Zif, Elizabeth and Mikey, and Carolyn and Lorenzo—sat together in the rows of two. Allison, Whitney, and Jeff huddled together in their three-person row. Stephanie read a thriller and ignored Hilary, who sat next to her and played on her smartphone. I found my aisle seat next to Faye and took out Karina's diary.

"What are you reading?" Faye asked, taking out her knitting needles.

She *never* asked what I was reading, even though I'd read the diary in front of her before. I hadn't expected the question. "Oh, just an old journal of mine." Faye gave me a funny look, shrugged, and put on her headphones.

Yesterday I talked with Lorenzo, one of the principals. We've been partners in several ballets and he's wonderful to work with. All the girls have a crush on him (me included) and probably a lot of the boys too. I'd go out with him in a second if he showed any signs of interest. I've been dating a nice guy named Jared, a dentist, so I doubt that's going to happen.

Lorenzo: "We have to have some talent but at the end of the day, that may only account for twenty percent of our success. Eighty percent is hard work. Ballet demands a great work ethic and determination. Everyone works their pants off to achieve their goals. I get a lot of satisfaction out of pushing that hard and feeling my body practically collapse at the end of the day. I feel powerful. We all think we're superhuman until something bad happens, like what happened to you, Karina. That scares the crap out of me.

I came from a small poverty-stricken town in Mexico. My parents had no education and they owned a small restaurant, so growing up I never had arts or cultural exposure. Ballet came to me as a total surprise and I had no idea what it was. All I knew was the poor people's lives in our village. Everyone suffered from malnutrition and there were many drug addicts. My brother was chronically ill and there was just no money to take him to the hospital or buy medicine. I was determined to find a way to get him the care he needed.

The day my life changed was in the middle of summer. I was playing basketball with some buddies and wearing my brother's shorts, which were way too big for me. These American gentlemen pulled up in a car and stopped to watch. They told us they were starting a dance school in Mexico City and wanted to recruit boys for the program. The tallest man said I had talent. Within a week I went to live in Mexico City to study ballet on full scholarship. My parents were thrilled I was getting out of there, and so was I. I didn't even know what ballet was, but right away I loved it and I knew I was good at it. I worked in the office at the ballet school and made money to send back to my family. Eventually my brother got the treatment he needed and we found out he had diabetes. Ballet changed my life and saved his.

You ask where I see myself in twenty years and I am struggling with that question. I would like to get married and have a family but it's hard to imagine right now. My primary relationship is with dance. I can't imagine dating a non-dancer because the girls in dance understand me so well. Most ballerinas are not ready to have babies, at least not at this point in their lives. I would like to see my family in Mexico more and I imagine I will teach or do something else in ballet when I retire. That's a long ways away though. I'm only twenty-six and think I have another ten years in me as long as I don't get injured.

It's hard to say how I feel about William. All the girls worship him and of course I admire him. He had an amazing career. Sometimes I feel he is competitive with the boys, at least the straight ones. He likes to own the girls and if I ever show much interest in one I can tell he bristles about it. His wife has been very ill with cancer and it seems to make him cling possessively to his dancers. He must be in a tough place personally, but that's another story. I try to stay out of that and just focus on my dancing."

It was already late when we arrived in Charlotte. After the company checked in at the hotel,

Faye and I dumped our bags in the room and headed out to dinner. We ended up in a group with Stephanie, Carolyn, Lorenzo, Ian, and Hilary because we all reached the lobby at the same time.

"I'm worried about Mikey," Ian said to Faye and me as we walked to the restaurant. "He's been drinking again and missing class. Last week he even showed up to a rehearsal drunk. Mikey is so frustrated that he's still in the corps after five years, with no featured roles or indication he'll ever become a soloist. Plus he's in a lot of debt. He spends his money frivolously on stuff like that ridiculous new sports car."

"Where's Elizabeth in all of this?" Faye asked. "She seems so together. Why doesn't she straighten him out?"

"Oh," Ian said, "Elizabeth tries. She dumps him because of his drinking every few months. She'll stay away for a few weeks and then she gets weak and goes back. That girl has everything professionally. It's a shame her relationship is such a mess."

"She seems like she really loves him too," I said. "I wish he could pull it together."

"He's selfish and immature," Ian said, "but she's no saint and she's not fully committed to Mikey either. He's in just as tough of a situation with her as she is with him."

"What does that mean?" Faye asked. As far as we knew, Elizabeth was perfect to the point of being annoying. Ian started backpedaling when he saw our confused faces.

"I didn't mean anything," he said. "Just that Elizabeth didn't get to be Elizabeth without some sacrifices, that's all. You two are new. Over time you'll get the picture." He held the door open at the restaurant and we filed inside, the conversation lost as we found our way to a warm table.

On opening night we had class onstage, followed by the dress rehearsal. There was barely enough time to eat a quick snack before we had to sign in for the half-hour call.

The girls' dressing room buzzed with activity as I pinned up my hair and applied makeup. I watched carefully to see what the experienced girls did to prepare. Makeup, hairpins, tights, and pointe shoes exploded all over the room as we made ourselves at home.

While I worked on my hair I thought about Ethan, just like I thought about him every night before I fell asleep. I felt sure I'd see him again, and what would I do then? Maybe he just thought I was a way for him and his friends to meet ballet girls. I wasn't sure he'd even prefer me once he met my pretty friends. If he was even interested in a ballerina, that is. He probably had a ridiculously smart girlfriend from Stanford who was over twenty-one and on the path to become a powerful CEO. As much as I tried to discourage myself, I couldn't stifle the thought of running my hands through his thick brown hair.

I was only in the last ballet so I had a lot of time to get ready. The dressing room emptied out once the show started. "Is my makeup okay?" I asked Carolyn. She inspected me. "I'd add more blush and darken the eyeliner," she said. "Let me help you." Carolyn wasn't dancing at all and was just there to cover in case someone got hurt. If she felt badly about it, she didn't let it show. She was as gracious as could be.

I put on my black tights, a pair of warm slippers, and the saloon girl costume for *Frontiers* and found a corner to warm up in backstage. While I stretched, I peeked around the back wing. The show was in progress and I could see the sweat, hear the cursing, and watch the dancers collapse in exhaustion as they came offstage.

The curtain fell on the second ballet and I went over to the rosin box to put on my dyed black pointe shoes. It felt strange to wear black shoes instead of pink. I rubbed both my heels in the yellowy-white powder to help keep my shoes on. The other corps girls sat and crowded in towards the box so I scooted out of the way to tie my ribbons. Faye gave me a hand up and I stood and rolled up and down on my pointes to see how the shoes felt. She nodded her approval.

"Places, please," Greg, the stage manager, called, and the overture to *Frontiers* began. I loved the Copeland piece because it was happy and evoked the Old West. After weeks of rehearsal, the melody was like an automatic cue to dance. I felt jittery and jogged in place to stay warm.

When I was little, I used to put on performances for my grandmother at her house. I'd go in her bathroom and try on all her makeup, even spritzing myself with her expensive perfume. She didn't mind, even when I put on one of her beautiful negligees for my "show" and as I was twirling I tripped on the skirt and fell flat on my face, ripping the sheer fabric. Other women might have been mad, but my grandma clapped until her hands hurt. "Do it again, you were beautiful," she would say enthusiastically as she restarted the music. I would begin again, leaping and waving my arms as if I were a butterfly.

That feeling of excitement and pleasure remained with me as an eighteen-year-old about to make her professional debut. As a child, I was utterly confident my performance would please my audience, and that feeling lingered years later. There was something about the moment right before the curtain went up that gave me such a rush. I knew I was bringing something good into people's lives. Grandma taught me that from an early age.

Faye squeezed my arm. "*Merde*," she said, which was a French curse word and the standard way dancers said good luck. All the ballet terminology was in French, so why shouldn't the slang be too?

"*Merde*," I replied and gave her a hug.

"Break a leg, you two," Hilary said, putting her hands on our shoulders. Actually *saying* "break a leg" was considered bad luck in the theater, and as usual she rubbed me the wrong way. Hilary wasn't even in our section and she didn't go on until later.

"Ditto," Faye said, patting Hilary's shoulder awkwardly. "Same," I chimed in to be polite. Rebecca and Allison congregated behind us, whispered their "*merdes*", and prepared for our entrance. Ryan gave Rebecca a kiss on the lips. "*Merde*, babe," he said to her. "*Merde*, ladies," he said, nodding to us. He was my partner for the night.

"Oh thank you!" Hilary piped up.

Faye looked at me and rolled her eyes.

Rebecca, Allison, Faye, and I lined up in the second wing. We were all wearing the same costume and to people who didn't know us, we looked identical. On the count of eight, the four of us stepped down on the right foot. The new phrase of music began and we marched onstage in unison, checking that we formed a perfect diagonal line. After four steps, we simultaneously posed with our weight over our right pointe shoe. Each girl put her right hand on her right knee and bent forward. As we arched our backs, I smiled at the audience. Adrenaline raced through my body.

Ryan, Marcus, Mikey, and Ian marched in from the opposite wing, synchronized and in line. Ryan faced me and posed with his arms crossed over his chest. The boys looked formidable in their spurs and cowboy hats. It was easy to smile at Ryan and interact with him onstage. He clearly liked to perform as much as I did.

We danced and I worked hard to stay in line and be on the music. Everything seemed to happen twice as fast as in rehearsal.

Out of the corner of my eye, I noticed William appear in the front wing. He stood so close to the edge that he was almost onstage. Even as I concentrated on my performance, I felt the acute awareness that William was there. He remained ever-present in my mind's eye as I danced.

Our section ended and Ryan held my hand as we ran offstage. "That went well. See you at the finale," he whispered. He squeezed my hand before he let go. "Thanks." I felt pretty good.

Faye was at the water cooler and I went over to get a drink. "How was it?" I asked. "It was okay, I think," Faye said. Her makeup already looked like it was melting off. "I didn't mess up," she said. "You?"

"So far so good," I said, already feeling addicted. I filled a paper cup with water and admired how happy everyone looked out onstage.

"There's so much energy out there," Faye whispered. A thin line of sweat ran down her cheek and onto her neck.

"We're so lucky," I said, feeling a rush of gratitude towards William.

She nodded toward me as her eyes stayed fixed on the stage. "I know," Faye said.

We moved closer behind the second wing to watch. Four girls posed onstage in a perfect square. Natasha was the second movement principal and her powerhouse style translated better onstage than in the studio. She traveled forward on her toes, flanked behind by the corps. In performance, she had to tuck her pink tights into her pointe shoes, which made her legs look much longer than the black cutoff tights she usually wore in rehearsal.

Adam was Natasha's partner and she was only a smidge shorter than him on *pointe.* They made a good pair. I would never guess Adam was anywhere near forty from the way he looked onstage, especially in a tasseled shirt and black cowboy hat. He looked like a kid. The only giveaway was if I looked closely, I could see dancing was an effort for him.

Natasha stepped forward with her leg behind her in arabesque and Adam moved in to hold her waist. They looked like seasoned professionals. She raised her arm over her head, tossing her nose up with dramatic flair. A feather in her French twist went right up Adam's nose.

I couldn't help myself—I laughed. Faye giggled. "He's going to sneeze," Ryan said behind me. "Oh no. Don't do it. Don't do it, man."

Adam walked Natasha around in a circle while she balanced on one foot. If he used his hand to move the feather, he would call the audience's attention to it, so he smiled and kept going.

"Adam won't sneeze," Lorenzo said, standing up from his stretch on the floor. "The man has been a principal dancer with LABT for a decade. Professionalism. Watch it in action."

Lorenzo was right. Adam didn't sneeze even though we could all tell he was fighting the urge. "He looks like he might explode," Ryan said, chuckling.

Natasha stepped away and Adam's nose was free at last. "No sneeze," Lorenzo said. "Told you." Adam ran into the wing and gave Lorenzo a triumphant high five.

"That was brutal," Adam said, laughing with us.

Natasha came off and put her hand on Adam's shoulder. "We should have practiced with the headpiece," she said, laughing. "No matter, darling. You were magnificent." She kissed Adam's cheek.

The second movement corps came offstage and Faye and I moved back to get out of their way. "Okay, cowboy," Ryan said to Lorenzo. "Show us something good out there." He lightly punched Lorenzo's arm.

"Don't worry, buddy." Lorenzo said, putting on his cowboy hat. He looked over at Faye and me and winked. "Watch and admire," he said to Ryan.

Onstage, Elizabeth balanced on her left leg and rose up and down on *pointe*. She looked unbelievably glamorous. Elizabeth's usually reserved demeanor had disappeared and she displayed a playful attitude I had never seen. Her energy was contagious. The eight *corps de ballet* boys and girls grinned as they posed in a diagonal line behind her, making a tableau behind Elizabeth as her long right leg flew up repeatedly next to her ear.

The audience clapped as she whirled across the floor. She struck a pose near the wing, hands on her hips and one knee bent. Lorenzo ran on. He winked at Elizabeth and launched into a showy series of consecutive turns and jumps, growling through clenched teeth. His sweat flew all over the stage.

"Ready?" Ryan asked. "Let's do it." He took my hand and led me to the back wing for the finale. Marcus brought Faye up behind us for the entrance. Across the stage in the opposite wing, Mikey waved at me while Rebecca held his other hand and jogged in place. Allison stood behind Rebecca, her arms crossed. Ian smiled and gestured animatedly as he talked to Allison and she just stared at him with a bored expression.

The music changed and we ran onstage on the new phrase, smiling at each other. We spaced ourselves evenly across and Faye, Marcus, Ryan, Rebecca, Mikey, Allison, Ian, and I barreled forward down the stage, our bodies doing exactly the same thing. After sixteen counts of dancing, we ran to the side and posed.

The whole company was happy about the same thing at the same time. No one was angry about casting, depressed over how they looked, envious of someone else, or worried about the future. There was no time or energy to think of anything else while we danced. We dove into the final steps of the ballet, dripping in sweat and faces glowing. The stage shook under all the feet as we executed the choreography in unison.

Faye accidentally knocked me in the eye and my fake eyelash came unglued. I blinked and prayed it would hang on until the end. All I knew was that I had to keep dancing. Stay in line behind Natasha, I told myself. Keep going. Keep going.

Rebecca and Faye danced on either side of me and I forced myself to stay even with them, pushing myself as hard as I could. The curtain fell on a frenzy of dancing as the music came to a dramatic end. Applause exploded over the final drum roll. I hurriedly fixed my eyelash.

We snapped to place as the curtain flew back up and I bowed my head along with everyone else. At the instant the curtain hit the ground again, people ran for the wings.

Ryan grabbed my hand and pulled me backwards because we were the first group to bow. "They loved us, as usual," he whispered. "Congratulations, Anna. Now you're an official member of Los Angeles Ballet Theatre."

"Thanks," I said. My heart filled with pride as I walked forward to curtsy.

The applause continued and the soloists took their bows. I felt Ryan's free hand fiddling with the back of my costume. "Hey. Are you unhooking me? Should you do that?" I squeezed his hand.

"You'll get out faster," he said. I felt his warm breath on my neck.

"Okay," I said, unsure if it was professional behavior to unhook a costume onstage.

Lorenzo led Elizabeth forward, their faces triumphant. The audience rose to its feet. "Bravo! Bravo!" people screamed. Someone threw a bouquet of flowers that landed at Elizabeth's feet. She picked it up and nodded her head graciously towards the crowd.

"Won't the audience notice if my costume falls open?" I whispered as Ryan worked more of the hooks open.

"Hate to break this to you," he said. "We're in the back row. No one looks at us." I glanced up at him and he smiled amiably, oblivious that his comment had made me feel bad.

"Bravo! Bravo!" they shouted.

Lorenzo stepped back as Elizabeth ran to the wing to bring the maestro out on stage.

"When you're onstage, you never know who might be looking at you," I whispered to Ryan.

"True," he said. The last hook on my costume popped open in his hand. "But probably it's your mother and that's it." I resented the way he diminished the importance of my first performance. If Ethan came to the ballet he would look for me in the back. I knew he would.

There was a collective exhale as the curtain fell and Ryan stepped away from me. Dancers streamed past us, heading to the dressing room. I turned to follow the crowd and noticed that every corps costume hung open as we shuffled off the stage. Ryan was right. No one noticed us.

Ryan caught up with Rebecca and put his arm around her shoulder as they walked offstage together. I followed, pulling pins out of my headpiece. Faye caught up to me and we nodded at each other, relieved that we survived our first performance. The artistic staff was deep in conversation by the front wing.

It was like everyone lived life for show. We spent all our time training to be extraordinarily self-aware, practicing the same movements every day for others to observe. As dancers, we were constantly on display, but we rarely spoke to the people watching us or made decisions at work, except about what we did with our own bodies. We were great at following instructions. And yet I struggled with how invisible I felt. I longed to know that at least one person saw the real me. I wondered if our dancing said enough about what we had inside, and even if it did, did that matter if no one noticed those of us in the back row?

Five

Elizabeth has been a principal here a long time, and most of us would kill to look like her. William is obviously infatuated with her and always perks up when she's dancing. I know he admires and respects Adrienne but he doesn't seem to have a romantic interest in her. With Elizabeth it's different. Everyone knows he wants her outside the studio. She's generally nice but hard to get to know, so a lot of us think she's stuck up. I can't say she was all that supportive about my promotion and I think she worried I would get some of her roles. Well that didn't happen because I hurt myself, and since then she's been a lot nicer to me. I hate to think that's the reason. She just plays her cards very close. Elizabeth had a boyfriend outside the company for a while but I think that ended recently. Who knows why but she's always had a thing for Teddy. He's nice, but why would anyone get romantically involved with an alcoholic? He's lucky to have her. She's a big presence in the company and the whole reason people tolerate Teddy's erratic behavior is because they respect her.

Elizabeth: *"I've been fortunate. I was able to move to New York when I was fifteen and train at the School of Ballet New York. I joined Ballet New York when I was seventeen and danced there for three years. It's cliché, but being in BNY was a dream come true. When William took over LABT he asked me to join the company as a principal. I didn't think I'd ever get out of the corps in New York and I knew it was a good opportunity. My family is in the Bay Area too so I liked the idea of moving back closer to them. William was enthusiastic about my dancing and that was good for my ego. I didn't think much of myself when I left New York. Everyone there was thin and gorgeous and special and it was impossible to stand out. I came here and started dancing these amazing roles right away. I was only twenty-one.*

I've had a problem with self-confidence. To actually know you were chosen to do this boosts your self-esteem because the staff believes in you. Also people are looking at you as a soloist and you can show your stuff. When I perform, it's just me. I can do what I want to do. That's helped me shake my fears and worry that people are looking at me to be a little more mature. It's been a blessing for me as a person and a dancer. One of my favorite things is getting flowers on opening night. That's a big deal because it symbolizes so many things, especially your hard work. I hold those flowers and I think, wow, I earned this.

As younger people joined the company I gained seniority and seasoning. I was more confident in my role as a principal dancer. One thing I think is really interesting is to see how excited the younger generation is about ballet. The kids coming in were so passionate and I think the setup here with the windows made us more accessible. They had friends outside the company and their youth and excitement drew people in. I was passionate but never outgoing, I didn't know how to do the outreach except to the seniors who already knew they liked the ballet. That's always a challenge, getting younger people more interested in what is really a classical art. The thing with ballet is that it's really like being a professional athlete. There are a limited number of really great ballet companies, particularly here in the United States, so to get a spot in a big company is really an honor.

For any young girl—or boy, but not as much—if she really wants a ballet career, it has to come from her. She can't be pushed into dancing by a teacher or parent. It has to be a love, because it really is a grueling life, and if it doesn't come from you it isn't worth it. No matter how many times you're told no, if you believe in yourself you can keep going and it gives you a wonderful confidence no matter how many times you are criticized."

All I saw of North Carolina during our visit was the hotel, the theater, and the closest restaurant. I was too tired to care. My skin was raw from the stage makeup, and I realized I hated repeatedly putting all that stuff on and then rinsing it off two hours later. The hairspray refused to come out of my hair, even after three shampoos. My scalp ached from the many bobby pins I used to hold my hair in place. The more I performed, the more I could see that we were in the business of deception. I felt nothing like the smiling and weightless dancer the audience saw when I performed.

The bus dropped the company at the airport. We collected our bags and I groaned because my carry-on was so heavy it hurt my back. People wandered off as soon as they checked their baggage at the curb and I walked in with Stephanie since I sat with her on the bus. We split up at the magazine stand. I wanted food and Stephanie was on a diet.

After downing a lousy airport bagel, I checked my watch and realized I was late for the plane. I ran for the gate, praying I hadn't been so stupid as to miss the flight.

To my relief, the forty-four other dancers and the artistic staff were still there. I hurried over to where Faye, Carolyn, Stephanie, Hilary, and Ian sat in the terminal. Hilary tried hard to make friends on the tour, maybe because she realized that no one wanted to be around her. I never thought that bothered her but maybe I was wrong.

"When does our flight board?" I asked.

"Flight's delayed," Ian said, looking up at me from his cross-legged position on the floor. "You can relax." He patted the floor next to him. "Your bag looks like it's going to explode. Why didn't you send most of your stuff on the truck with the theater cases? They drive the sets, they might as well drive your other stuff too."

"I did send my theater case," I said, embarrassed. "I just packed too much. This is my first tour. How was I supposed to know what I'd need?"

He laughed. "You'll learn."

"Have a seat," Faye said. I dropped my bag and sat down between Ian and Carolyn, who had a needle in her mouth while she stitched ribbons. We were always sewing pointe shoes.

I stared out the window as we waited to board. I liked performing because I was free to dance without the mirror. Years of training gave me an innate sense of right and wrong, but that was the only guide I had. Performing helped me trust my instincts. The mirror that we looked in every day for class and rehearsal was merciless, so there was something wonderful about being free from my reflection.

In Pittsburgh, I felt anxious as I prepared for my first performance of *Violins*. I worked on my hair and makeup for an hour. I wanted to be all ready before I went up to the stage to put on my pointe shoes and stretch. Before I scampered upstairs, I gave myself a long look in the mirror and thought, *don't screw this up.*

"*Merde*, Anna," Faye said, walking up to me in the wing as I did some *tendus*. She had the night off.

"Thanks. Do I look okay?" I looked down at my white leotard, white skirt, and pink tights. It was such a simple and elegant costume. "I've never been onstage for twenty minutes nonstop. Every other ballet I've performed had exits. What if my nose starts to run?"

"Don't wipe it, whatever you do," Faye said. She pulled a loose string off my skirt. "I'm going out to the house to watch from the front."

I wished I could see what I looked like from out front. "Oh, cool. I'll be curious to hear how it looks from out there."

"Sure," said Faye. We watched Allison and Sasha practicing onstage in white costumes identical to mine. They both looked very serious. Hilary came barreling across the stage practicing her *grande jetés*. Sasha jumped out of her way, annoyed.

"Do you think it's a bad sign that I'm not dancing tonight?" Faye asked. "You don't think that means I won't get a corps contract, do you? Hilary said it was weird that I'm off."

I peeled off my leg warmers and threw them under a table backstage. "Don't be ridiculous. You know better than to listen to Hilary. Dancing *Violins* doesn't mean anything. Plenty of people aren't in every ballet." Faye was my closest friend in the company and it would be devastating if she didn't get a contract. "You're doing fine."

"Thanks for the reminder," she said. "I don't know how I would have gotten through the past few months without you."

"Ditto," I said, giving her a hug.

"Five minutes. Five minutes, please," announced Greg over the loudspeaker. He peeked around the wing at Faye and me. "Did you hear that?" He was always meticulous about doing his job.

"Yep," I said. "Thanks." He nodded, adjusted his headset, and walked back to his position in the front wing. William would be standing there in a few minutes when the performance began.

"I'm going out front," Faye said. "Have a good show."

I waved and walked back onstage to continue my warm up. Adrienne and Zif practiced a lift near the curtain. He gently lowered her to the floor and they whispered to each other softly, his hand on her lower back. The whole cast trickled onstage and the seven other corps girls congregated in a circle center stage.

"Anna," Allison called. "Come here. We're having a huddle." She waved me over.

"We need our eighth girl," Rebecca said.

I joined the circle between Rebecca and Whitney. All eight of us linked hands and I caught Hilary's eye across the circle. She gave me a grudging half-smile and I smiled back.

Rebecca and Whitney's hands were warm and I could feel the energy between us. We closed our eyes. In the dark, I felt my breath synchronize with the others and I envisioned us breathing as a team.

"Wait for me," Adrienne interrupted.

"Of course!" Allison said apologetically. "Join." She dropped hands with Hilary to let Adrienne into the circle. Adrienne's presence felt comforting and I was glad she was there. Natasha or Elizabeth would never have joined us.

"*Merde*," Adrienne said as we opened our eyes.

"*Merde*," we whispered.

"Places, please," Greg called from the front wing.

I walked to my spot on stage left. Three girls lined up directly in front of me on the quarter mark. On stage right, the other four formed an identical line.

Allison was my opposite and she caught my eye across the stage. "I'll watch you out of my peripheral vision. Try to stay directly across from me. We sometimes get out of line in rehearsals," she said.

"Okay," I said to her, adding "bossy" under my breath. Allison was always telling me what to do.

Greg's voice boomed over the loudspeaker. "Good evening, ladies and gentlemen. Welcome to this evening's performance. At this time, we ask that you turn off all pagers and cell phones. We would also like to remind you that for the dancers' safety, the taking of flash photographs is not permitted. Thank you. Enjoy the show."

I faced the curtain with my left foot flat in front of my right foot. My toes pointed out into the wings. As I inhaled, I placed my arms in a perfect circle with my fingertips just in front of my thighs. I clenched my teeth and pulled every muscle in my calves, knees, thighs, butt, and stomach up towards the ceiling. At the same time, I pushed my shoulders down and lengthened my neck without swaying my back.

The seven other girls did something similar to prepare their own bodies. Each of us had personal physical intricacies to sort out over years of daily practice, but at that moment, we had to look the same.

Adrienne and Zif pressed their foreheads together for a moment of silence before they walked off the stage to let us open the ballet. Their dancing always seemed deeply connected to their love for each other.

The curtain went up. I saw the conductor illuminated by one small light on the music stand. He raised his baton.

All eight of us bent our knees and launched into the opening steps. The music sounded powerful and immediate. I focused on staying on the counts and making my movements crisp.

We danced into a circle formation and opened out into a line. I took Adrienne's hand. She smelled like sweat mixed with lilac perfume. I turned to let my arm wrap around my torso as I stepped back to face the audience. On the next count, Adrienne offered her other hand to Sasha, who mirrored my movements on Adrienne's other side.

I looked at the people in the front row and the few faces I could make out look deep in thought. For one full count, Sasha, Adrienne, and I stood there locked in our chain of arms. As the music climbed, we raised our right leg behind us to create a chain of *arabesques.* It was my favorite moment in the ballet.

Sasha and I rejoined the corps to walk in one line with our hands joined. We melted into two lines of four across the stage behind the principals. In unison, the entire cast travelled downstage on pointe towards the audience. Everyone bent their knees and jumped. My legs crisscrossed three times in the air. I landed on my right knee at the same moment the music came to an end.

Applause. The curtain fell. I looked over my hand into the front wing and stared right into William's eyes.

Faye greeted me as I came out of the shower in my towel. "You've got to watch from the audience,

Anna," Faye said. Her face glowed. "I was blown away. What we see in rehearsal is nothing…it's different than when we used to go to watch Ballet New York when we were in the school. It's so much better to see your own company."

"I bet," I said, excited to hear that the show looked that good. She seemed genuinely moved.

"Adrienne and Zif were unbelievable," Faye said. "You looked fine. Try to keep your shoulders down. They tend to creep up when you get tired."

"Okay," I said, "Thanks." I was grateful for the feedback. Corrections were a compliment because they meant someone was paying attention. We hungered for our teachers to correct us in ballet school. In the company, if the artistic staff corrected us it was almost always about the choreography or something stylistic, not our basic technique. By the time we became professionals we were supposed to have the basics all figured out, but there was always room for refinement and improvement. There just wasn't much time or energy anymore when there were so many ballets to perform.

I was tired and hungry when we left the theater. The shows drained away energy and left me with a sense of accomplishment. Every time I performed, I wanted to do it more.

George arranged for a restaurant to stay open late just for us, since almost everyone preferred to eat a bigger meal after the show. We needed to be able to hold our stomachs in while we danced. I never ate much before a performance, but often everything closed by the time we left the theater so it was nice of George to look out for us on tour. Eating disorders were a ballet cliché, but honestly, it was impossible to do the job without food. Most of the hard-core anorexics and bulimics I knew in ballet school never made it to a company at all.

Two days later we flew from Pittsburgh to New Jersey. I had a performance off so I could finally watch from the front. Faye wasn't dancing either and we sat in the audience together on opening night. The ballets and the dancers looked markedly different from the house. I never saw half the stuff that happened when I was up there dancing. Even watching from the wings gave a totally different sense of the way the bodies were working—like machines.

From down in the audience, I saw the facial expressions, the way the dancers came across onstage, and how personality quirks appeared in the way people moved. Mikey had sloppy technique and a sleepy smile, Ryan looked energetic and charming, Allison made angry faces and moved harshly, and Rebecca floated through everything like her mind was far away. The principals appeared more mature and complex. Lorenzo was a masculine and powerful presence, Elizabeth appeared elegant but strangely vulnerable, Jeff was intimidating and remote, Natasha was unabashedly overconfident, and Adrienne and Zif looked like royalty. They were all formidable. My hands hurt from clapping when the curtain fell for the last time.

"I wonder what Carolyn did tonight," Faye said as we crossed the street on our way back to the hotel. Carolyn hadn't performed yet on tour and because I still stood next to her at the *barre* every day, I could tell she felt down. Everyone knew Carolyn's situation was bad because the apprentices shouldn't have been dancing more than a senior corps member, and in her case, we were. The only thing Carolyn would perform on the entire three-week tour was one show of *Tidal Moods*. Other than that, she would only get to dance if someone got injured.

"She left at half-hour, before the show started," I said.

"It surprises me that the company would hire someone and not put them onstage," Faye said. "The casting is so imbalanced. Allison does three corps roles in one night when Carolyn doesn't dance at all. The less Carolyn dances, the more out of shape she gets and the harder it is for her to lose weight."

"I know," I said. "I wonder if that's more William's idea or Lila's." The common understanding was that William told Lila which corps dancers he liked and she did all the corps casting. He only bothered with the principals. People were always more frustrated with Lila than with William. She received the brunt of everyone's anger for William's decisions because she worked more closely with us, but we never knew exactly what went on during the artistic staff meetings.

"I'd love to be a fly on the wall when they do the casting," Faye said. "Well, it's good the hotel is so close. Carolyn was stuck at the theater in North Carolina. Here, if someone gets hurt or sick it would only take five minutes for her to run over." If we were off and left at half-hour, it was in our contract that we had to be close enough to get to the theater and be onstage in thirty minutes if someone became sick or injured.

"Right," I said. We both yawned as we stepped into the elevator.

"Press five," Faye said.

From down the hall, a male voice called, "Hold the elevator, please."

I put my hand in the doors and William squeezed through. He still had his black tuxedo on from the evening's performance and his bow tie hung open around his neck. I felt a similar sense of heightened self-awareness that I felt that day on Ethan's front porch. William's presence gave me a sort of thrill.

"Good evening," he said and we nodded politely. "Very nice job tonight, ladies." He smiled at us, running his hand through his thick silver hair. The image of his eyes fixed on mine at the end of *Violins* appeared in my head. Faye studied the floor numbers over the elevator door and said nothing.

"Thank you," I replied, and realized that William didn't know that Faye and I hadn't performed. The doors opened on the fifth floor. "Good night."

"Bye," he replied.

We walked down the hall as the elevator closed and William disappeared.

"Well, then," I said.

"At least he said good job." Faye laughed cynically.

"Does he even remember who we are?"

"Who knows?"

"That's depressing," I said, knowing that either the director thought you "had it" or you didn't. Promotions were often arbitrary and opinion-based. Everyone had great technique and stage presence, so casting depended solely on if William liked you or not. If I wanted to go anywhere in the company, I needed to make sure William at least knew when I danced.

I went to bed feeling discouraged. How could I get Ethan to take me out on a date? How could I catch William's eye? What I needed was Adrienne's secret, whatever it was she did to make everyone fall in love with her.

Six

"*Nutcracker* is awful," Stephanie told Faye and me over dinner at a local brewpub on our first night back in town. "You'll earn every inch of that corps contract you want so much."

"It's that bad?" Faye asked skeptically.

"Thirty-five performances," Stephanie said. "*Nutcracker* is the holiday cash cow. You can never get the music out of your head. Every store you go into plays the Sugar Plum Fairy variation on loop. Dink dink dink, dink dink, dink, dink-dink-dink...There are a hundred screaming kids backstage with their ballet mothers lurking around. In the party scene all we do is stand there. There's no dancing. The guys have to wear those putrid mouse costumes twice a day. The audience isn't the regular crowd that comes throughout the year because they know better. Families come as a holiday thing, or parents of the kids in the show."

"I like *The Nutcracker*," I said. "How can you not appreciate when the tree grows and it snows onstage? It also means we get to be in every single show." The apprentices danced every performance of Snow, Spanish, Waltz of the Flowers, and sometimes Marzipan if we were lucky.

"You're fresh blood," Stephanie said. "Let's talk after the twentieth performance, Anna. Then you tell us how magical *Nuts* is."

"Nice nickname," Faye said.

"*Nutcracker* isn't a real ballet," Stephanie said. "There isn't even real dancing until the second act. If they're going to come to the ballet, people should see something like *Tidal Moods*."

"I hear you," I conceded as our food arrived. There was no arguing with her. The place had started to fill up.

"Hey," I said, "isn't that Ari?"

"It is," Faye said, and I could see the excitement in her eyes. She felt about the Ari the way I felt about Ethan.

"Oh great," Stephanie said, rolling her eyes. "Ryan's surfing sidekick." I raised an eyebrow at her but she didn't say anything further.

Ari spotted us and made his way over to our table. "Seen Ryan?" he asked casually. He had on a ratty t-shirt, an orange knee-length bathing suit, and flip-flops. His bleached hair stuck out in every direction.

"Ryan's not here yet," Faye said. "Rebecca mentioned she was meeting him at seven. They should be here soon."

"He missed some good surf while you guys were on tour," Ari said as he scoped the room. He had a detached manner that made it hard to tell if anything was going on in his head. "How was the trip?"

"Great," Faye said. "The company got amazing reviews." Ari looked at her and offered a lazy half-smile. Her eager face made it obvious how she felt about him; maybe too obvious because he turned to Stephanie. "What's new with you?" Ari asked.

"Nothing," Stephanie said sourly.

Ryan appeared behind Ari and Rebecca followed behind. "Hey man! What's up?" Ryan said. He slapped Ari on the back. "Hi ladies."

"Yo," Ari said to Ryan. "There you are."

"Dude," Ryan said, giving Ari a high-five. "Good to be back." Rebecca waved hi to us and slipped her arm possessively through Ryan's.

"C'mon man, let's get a drink," Ari said, nodding his head towards the bar. Ryan looked at Rebecca and she nodded. Ari called over his shoulder, "Anyone want anything?"

"I do." Faye said. "I'll come, wait up." She practically leaped out of her seat.

"Alright," Ari said, taking a longer look at Faye. "How old are you again? Never mind. Let's do a shot." He took Faye's hand and led her to the bar.

Stephanie and I looked at each other. "Maybe I should say something to her," Stephanie said.

"About what?"

"About Ari," Stephanie said. "He's already been around the company. I dated him and so did Whitney."

"Seriously?" I said. "I didn't know that. I've only met him once." I glanced over at Faye. "What happened?"

"Nothing," Stephanie said, "He's a flake. It was all good and fun as long as I didn't want a relationship. Same with Whitney, I assume. She got involved in that mess more recently than I did. We don't talk about it. I've been done with him for a while and after all of his garbage I swore off dating completely."

"That's a shame," I said, wondering if Ethan was like that too.

Over at the bar, Faye had her arm around Ari's neck and he leaned in to whisper something in her ear. Rebecca and Ryan looked like they were having a serious conversation. I focused on our plate of fries and shoved a few in my mouth. Stephanie looked at me funny. "I think someone is watching you," she said.

"Really?" I said through a mouthful of food.

"Don't be obvious," she said, and of course then I had to turn my head to see where she was looking.

Ethan was there, sitting down with three other guys just a few tables away. When thoughts of him floated in my head, which they seemed to frequently, I felt warm and painfully hopeful. The sight of him confirmed and reinforced those feelings. Stephanie was right, he was looking at me, and our eyes met across the room.

"I know him," I said.

"You do? He looks like a guy who likes dogs and knows how to fix things," said Stephanie. "Hot."

"All that and he designs buildings," I said. "Here he comes."

He ambled up to our table. "Hi Anna," Ethan said, "Nice to see you again." I wondered if he'd been hoping to run into me as much as I wanted to run into him.

"Hi Ethan," I said casually. "This is my friend Stephanie. How's it going?"

"Things are good. I don't mean to interrupt you, I just wanted to check that your head was ok."

"You're not interrupting. It's fine, thanks." I turned to Stephanie, "This is the guy that dropped a branch on my head."

"Oh." Stephanie smirked. "Nice going."

"Not my best moment," he admitted. By then, I had taken a full inventory of his thin blue cotton sweater, khakis, sandals and day-old stubbly cheeks. My ability to talk comfortably with him was already gone. I desperately wanted him to sit down with us and at the same time hoped he would leave. We looked at each other awkwardly. "Well, good to see you," he said. "I better get back to the guys."

"Okay," I said. "See you later." My heart fell as he walked away.

The evening wore on, and while I chatted amiably with Stephanie, I never stopped observing the way Ethan listened to his friends, gave a rare subdued laugh, and slowly downed his meal. Every once in a while he would glance over and catch my eye and we would smile at each other.

"Hey," Faye said, reappearing at our table. "Ari and I are heading out. He wants to lend me a book."

"Faye," I whispered, "Ethan's here."

"What? *The* Ethan?" She subtly turned and followed my gaze.

"He already came over and said hi. You missed it."

"This is so great," Faye said, grinning. "He's cute. Don't leave without giving him your number."

"Faye," Stephanie said, "You know that I used to date Ari, right?"

Faye paused. "No, I didn't." She looked uncomfortable. "Seriously? Are you mad at me? I honestly had no idea. How long ago?"

"Oh no, of course I'm not mad. It's long over," Stephanie said lightly. "Just be careful, ok? He's not looking for a relationship."

"I get it," Faye said, flinching. "Do you mind if I at least see for myself?"

"Be my guest," Stephanie said. "Guys get away with whatever they want."

Faye looked over at Ari beckoning her by the door. "I better go." She waved at us and went to Ari, letting him open the door for her. Stephanie looked decidedly disapproving, despite claiming that she didn't care.

"As if that's not bad enough, I bet Ryan dumps Rebecca for someone else before the season's over," Stephanie said. She motioned to the waiter that our check was ready.

"Why?" I asked. "She seems to really like him."

"That's the kiss of death," Stephanie said. "I know I sound bitter, but it's the truth. Trust me. Are you ready to go?" She slid out of the booth.

"I guess." I glanced over at Ethan's table and saw he was deep in conversation with the guy next to him. There was no way I had the nerve to give him my number, especially not after everything Stephanie had said. I felt silly even hesitating with her eagle eyes on me, so I followed her out so we could walk most of the way home together. Stephanie left me feeling discouraged, and when I walked into my apartment, I found it especially lonely and depressing without Faye.

Ari better treat her right, I thought, and regretted leaving without saying goodbye to Ethan. Maybe I was nobody to him. I desperately wanted someone who would think I was more than just another girl in the corps. I wanted someone who thought I was special, and beyond that, I wanted Ethan to be that person.

Seven

Sasha has only been in the company a year and she's one of the youngest dancers in the corps de ballet. Her technique is rather weak, but she has wonderful stage presence and an unusually confident demeanor for someone her age. She's also one of the ones who always know every count in every ballet, so the other girls always ask her to go over the choreography with them. A lot of people think she's going to have a big career here, but personally, I'd be amazed if she makes it past soloist. She's popular but I don't think she's cutthroat enough.

Sasha: *I feel like I've been in a relationship with ballet for most of my life. I'm from a small town in Virginia and my studio was only ten minutes from my house. I went there since I was two. It was a really small school and I'm the only dancer in the company who didn't come from a big famous ballet institution. William taught a master class in Washington D.C. when I was seventeen and my mom drove me into the city to take with him. After class I asked him if he was hiring. He said he would consider me for an apprenticeship if I flew out to LA and took class with the company. So I did and he offered me a job.*

I like being in LABT but sometimes I feel like I'm missing out on a lot. Our lives are so sheltered and it makes me frustrated. I don't think William takes much notice of me. He's probably glad I'm here to be a solid member of the corps, but he's certainly not taken with me the way he is with Elizabeth. If I knew how to catch his eye I would. We all think that maybe one day out of the blue he'll suddenly look at us differently and say, 'Wow, she deserves more.' It's how we keep ourselves going, that hope. It's not true. How he sees us from the beginning is pretty much how he'll always see us.

The ballet season opened in Los Angeles in November, and before every show William gave a free pre-performance talk. The hard-core patrons rushed to get to the ballet early so they could see William Mason in the flesh. He was greatly admired and the society women savored his every word.

William's voice boomed over the loudspeaker into our dressing room on opening night. "Roizman's point of departure for *Rhapsody* was a student who fell asleep in the corner of the studio," he told the audience. "It was the first ballet he choreographed and he was frustrated at the lack of drive in the dancers, so he challenged them with difficult steps and caricatured their personalities. Roizman let the natural occurrences in the studio become a part of the ballet. One girl walked in late; another girl forgot the steps and gave up; and one was so enraptured with dancing that she couldn't stop. Roizman put it all in the choreography."

"He milks this for all it's worth," Carolyn said, rolling her eyes. She had managed to drop a few pounds and they'd cast her in the matinees that weekend. Most of us were relieved. When one person in the corps was suffering, it affected everyone's morale.

"From there, our program segues into *Georgia On My Mind*," William continued. "The point of departure for this piece is the nostalgia we feel for specific places..."

"If William doesn't stop overusing that 'point of departure' phrase I'm going to scream," said Allison. I laughed, smudging my eye shadow while I was trying to apply it. We mocked him, but we all knew William kept the money coming in with his star power.

Allison flipped her hair over her head and brushed it into a ponytail. She was noticeably bitter towards the artistic staff because she wasn't first cast in one of her roles. I had become increasingly conscious of how much everyone's emotions, including mine, were so dependent on casting. The stakes were higher for the older dancers, so while Faye and I felt grateful we had one performance of one little part for the whole weekend, Allison was furious if she danced every night but wasn't first cast for everything.

Blasting music over my headphones did little to block the world out. I looked tired and pale from working so hard. In half an hour, the girl in the mirror would be made-up, dressed, and smiling like someone without a care in the world. Until then, she looked like someone who was so exhausted all she wanted was to crawl under the covers and fall asleep.

"Now I'd like to open it up to questions," we heard William say to the crowd. This part was interesting and we always liked to hear what the audience asked. The loudspeaker crackled.

"What are the dancers' day jobs?" asked a man from the audience. "What do they do in real life?"

"No!" said Rebecca. "Someone did not just ask that."

"Is that a joke?" Sasha asked.

"Ballet is their day job," William said with a sigh. "Our dancers rehearse and perform for eight hours a day, six days a week." He handled the answer graciously although we knew the question irked him too.

"That question is offensive," Whitney said.

"William, when will you perform with the company?" a woman asked.

Stephanie snorted.

"I don't think you want to see a sixty-year-old man on the stage in tights, so that won't happen anytime soon," he said. "Thanks for asking." William enjoyed that kind of attention and even though we couldn't see him, we knew he had a smile on his face.

"Why does your company focus so much on Roizman ballets?" asked a male audience member. "A lot of us want to see a classic, like *Swan Lake*."

"Oh, brother," said Allison. "He hates those questions."

"My background is in Roizman," William said. "Not to mention that a production of *Swan Lake* with full sets and costumes costs a lot more than a production of *Tidal Moods*." He hated to discuss financial issues. "The dancers in *Tidal Moods* wear leotards and tights. There are no sets. *Swan Lake* requires elaborate costumes and scenery. But hey, let me know if you want to finance it." The audience chuckled at the jab, perhaps taken aback by William's bluntness.

"It's frustrating," Rebecca said. "That people don't understand how much money these productions costs or how hard we work. No wonder ballet companies are broke."

"At least there are so many people that do support us," I said. "The arts always have trouble.

Performing on a shoestring budget comes with the territory."

Another woman in the audience gushed, "Oh William, I remember when you danced the lead in *Fire*. You were like a dream. It's such an honor to see you in person. Do any of the up-and-coming dancers in LABT have that certain, you know, *je ne sais quoi*?"

The dressing room fell silent. I remembered one of my first ballet teachers, Madame Androvichevsky, who had a thick Russian accent. She used to tell my mother, "Anna vil be prima. She vil never be in ze corps," and my mom had quoted her many times over the years, hanging on that line as a mantra or just a reassurance that we were going through all the stress, heartache, and expense for a good reason. If my mom or a dolly-dinkle ballet teacher said something like that, the comment was sweet but could be dismissed. All of us had heard that from our mothers and early teachers. To hear it from William Mason, though, now *that* would mean something.

"We have many talented dancers," William said. "You'll have to watch and pick your favorites this season. I have my eye on a few." He paused and we waited breathlessly, hoping he would be more explicit.

"Thank you for coming today," he finally said. "I hope you enjoy this evening's program." The audience applauded politely and the noise over the intercom reverted to gentle voices and instruments tuning. There was a collective—and audible—exhale in the dressing room.

The company travelled to Palm Springs for the weekend and I took a *barre* spot onstage by Ryan for company class. "Aah, Palm Springs," Ryan mused, resting his elbows on the portable *barre*. "The last time we did *Fire* at this theater, an ambulance was in the parking lot after the show. The ballet was so exciting we gave someone a heart attack."

"For real?"

"Would I make that up?"

Class and tech rehearsal rushed by and I prepared myself for a performance of *Violins* and *Frontiers*. At half-hour I already had my makeup and hair done. Faye sat next to me in the dressing room, staring at her reflection. She looked tired and I knew it was because of Ari. He had even driven her down from LA. They'd been inseparable the last few weeks, so much so that he had come to Palm Springs to watch that evening's performance and keep her company. Whatever Ari's pro surfing gigs were, they weren't happening at the moment. He appeared to be unemployed. I was getting rather tired of him sitting on the couch in our apartment, although he did seem serious about Faye. Maybe Stephanie had been wrong about him.

"I used to always worry I wouldn't find a guy who understood what we do or why we do it," Faye said. "But I think Ari kind of gets it."

All I could do was sigh. I still worried about the same thing. Who didn't? I was about to open my mouth and let all my longing for Ethan pour out, but before the conversation went any further, Ian barged into the dressing room unannounced. "You won't believe what just happened," he said.

"Hey!" said Rebecca. "What if some of us weren't dressed?"

"Whatever, Rebecca," Ian snapped. "I'm gay. Besides, this is important." I had never seen him look so serious about anything and a sick feeling rushed through my stomach. "What's wrong?"

The pre-performance rituals ground to a halt. We were used to Ian coming in our dressing room, but everyone could tell by his tone of voice and facial expression that for once he wasn't there to watch us do our hair.

"Someone got hit by a truck," Ian said. "We were outside smoking and saw the whole thing. One second he's crossing the street, the next, he's lying still and limp in the middle of the road."

"What are you talking about?" asked Faye, snapping out of her reflection-induced trance. I put down my hairbrush.

"We were outside for the pre-show cigarette. A guy cut across the major street behind the theater. We were far away so he was just a silhouette, but he had a backpack, probably a college kid. A huge truck barreled around the corner out of nowhere. The driver didn't see him. Elizabeth screamed so loud I went deaf in one ear."

"You're joking, right?" Rebecca asked.

"It's true," he said. "We watched the whole thing. Lorenzo took off running to try and give him CPR before the ambulance came."

"When did this happen?" I asked.

"Now," he said. "Just now. I ran in here just after it happened. I was too scared to follow Lorenzo over there. Everyone's congregating outside." He gestured for us to follow him out of the dressing room.

The regular smokers were already gathered in the hall. Teddy had his arms around Elizabeth in a protective hug and her slim torso practically disappeared into his wide chest. Jeff was talking fast and gesturing dramatically to Allison. Marcus and Stephanie stood next to each other looking dazed. The door at the end of the hall flew open and Lorenzo came walking in. Carolyn rushed to him. "Are you okay?" she asked.

"Not even close," Lorenzo said. "The ambulance took him away, but he was already dead. He never knew what hit him. Where's Ryan? Where's Faye?"

"They confirmed he was dead?"" Stephanie asked.

"Fifteen minutes, boys and girls," Greg interrupted over the loudspeaker. "This is your fifteen minute call."

"I'm here," Faye said behind me. "Why?"

Lorenzo crossed his arms and steeled his expression. "It was Ari."

Stephanie let out a moan and Faye fell to her knees. The moment seemed to stretch on forever. I hoisted Faye to her feet and tried to steady her. Her body felt like a limp rag. All I could think was that this wasn't right; this wasn't fair; this was a mistake.

I led Faye back to the dressing room and she collapsed in a heap on the floor, sobbing. Thankfully she wasn't in the first ballet. I watched helplessly while she reached for her cellphone and called the hospital.

Ten minutes later the curtain went up. People paid to see the show, no matter what happened in the outside world, and we were professionals. We gave a solid performance of *Violins*. Our bodies move soundlessly through the choreography, using the dance as a vessel for our grief.

There was a funeral for Ari when we returned to LA. I was still in a state of disbelief and shock as we stood on the outer circle behind his family and the surfing community. I hardly knew him and felt awkward being there. Faye wanted to attend but seemed uncomfortable too. Ryan, Rebecca, Ian, Allison, Jeff, Lorenzo, and Carolyn were the other dancers present. Stephanie opted not to come.

Ari was the first young person I knew who had died, and his was the first funeral I ever attended. His death had been so sudden.

Faye reached for my hand and we clasped fingers. "I don't want to be alone," she whispered while Ari's mother gave a tear-filled eulogy. "I know," I said, bowing my head. I wanted to say something more that would help ease her grief, but the right words wouldn't come.

We both found it so hard to look at Ryan's face. He had known Ari the longest and the best. In the harsh sunlight, he looked strangely pale and lost. In the days since Ari had died, everyone suddenly had memories of him to share, so much that it almost seemed we were pretending we knew him better than we actually did. Ryan had said nothing. He looked like his grief kept hitting him again and again, like waves.

The *Nutcracker* grind began the day after Thanksgiving, making it impossible for most of us to go home for the holiday. Carolyn invited Faye, Ian, and me over for dinner at her place and she and Lorenzo cooked the turkey. We had a nice, mellow evening.

Stephanie was right about one thing: *Nutcracker* may have been fun to dance in as a kid, but as a company member, it was a circus. I had been in the *Nutcracker* since I was nine and knew I'd always feel nostalgic about it, no matter how crazy things became. There were so many dancers I looked up to in my old hometown production, and it was strange to have become one of those older dancers. I felt a responsibility to make the experience fun for the kids, the same way generations before had done for me.

The *Nutcracker* story centers around a young girl names Marie (sometimes called Clara) who receives a Nutcracker from her Uncle Drosselmeyer at a party on Christmas Eve. After everyone has left, she sneaks out of bed and falls asleep under the Christmas tree holding her gift. She has a strange dream that night. Drosselmeyer reappears and makes the Christmas tree grow to an enormous height. Her Nutcracker and toy soldiers come to life to do battle with some evil mice, led by the Mouse King.

The Nutcracker and the Mouse King engage in a sword fight, and Marie throws her slipper at the Mouse King and helps the Nutcracker defeat him. After their victory, Drosselmeyer turns the Nutcracker into a handsome prince.

The prince takes Marie on a magical journey through the Land of Snow and to the Kingdom of the Sweets, where the Sugar Plum Fairy welcomes them to her court. The characters of the court perform for Marie and her prince, and at the end, the prince takes Marie home in a sleigh. She wakes up and marvels at her incredible dream.

The story of the *Nutcracker* was ridiculous and yet, an audience favorite year after year. There were many parts for children and it was such a holiday cash cow that no company could afford not to perform *Nutcracker*. More than any other ballet, *Nutcracker* was an intrinsic part of all dancers' lives.

On opening night, I sat on the couch onstage before the curtain went up. Marcus, dressed like an army general for the opening party scene, came over to me, his mustache hanging crooked off his upper lip.

"Lookin' good, Grandma," he said. "Who's your Grandpa?"

"Mikey." I looked down at my nineteenth-century purple dress. With all the heavy makeup and my silver wig, I looked like an eighty-year-old woman. When I'd first been cast as Grandma I'd resented the role. The taller girls played the mothers in the party scene and wore beautiful gowns. Now that I was there in full get-up, it was actually kind of fun to be a quirkier character.

"You know they like you if they think you have what it takes to be Grandma on opening night," Marcus teased.

"Gee, thanks," I said and rolled my eyes.

When the overture began, I stood in the wings and waited for my Grandpa to show up for our entrance. Mikey had been the Grandpa in the party scene for years.

A little girl in ringlets and a pink dress came up to me. She was probably ten and played the role of the grandchild. "Are you my Grandma?" she asked.

"Yes," I said, "I'm the youngest grandma you'll ever have." She laughed and skipped over to her friend. I remembered being that girl. Her eager face, brimming with potential, was one of the reasons I loved the *Nutcracker*. She'd have lifelong memories of the experience.

Mikey appeared just in time for the cue, and we made our entrance. Most of our choreography involved sitting on the couch and smiling at the children. As soon as we sat down, Mikey pretended to fall asleep. The little boy who played Marie's brother unexpectedly puked onstage during the soldier dance. I felt bad for him, but it was so hard not to laugh, especially when Rebecca, who was the maid, had to go over and clean it up. She hurried offstage with puke on the bottom of her apron and a look of disgust on her face. The Grandfather's Dance marked the end of the party scene and Mikey led me to center stage for our few counts of shuffling. I kissed my "grandkids" goodbye and hobbled off into the wing.

The minute I came offstage I ripped my wig off. People cleared out of my way as I rushed down the stairs. I dreaded this part of the ballet. The corps girls' dressing room was far away from the stage and the heeled character shoes I wore as Grandma made it hard to run fast. I could do anything in pointe shoes, but high heels were not so easy.

By the time I made it to the dressing room I had taken off all my purple accessories. A female dresser unhooked my purple dress while I frantically scrubbed off my old lady makeup. The costume fell off and I hopped out of it. The new layer of makeup to make me young and pretty went on next. I raced to fix my bun where the wig had messed up my hair. I rushed as fast as I could, scared I might not make my next entrance. The rest of the girls were already upstairs for Snow scene. I heard the Fight scene music over the intercom and knew time was running out.

With only a few minutes to go, I jammed pins into my tiara to anchor it to my head, put on my pointe shoes, changed my earrings, put on my silver tutu, waited for the dresser to hook my costume, and ran for the stairs. When I appeared in the wing, the snow was already falling onstage. I was freezing cold, panicked, and miserable, but I had made it.

Allison led my line of snowflakes onstage. Paper snow flew up my nose and into my throat and I held on to my silver wands with a death grip. Faye dropped one of her wands and Sasha kicked it offstage. Snow was my favorite scene and despite the chaos, I enjoyed being part of it.

In the second act, I changed costumes between the Spanish Dance, Waltz of the Flowers, and then back to my Spanish costume again for the finale. By the time the heroine Marie and her Prince flew away in the sled, I had used up every ounce of my energy. I was as tired from the constant change of identity as I was from the dancing.

After we showered and put on our street clothes, Faye and I left the dressing room together. As we reached the stage door, Greg, the stage manager, walked over. "Anna," he said, "you have a fan letter."

"I do?"

"Here," he said, handing me a note, folded and obviously scribbled on the back of a program. "Some guy dropped this off for you right after the curtain came down. He said he couldn't stay but wanted you to know he was here."

"Thanks," I said. Greg nodded and hurried back to the crew.

"Open it," Faye urged. I unwrapped the note.

Hey Anna,
   You looked great tonight. I brought my ten and twelve-year-old niece and nephew to the show and they loved it. It was amazing to see you up there. I'm sorry I couldn't stay to talk to you in person and I know this is a busy time of year for your company. Hopefully we'll cross paths again soon. Happy holidays.
   Best, Ethan

I couldn't believe he had come and left me a note—that note. He still thought about me. I wondered if he still thought about *dating* me. I was so disappointed that I had missed seeing him.

Faye clapped her hands. I hadn't seen her smile like that in ages. "I knew it," she exclaimed. "He likes you as much as you like him."

"Do you think so?" I asked, giddy he'd seen me perform, even if I had been dressed up as a grandma. "He didn't leave his number."

Faye shook her head at me. "It's obvious."

"Once Nutcracker is over, I have to find a way to run into him again. How am I going to manage that?"

"We'll figure it out," said Faye, grinning.

On Christmas Eve, I stood onstage before the curtain rose on our twentieth performance of *Nutcracker*. We'd given two performances a day for the past two weeks. Marcus walked over in his army general costume, his mustache still hanging crooked off his upper lip. The performance ran perfectly by this point in the run, down to a science. I didn't understand how people could stand to dance the same thing night after night on Broadway for years. The repetition wore on me and I had become bored with the whole show.

We were all in a festive mood and I had gone a little crazy on the makeup. If I crossed my eyes, I could see the giant mole I had painted on my nose. I had even glued a few eyelash hairs in it.

"Linado. That's repulsive," Marcus said, chuckling.

"Not any worse than this." I held up my right hand, which had a sixth finger. "I found this fake finger at a Halloween store." We grinned at each other.

Mikey appeared dressed for Grandpa. "Here we go again," he said. He bowed and led me into the wing as the overture began.

As the party scene continued, Rebecca, in character as the maid, carried on a tray of drinks for the choreographed toast. For Christmas Eve, Ian had filled them with champagne.

Sasha, as Marie's mother, held my arm as I tottered over to the couch and put my purse on Mikey's seat next to me. He sat down a moment later and the whoopee cushion inside deflated with a bang, right in time to the music. Ian, Marcus, and Sasha were close enough to hear it and erupted with laughter. Everyone was having fun. As I rushed off for my quick change after the party scene, William and Lila were in the wings and they were laughing too.

At intermission, we were giddy with anticipation for the holiday and the dressing room buzzed with energy. "Christmas Eve is always my favorite *Nutcracker* performance," Carolyn said as she pinned in her headpiece for Waltz of the Flowers.

The door to the dressing room flew open and Lila walked in. It was a rare appearance. She always spoke to us up by the stage, never while we were changing. Most of us spent the intermission picking paper snow out of our hair and the last thing we wanted to deal with was a member of the artistic staff.

"This is a professional ballet company," Lila said in an angry tone. "You do not have the right to take liberties with the party scene. If anything like that happens again, someone's going to get fired." The threat hung in the air as she took the time to glare around the room. My mouth twitched, but I knew the worst thing I could do at that moment was laugh. I bit the inside of my cheek.

I don't know how we had developed the urge to challenge Lila's authority. Maybe because we were so burned out by *Nutcracker*, we had reached the point of not caring. Lila was smart enough to know she was losing control of us, and I knew deep down we'd been inappropriately silly for a professional ballet company. It was beneath us. Even though we knew the rules, we were just kids. Once in a while, we just desperately wanted to goof around.

Needless to say, the second act was a much more somber affair. I left the theater feeling ashamed.

I flew home to Rock Island for five days after *Nutcracker*. All I did was eat, sleep, and read Karina's journal. My parents' familiar presence had a nurturing effect. Sometimes, I didn't realize how exhausted I was until I stopped dancing for a few days.

Adrienne is hard to get to know because she and Zif seem to live in their own private world. I was surprised at what she told me since she's always upbeat in public. I would never have guessed she felt poorly about herself.

Adrienne: *"I'm still not always sure I'm cut out for ballet. I could stand to weigh a little less and have a smaller chest. Dancer thin is not like thin on the street. We're talking about fifteen percent below the ideal weight for your height, which is basically an anorexic weight. If your career is on the line, if the roles are on the line, whether or not you will ever reach that ideal, you will do practically anything. When I look in the mirror on bad days, I see somebody who is fat and ugly and a disappointment."*

We opened *Elements* in Los Angeles in January. *Elements* had three sections: *Earth, Wind,* and *Fire,* and on my birthday I danced in the corps of *Fire* for the first time. *Fire* was still my favorite ballet and the lead was still my dream role, the one I understudied but didn't get to perform in the SBNY workshop. I was just thrilled to be in the corps. The choreography was even more fun to dance than it was to watch.

I studied Adrienne and Zif from the wings as they performed the *Fire pas de deux*. Their lives looked perfect to me. I couldn't understand how someone as incredible as Adrienne could feel the way Karina described in her journal. It was the saddest thing I'd ever heard. If even Adrienne couldn't feel adequate, how could I hope to be good enough?

"Hi," Faye whispered from behind me. She had changed since Ari's death. Even if she could forgive herself for being the reason Ari had been in Palm Springs, it wouldn't bring him back. She had gone to see a therapist and that seemed to be a good thing.

"I've been meaning to ask you," Faye started, "when you're going to find Ethan."

My heart skipped a beat. I'd been wondering the same thing myself. It was unlikely I was going to be lucky enough to casually run into him, and the more time that went by the less I felt like I knew him at all. The only real option was to walk right up to his front door and knock. Then what would I say?

"I'll do it soon," I said, knowing Faye was tired of my cowardly excuses.

"We'll do it tomorrow on our day off," she said firmly, and even though I was scared, I was grateful for her conviction.

Faye practically pulled me down the street towards Ethan's house the next morning. She marched me right up his front walk and rang the bell. I was amazed at her confidence. "I don't regret the time I spent with Ari," she said. "But you might regret all the time you wasted not being with Ethan." There was no arguing with that.

We heard a rustle after a moment and Ethan cracked the door. To my great relief, his face lit up when he saw me. "Hi," he said, pushing the door open wide. "What are you doing here?"

The reality of Ethan was jarring after imagining him in my mind for so long. My memories hadn't done him justice. I had forgotten how ruggedly handsome he was—it didn't seem possible that he could be even more attractive in the flesh.

"Hey," I said. "We were in the neighborhood and I've been meaning to thank you for the note you left after the *Nutcracker*. I hope we're not interrupting. This is my friend Faye. Today is our day off and we're on our way to brunch. Want to join us?" I gave the speech so fast I ended up sounding like a deflating balloon.

He gazed at me, concentrating, as if trying to read my thoughts. "Well, I have a lot of work to do today, but I guess it can wait. A guy needs to eat."

"Absolutely," Faye said. I couldn't believe this was really happening.

"Come in for a sec," Ethan said. "I have to find my shoes." We stepped past him into the foyer while he rummaged in the front closet. The house still had his mother's touch, with doilies and wallpaper in the dining room. "Don't worry, I'm working on changing up the interior style," he said apologetically. I laughed because the décor only emphasized his masculinity. "Ready?" he said, holding the front door open.

As we walked to the restaurant, Ethan remained silent. "Tell us about your job," Faye urged. "We so rarely get to hang out with non-dancers." I was eager to hear more and waited quietly, grateful Faye could fill the gaps when I felt so tongue-tied.

"There's not much to tell," he said. "It's a lot of problem-solving and figuring out how to get buildings up to code. I like managing projects and seeing a building through to completion. I'm still pretty new, so it's all a learning process."

We settled into a corner booth, surrounded by the smell of fresh bakery and coffee. Faye and I shared a bench and Ethan sat comfortably across from us.

"So tell me what life in the ballet company is like," he asked. "I'm curious. It's a whole different world. Is it as competitive as it seems? How did you get into it?"

"Probably more," Faye said. "Where do we even start?" She looked at me expectantly, and I realized I was going to have to say something or he was going to think I was trying to fix him up with Faye.

"The company is great," I said, "It's just a lot of hard work and yes, it's very competitive."

"Some of the moves you did in *The Nutcracker* were pretty crazy," he said, focusing on me. "How did you get serious about it? How does someone actually become a ballerina?"

I paused and looked at Faye. She waited for me to continue. ""Has anyone ever told you that you ask a lot of questions?" I asked, feeling put on the spot.

"You're the first," he said, his voice husky. "I must find you interesting."

I did my best to remain immune to his charm and struggled not to show he was winning me over. "Fine. Well, I started dance classes by the time I was three. Every year I just got more and more serious about ballet and started going away for six-week summer sessions when I was thirteen. I stayed at the School of Ballet New York for my junior year of high school. Faye and I were in the same class. I wanted to join Ballet New York but I didn't grow tall enough. The girls who were too fat could at least starve themselves or whatever, but if you're not tall enough, you're just not tall enough. Fortunately all the directors in the country come to the school's annual workshop, and William offered me a job after he saw me perform. Faye got in too so we started at the same time. We have an apartment together."

"I see," he said, his voice filled with admiration. "I didn't realize there was a height requirement."

"Well, some companies are taller than others," Faye said. "You can't have a row of swans with one swan three inches shorter than the rest in the middle of the line. It looks terrible. LABT is a shorter company."

"That makes sense," he said. For a moment we stared at each other and I felt an actual *pull* in his direction. That's how strong our attraction was—it was practically a magnetic force. "So how much do you dance now?"

"Oh, about eight hours a day, six days a week, I'd say, sometimes more with performances," I said. "It's pretty brutal."

"That sounds crazy." He looked vulnerable then, like he was processing how different we were than normal people. "You must really love what you do."

"Yes," I said. "You have to or there's no way anyone would do it." I put a forkful of pancakes in my mouth.

Ethan grinned. "I'm glad to see you eat."

"Anna has no problem eating," Faye said with a laugh. She knew I ate more than twice what she did and still weighed less. The conversation turned after that, and I was relieved to have the dynamic move beyond the getting-to-know-you interview. The three of us compared favorite bands and movies, analyzed a congressman's recent affair, and lamented the death of indie bookstores. When the check came, Ethan swept it up before either of us had the chance. "Let me," he insisted, waving away our gratitude.

"I'll get the next one," I offered, and immediately regretted the presumption when I saw a cloud pass over his face.

"I'm afraid it'll be awhile then," he said, "My work is sending me to Switzerland for the next year. Can I take you up on that when I get back? You might be too busy with new boyfriends by then." He said it to both of us and at first I thought I hadn't heard right. Maybe Faye was the one who he was interested in? Had he said *Switzerland*? Seriously?

"Oh no," Faye said. "Hang on, I'll be back in a minute." She made a quick exit for the ladies' room.

The disappointment must have shown on my face because Ethan reached across the table and grabbed my hand. "Hey," he said, lowering his voice. "Forget the Switzerland thing for a second. If I weren't leaving town, would you go out on a real date with me? Without bringing a bodyguard?"

"I thought you said I was too young for you," I said.

"You are," he said, "but I think that's beside the point."

"Then yes, I would." My hand started trembling and I pulled it away. I hugged myself with my arms, wishing I could curl up in a ball and cry.

He let go of me and let out a heavy sigh. "You don't want me, Anna," he said.

"Why did it take you so long to ask me out?" I asked. "I'd been hoping you would since we first met and it's been over six months. Why did you leave the theater before I came out that night? Why did I have to be the one to come back to you?"

He put his head in his hands and ran his fingers through his thick dark hair. "I don't know," he said, staring down at the table. The anguish in his voice was unmistakable. "I was stupid. I thought you would say no. You seemed like you were so wrapped up in your ballet life. I regret it now."

"I'm not so wrapped up that I didn't notice you," I said. "I've never met anyone like you. When do you leave?"

"Thursday night on the red-eye."

"You're kidding, right? Shouldn't you be packing or something?" I was amazed he'd come out to brunch like this. That's when I realized just how much he must like me.

"Yes, I should be packing, but I wasn't going to pass up the opportunity to spend time with you."

"Oh," I said breathlessly. I had never felt a man look at me the way Ethan did. He made me feel like I could be his whole world if that was what I wanted.

I saw Faye coming back out of the corner of my eye, so I quickly grabbed a pen and scribbled my phone number and email. "Here," I said, shoving the napkin across the table. "Why don't you stay in touch? Assuming I get my company contract for next season, I'll still be here when you get back."

He took the napkin without taking his eyes off mine. We were still staring at each other silently when Faye reached the table.

"Ready?" she asked. We nodded. Outside the restaurant, Ethan gave us both a hug and we thanked him for brunch. We parted ways with so many unspoken words hanging between us. Faye and I headed off to catch a matinee at the movie theater, and as soon as the lights went down in the theater, I let the tears roll down my cheeks. I knew with my schedule of rehearsals and evening performances that I wouldn't be able to see Ethan before he left.

His email appeared in my inbox later that night. *Don't forget me.*

In the middle of March, George announced that next season's contracts were going out in the mail. Faye and I were a wreck all week. No one had said a word to us about how we were doing and we didn't know if William and Lila liked us. All we knew was that they had let us perform.

Faye pulled the envelopes out of the mailbox a few days later. My hands shook when I reached to take mine. "So if you don't get a corps contract, what's your plan?" Faye asked.

"I don't know," I said. "I guess I'd look into college." I felt sick at the thought. "Or maybe I'll try to audition for other companies, but it's too late to audition this year. I'd have to move home and try to stay in shape for nine months. What would you do?"

"No idea," she said. "This year has been so hard I can't think beyond the next day. Let's find out."

We ripped open our envelopes. To my relief, I pulled out a full-fledged corps de ballet contract with my name on it. When I raised my eyes to meet Faye's she smiled at me. We had both made it.

"Congrats on your contract," Ian whispered to me across the *barre* before class. "I'm glad you and Faye and Hilary got them. You all deserved it."

"Thanks."

"Adam didn't get one," Ian continued. "William is forcing him to retire."

"I can't believe that," I said. "Adam has been in the company for twenty-one years. It's sad for him to leave this way."

"Well, probably better than William letting him dance past his prime so the audience remembers him as an old man."

"I guess."

"Carolyn got hers," Ian said. "I guess they decided she lost enough weight. Did you know Stephanie got promoted?"

"I heard. She did the roles, she earned a promotion."

"Yeah," he agreed. "Can you believe Whitney's leaving? I don't think she even knows what she's doing next."

"I didn't know about Whitney. Wow. That's brave." Whitney had been in the corps for seven years and had lost her momentum. Still, it was sad.

"She's moving back home to Idaho to live with her parents," Ian said. "She must have been really unhappy."

I looked at Whitney across the room, quietly tying the ribbons on her pointe shoes. I felt like I didn't know her at all and couldn't imagine making that decision. I admired her courage to move on. It was amazing how the hierarchy could change with such ease. In the company, we were whatever William said we were. In the world outside, maybe we could be whatever we wanted.

The company contract didn't mean financial security. The season only lasted thirty-five weeks out of the year and we were unemployed for the remaining seventeen weeks. In Europe, most dancers danced all year and didn't have layoffs. They were lucky to have such steady employment. For us, as well as the other companies in the United States, we had no salary during the breaks. Everyone collected unemployment.

The energy at work lagged the last few weeks of the season. With Ethan gone and no further emails between us to sew up that hole in my heart, there wasn't much left to motivate me. I vowed to forget about him and focus hard on my career. The dancers were less serious and more carefree in class and rehearsals, like kids about to end the school year. Allison and I were the last ones out of the dressing room on the final day.

"What are your plans during the layoff?" I asked her.

"Oh," Allison said, "The usual. My family only lives an hour away so I'll go see them for a few days. I'm going to do a road trip to Seattle with some old friends too."

"That sounds nice," I said. "I need to find something to do after I get back from visiting my parents in Rock Island. That'll get old fast. Do you ever get another job?"

"No," Allison said. "I tried that my first year. It was a waste. Waitressing paid less than unemployment and I needed time to take class. Just because we're laid off doesn't mean we don't need to keep up our technique. William would be furious if we came back totally out of shape. The principals are lucky and usually have gigs lined up. Jeff has one for a week with Ballet Nevada and I was hoping he could get me a job there too, but it didn't work out this time. I have to keep taking class regardless. Miss one day and you know. Two days your teacher knows. Three, everyone knows."

"Ouch," I said, knowing she was right.

Faye and I packed up our apartment. Our nine-month lease was up, and we had decided to get our own places. We both needed somewhere to get away from work. Since we would both be in the corps next season and making a little more money, separate rents would be manageable.

I went home to Rock Island for three weeks and took class at my old ballet school. They invited me to teach a few classes too. It was a nice break and good to see my parents. By the time my visit ended, I felt refreshed and ready to go back.

Eight

My layoff days in LA started with morning ballet class. The senior company members took turns teaching class during the break, depending on who was in town. In the afternoon, I went to the beach and swam, and at night I read novels or hung out with whichever friends were around. The slower pace was a welcome change, even if I felt anxious from time to time about what I was doing with my life.

On the first day back to work, I stopped at the bulletin board to check the schedule. There was a rehearsal for *Afternoon Symphony* at noon that listed every corps girls' name except mine. "Allen, Linado," appeared next to the two-thirty *Afternoon Symphony* rehearsal. *Afternoon Symphony* wasn't on the performance schedule until the end of February, eight months away.

"Allen" meant Natasha Allen, so I was called to a rehearsal at lunchtime with a principal. I still didn't know Natasha very well. Lorenzo and Jeff joked around with her the most, but she rarely talked to Elizabeth and Adrienne and all her conversations with the corps dancers were just a litany of complaints. I wasn't even sure she remembered my name.

I had seen *Afternoon Symphony* once during my first year at SBNY. It was a Roizman ballet and there were twelve corps girls, a principal couple, and one female soloist. The soloist role was all complicated footwork and impressive leaps. It was exactly the kind of part they always cast Natasha in because she had a huge jump and beautiful feet.

After class, I had two hours off because all the other girls stayed for the *Afternoon Symphony* corps rehearsal. It was my first day as a full member of the corps de ballet and it felt strange not to be at the corps rehearsal.

I passed by Hilary as I was leaving the studio. "Have a nice break," she sneered, giving me an icy look. I smiled awkwardly.

At two twenty-five I walked into one of the small studios and started to warm up. Natasha appeared at two thirty-one. "It's been a few years since I danced this," she said, switching on the screen at the front of the room so we could watch the opening to *Afternoon Symphony*. She was the soloist on the film. "I think this performance is from four years ago," she said, pulling her hair back into her usual ponytail.

After we watched, she walked to the center of the room to start teaching me the steps. I followed and stood behind her.

"So you have eight counts to walk in," she said. I nodded and we dove right in to learning the choreography. The time flew as we worked. She taught me the entire role in fifty minutes, and at three twenty-five she asked, "Want to run it for me once?"

"Sure," I said. My brain felt overwhelmed with musical counts, arm positions, and the sequence of the steps. When I learned corps roles, at least I could confer about the choreography or go over counts with my friends. Not anymore. I was on my own.

I walked to the back of the studio and Natasha stood at the front. She hit play and we counted to eight together. She quit counting then and I danced the role for her the best that I could remember it.

At the end she nodded and hit stop on the music. "Not bad," she said, looking pleasantly surprised. "You'll have to practice the *brisés*. At least now it's in your head."

I nodded and practiced a few more *brisés*, a small jump where I crossed my back leg in front of my front leg, bending over my extended legs while I was in the air and returning the leg to the back and straightening up as I landed. I needed to start thinking about style and musicality.

I thanked her and left for my next corps rehearsal, feeling confident I could work hard and do the part well. My legs weren't as powerful as Natasha's, but my jump was light and would bring a different quality to the choreography. It was a luxury to not have to worry about staying in line. I would finally have the opportunity to show off what made my dancing special.

Carolyn and Stephanie invited me to lunch. We picked an outdoor café and basked in the nice weather.

"I never got to say congratulations on your contract," Carolyn said.

"Thanks. I am so relieved. You too. And congrats, Stephanie, on your promotion."

"Thank you," said Stephanie. She looked content these days.

"Well deserved," Carolyn said. "I was feeling good too, until William sent me the letter."

"The letter?" Stephanie asked.

"Oh, you know," said Carolyn. "The same as all the other letters—that I have an unacceptable aesthetic line. I've been getting them for ages. At least he didn't threaten to fire me this time. I'm so tired of it."

"What do they want from you?" I asked. "You already lost weight this year. What does Lorenzo think of all this?"

"Oh, he's frustrated for me," she said. "But after a certain point there's only so much I can do. I don't want to go to another company, and if I'm as fat as William thinks how could I even get another job?"

"That's not true," Stephanie said.

"Isn't this a lawsuit waiting to happen? Remember that dancer in Boston who died from anorexia? I thought her family tried to sue the company for telling her to diet."

Why did William hire Carolyn if he didn't like what she could offer? He could ascertain her body structure in one glance. She was bigger-boned and womanly, but she wasn't fat by any means, and her shape wasn't going to change all that much no matter how little she ate.

"I remember," Carolyn said. "The family didn't win the case, and she was already dead. Let's face it, a lawsuit is a good way to get blackballed from every ballet company on earth."

"I can't argue with that," Stephanie said.

"True."

"Anyway," Carolyn said. "Congrats to you, Miss *Afternoon Symphony*. Looks like you're William's new favorite."

"I'm not so sure about that, but thanks," I said, embarrassed to be talking about my opportunity.

"You are," Stephanie said. "That's how things started happening for me."

"Were you nervous when you did your first soloist role?" I asked.

"Of course," Stephanie said. "William stood right in the front wing and everyone was watching. I felt prepared and had rehearsed a lot. Actually, I was proud of myself. I worked hard and just tried to be in the moment and savor it. That's what performing is, just being in the moment every second we're out there. We have to be more alive than anyone in the audience. People live through us when we're up on the stage and it's our job to make watching us worth their time."

"Exactly," Carolyn said.

"It's not about who can do the steps, because we all can," said Stephanie. "Ballet school is about perfecting our technique before we get here. William doesn't have time to teach us how to dance."

I nodded. I was surprised at my own reluctance to be seen as a rising star, even though it was what we all dreamed about. My heart filled with reservations. Responsibility came along with the opportunity, and it was up to me to prove I deserved it.

"Once you perform a soloist role, you have to become more than just a dancer," Stephanie said, taking a sip of her iced tea. "This is going to help turn you into an artist. Dancers in the corps learn how to stay in line, blend in, and be a part of something larger than just their own dancing. But principals know the art of individuality and self-expression in front of thousands of people. Honestly, I was only afraid before I walked onstage. You can't be a shivering chicken. If you want to be good, don't care what other people think."

"You can't think about anyone else," agreed Carolyn. "If I took all the negative things William and Lila said to me to heart, I wouldn't be here now."

"I worry that I'm not good enough," I admitted.

"We all do. Get over it. That's not your concern, and it's not for you to decide," said Stephanie. "All you get is the knowledge that William picked you. He doesn't have to, you know. There are plenty of other girls waiting—"

"I know— "

"You're the one he picked, Anna," Carolyn said. "You have a natural quality on stage. Even as an apprentice you stood out in the corps, always eager and passionate about what you were doing. Just work hard and wait. Don't care too much if the others hate you. There will be a long time when you feel like nothing comes together, and then one day it will. William knows what he's doing. He's been in this business a long time."

After a grueling *Nutcracker* run, I spent New Year's in LA with my friends. On the first day back in January we had a complete rehearsal of *Afternoon Symphony*.

"We'll run the first cast to start," Lila said, her pen and paper poised to note every mistake. "If there's time we'll run the second cast."

I stretched on the side while the corps danced the opening. Natasha was first cast of the soloist role and when her entrance came I marked behind her in the back of the room. I didn't have enough room to dance full out so I concentrated on my arm positions.

William strode into the room during the first cast run-thru and took a seat in the front by Lila. He crossed his arms and stared intently while Adrienne and Zif danced the *pas de deux*.

We grew more serious with William's arrival because the rehearsals seemed much more like a performance when he was around. Lila inspired fear because she yelled at us, but William inspired respect.

As the first cast finished the run through, I started to warm up again. "Second cast, from the top," Lila said. "Elizabeth and Jeff in the *pas de deux*. Anna as the soloist."

I nodded, trying to pretend William wasn't watching. My nerves were even worse than before a real performance.

The corps girls danced the opening while I jogged in place. My heart beat faster as the music to my part began and I made my entrance, posing in the center of the room. I had never danced front center with the company. Everyone was watching. It was the first time many of the dancers had paid attention to me since I joined the company.

I had thought about the role frequently over the past six months. At night in bed, I visualized it before I fell asleep. When I ate dinner alone in my apartment, I watched the DVD. Except for Natasha, no one had seen any of my work to prepare.

I moved my body through choreography I had studied diligently and internalized. William watched me closely. The movements weren't entirely comfortable yet and halfway through I became painfully physically tired. Thinking about and marking the steps was different than dancing the role full out without stopping. By the end, I felt myself slipping behind the music. My mind understood the role, but my body needed to build the stamina.

When my section ended, I walked off the floor and tried to catch my breath. Faye smiled at me encouragingly. I did my best to appear calm and confident, but inside I was a ball of nerves, longing for approval. To hide my anxiety, I made a production out of stretching out my calves while the corps finished the section. I glanced out the window, and to my amazement, there was Ethan. He waved and gave me the thumbs up. I smiled and waved back.

The events of the day overwhelmed me. How could he be back with so little fanfare? It was hard to believe it had been a full year, but my ballet life was so full that time sped by. I had thought of him less and less the longer he'd been gone, but when I experienced a longing for romance, it was always his face that appeared in my head. As much as I hated to admit it, I still liked him more than anyone I'd met while he'd been gone.

"Pretty good, Anna," Lila said, stopping the music at the end of the section. "Pretty good. Let's talk about those *brisés*." She beckoned me to her to go over corrections. I braved a glance at William and he gave me the briefest of smiles. I looked away, embarrassed, and when I looked back again his expression had turned as impassive as ever.

When the rehearsal finished, I gestured to Ethan to come around the back. I walked out into the alley still wearing my dance clothes and pointe shoes. He was waiting with his hands in his pockets.

"Hi stranger," Ethan said. "Good to see you again." He opened his arms tentatively.

I didn't hesitate and threw my arms around him in a giant hug. "You're back!"

"You were impressive in there," he whispered in my ear. It was the most meaningful compliment I had heard in ages.

"Your timing is perfect," I said. "You showed up just in time for the first rehearsal of my first soloist role."

"I suspect it won't be your last." He pulled back to look in my eyes.

"Thanks."

The door flew open and Hilary, Sasha, and Rebecca walked out on a break. I disentangled myself quickly, embarrassed, while they gave Ethan a full once over. In that moment, I saw him through their eyes, a normal good-looking guy. He noticed the excitement over his presence, but not in an obnoxious way. His manner implied he felt fortunate to be there.

"Hi," Hilary announced loudly.

"Hi," Ethan said, smiling politely at her.

"Who's your friend, Anna?" Sasha asked.

"This is Ethan," I said. "He's been away working in Switzerland for the year and he just turned up out of the blue. Isn't that nice?"

"Well hello, Ethan," Hilary said in a suggestive tone that irritated me. They all shook his hand. "We're just going for coffee," she continued, "Why don't you guys come along? Ethan, I would love to hear all about Switzerland. That sounds so exciting."

Ethan looked at me quizzically and I hesitated.

"Come on," Sasha pressed. "It'll be fun."

"Sure," he said at the same time I said, "I should get back."

"Don't be lame, Anna," Hilary said. "You can share him. We'll wait while you change."

I was annoyed that they had busted in on our reunion and felt I had no choice but to cooperate. Ethan was just being polite.

On the way to the coffee shop, he was a perfect gentleman. He told them how we met, chatted amiably with everyone, and paid for the whole group. He asked questions and listened earnestly. Everyone was in love with him by the time we returned to the studio.

"See you later," Rebecca said, and she and Sasha departed quickly.

"Come back and see us soon," Hilary said, squeezing his arm. "Maybe the two of us could grab coffee again sometime."

"Okay," he said lightly. I could tell he thought nothing of it but her comment bothered me.

"Thanks for coming by," I said, hoping she would go in first so I could talk to him alone.

"Well," he said, looking from me to the other girls and back. "It's great to see you."

"You too," I said and contemplated what to say next. I was determined not to let him get away before I knew for sure I was going to see him again. Before either of us came up with the right words, Hilary tapped my shoulder.

"We have to go, Anna," she said. She sounded like my mother. "We're going to be late to *Fire* rehearsal."

"You better go," Ethan said.

"Go on, Hilary," I said. "I'll be there in a second."

"Okay," she said, whining. "Hurry up though. Bye." She backed away slowly.

Ethan moved closer to me. "Got somewhere to be tonight?" he asked.

"Tonight?" I bit my lip. "No, I'm done at six and was just going to go home and do laundry."

"Perfect. Laundry can wait. Pick you up at six-thirty?"

"Okay," I said without hesitation. "I'll text you my address." He waved and I watched him walk away, my heart beating loudly in my chest. I wanted to spend time with him and talk about everything. We had waited long enough.

Inside the dressing room, the girls were buzzing. Sasha was telling Faye about the coffee trip.

"I can't believe I missed it," Faye said.

"He's so cute," Hilary said. "You better seal that up fast, Anna, before one of us steals him."

"I think he likes you," Rebecca added, and I smiled to myself. The *Afternoon Symphony* rehearsal had completely faded from memory.

I ran home at top speed after work. My small apartment, which I usually kept impeccably neat, became a disaster as I threw down my bag and began pulling clothes out the closet. Would he like my place? The furniture was simple but cozy, an overstuffed chenille couch, small light wood table and chairs, a sleigh bed, and framed black and white photography — mostly various city shots — on the walls.

I left a pile of bobby pins on the sink counter and jumped into the shower, lathering the hairspray and kinks out of my poor hair. Preparing for a date was a revelation. I felt liberated. There was something symbolic about putting on a dress and letting my hair fall in a long cascade over my shoulders.

He rang the buzzer just as I finished applying lip-gloss and I waited nervously while he rode the elevator.

I opened the door and Ethan stood there with his hands thrust into the pockets of his jeans. For an instant, before we jumped into something we'd both anticipated for such a long time, we had a moment that seemed so real to both of us, a spark of connection that we would learn to come back to again and again in the future. The warmth in his eyes and the promise of his smile bubbled around me like champagne. "Ready?" he asked.

We ate at a small Italian bistro with red-checked tablecloths and candles on the tables. In the flickering light, our voices rose and fell as we traded stories of our lives and the adventures of the past year. His voice lulled me into a kind of trance, and as he described a narrow road he took up a mountain on a ski trip in Switzerland, I thought, I could listen to this man talk forever. Watching him absorbed in his story, I marveled at his willingness to open up to me. He had never been this way before, and his vulnerability offered a feeling of safety. It occurred to me that he had spent a year building up the courage for this, or maybe it was me who needed that time to prepare. Regardless, we were finally together, and it felt perfect.

On our way home we stopped to stroll through an art gallery, and Ethan paused in front of a beautiful photograph of a woman on a horse. The conversation turned to the angle and lighting involved in the shot. I stepped forward to look closer at the image and in a moment Ethan moved in behind me, his fingers trailing lightly along the seam of my dress, warming my skin. Because of all the partnering I did at work, I was accustomed to being touched by men, but never like that. I held my breath.

"Do you like it?" he asked, his voice low and easy.

I let my breath out slowly, wondering if he knew how much I was longing for him. "I do."

He put his lips to my neck and kissed my skin. I nearly melted into a puddle at his feet, wanting more, but he stopped there, took my hand gently, and walked me home.

"I'll see you soon?" he asked outside the door to my building. "Maybe tomorrow?"

I nodded without speaking, and his hand pressed low on my hip, pulling me towards him. After a soft and insistent kiss, he disappeared quickly into the darkness.

Via text we decided that I would go to Ethan's house after work the next day. I took my time in the dressing room brushing my hair out and washing the sweat off my face. I felt flummoxed by our date the night before. It was so easy to imagine being with him, but the reality was different and I didn't know that I had the energy to sustain the emotional intensity I felt when we were together. It was hard to imagine reaching beyond my insular little world. There was no way I could afford to be this distracted all the time. Nothing had ever truly turned my primary focus away from ballet, and Ethan's consuming presence seemed to threaten the life I'd worked so hard to build.

When I reached his house, I found him in the front yard painting the fence. He was wearing paint-stained cargo shorts and no shirt. I liked the way he was concentrating on his work.

"Hey," I said.

He stood to greet me. "Hi." We kissed. I felt fragile suddenly, as if I had ceased to be the girl who had just rehearsed five ballets and could move to New York on her own at sixteen. The small muscles in his arms and shoulders flexed appealingly as he ran his fingers through my hair.

"So," I said, "want some help painting that fence?" I liked the idea of working with my hands, on a real home, on a project that wouldn't disappear the minute after I had danced it. That was the way I wanted to get to know him, by building something together, slowly, the way I'd built my ballet technique. I needed to see more than just what he did, but the *way* he did things, and what qualities he brought to his work. I knew how the other dancers moved, how they breathed when exerting effort, what was hard for them. Those were the things I knew about the people I saw every day, and I wanted to know even more about him. Those were also the things I wanted him to know about me.

His whole face lit up. "Really?" I had surprised him.

"Really. I'm dying to get my hands dirty if you need some help."

"I'll get you a paintbrush and a junky shirt," he said, hurrying off as if he thought I would change my mind.

He set me up and before sunset, we transformed the fence from a chipped and dirty cream color to a bright fresh white. It was the calmest two hours I'd had in ages and the smell of fresh paint brought back memories of painting my bedroom years ago in Rock Island. We spoke only to discuss the work or ask how things were going, and the time passed in companionable silence.

"I think this is the longest I've gone in months without thinking about ballet," I said. "It frightens me, actually."

"You're scared to have a life outside your work, aren't you?" he asked. I found his accuracy unnerving.

"Maybe. I worry that the moment I stop concentrating, it will slip away. I think it's amazing that once you build a building it's going to be there for years and years. I envy that. When we dance it's gone right after we do it."

"I never thought of it that way," he said. "Well, you better be careful then because I've got plenty more projects around here to distract you."

"Ethan, I need to go slow," I said, feeling inexplicably panicked. I rose to my feet and he stood and reached for me.

"It's okay," he said. "Don't be scared. Just eat dinner with me. I'm not leaving the country again. I've waited over a year to get to know you and I'm not leaving LA for work ever again if I can help it. So let's just spend some time together. I like being with you."

I reached forward and touched his chest, feeling the dip at his throat and the layers of muscle that formed his shoulder. As much as I logically thought I wanted to go slow, when I looked at him all I could say was, "Okay."

Before my debut in *Afternoon Symphony*, I was called to rehearse a new ballet. The dancers at the first rehearsal of *Spring Season Pas de Deux* included Adrienne, Zif, Elizabeth, Lorenzo, Natasha, Jeff, and me. I was a conspicuous presence and the only corps member at the rehearsal.

"William choreographed *Spring Season Pas de Deux* his first year as director," I overheard Adrienne say to Elizabeth as they stretched on the floor together.

Lila walked into the room and clapped her hands. "Let's go. I'll start with the girls." She ran her hand through her short hair and turned to inspect herself in the mirror. Zif, Jeff, and Lorenzo moved to the side of the room.

Adrienne, Elizabeth, Natasha, and I marked behind Lila as she showed us the steps. We all looked so different, with Adrienne's dark and sultry elegance, Elizabeth's beauty queen glamour, Natasha's overdramatic and in-your-face personality, and me, the youngest and most eager. Principals shared some roles, but usually they did different things because they were different types of dancers. *Spring Season* seemed to have been cast based on which girls were William's favorites.

William appeared in the doorway near the end of the rehearsal, and he and Lila took a moment to whisper. We discussed the steps while we waited for Lila to return and Adrienne explained some of the counts to me.

"This piece is about first love," William said, interrupting us. "Your movements and demeanor should portray youth and innocence." His eyes scanned the room. I turned to examine my reflection in the mirror. The way things had gone with Ethan in the month he'd been back told me everything I needed to know to dance the part. Even standing next to the likes of Adrienne, Elizabeth, and Natasha, I knew my presence best suited William's description.

The third rehearsal scheduled for *Spring Season Pas De Deux* caused a great deal of gossip because Jeff and I were the only ones called.

It seemed too easy. My first year as a true member of the company, and I had a rehearsal for a principal role. Many dancers spent ten years in the corps and never danced any featured parts.

Some dancers had a strong reaction to the casting news, but I had done nothing more than anyone else. I worked hard, I was never sick or injured, and I danced the best I could every day. True to his word, Ethan had given me plenty of space to stay focused on my work. Despite my resistance to over-involvement, it was often me who asked to see him more. Whenever I had a moment to myself, I wanted to spend it with him.

Jeff was warming up at the *barre*, carefully inching his legs in and out of fifth position in slow *tendus*, when I walked into the studio for the rehearsal.

"Hi," I said, determined to be friendly even though I was frightened to work with him. His small features and skinny legs were sleek and elegant, his brown hair and pale skin matched my coloring, and he was shorter than Lorenzo and Zif, so I could see why William decided we were well-matched as partners. I just wished he were *nicer*. Jeff ignored my greeting, but then again, he always ignored the corps girls.

Lila arrived and gave me a curt smile. "Let's run it and see how it goes," she said. I wondered if the latest gossip about her was true. Faye had heard from Ian that she was having an affair with a married movie producer. We had no idea how Ian got his gossip but he always seemed to be right. Lila never told anyone anything about her personal life, so it was fun to speculate about her.

Jeff and I began to dance the *pas de deux* and Lila watched, letting the tape run. We rehearsed the entire opening *adagio* for the first time. It was so different than partnering class at ballet school. We didn't stop and there was no room for error. Partnering required sensitivity, but Jeff and I were strangers and had no personal connection.

My body felt awkward as he guided me through the supported turns and small lifts. When we clasped hands, I sensed we didn't want to be touching each other. He wouldn't look me in the eye. Touching Ethan felt so right and natural, so why did dancing with Jeff feel the complete opposite? I needed him and all I had was the sense that he was annoyed at dancing with a girl in the corps.

William appeared and sat down in the front next to Lila. I had never been in this small of a rehearsal with him and wondered if the outcome could determine the entire direction of my career.

Lila stopped the music and walked over to us. "Anna," she said, "You need to hold Jeff's arm with a stronger grip. If you don't give him any leverage, he can't find your center of balance."

"Exactly, thank you," Jeff said to Lila. He turned to me. "Your arm is about as firm as a wet noodle." I nodded, pressured by the implication that I was making things difficult for Jeff. I was the novice and he was the principal, so if something wasn't right, I was obviously going to take the blame.

"Got it, Anna?" Lila asked briskly and moved on without waiting for my response. "Jeff. Let's run your solo." She walked back to the front to restart the music. I was taken aback. She had never been that curt towards me in corps rehearsals. William crossed his arms and leaned back in his chair, his expression cautiously optimistic. Did Lila agree that I should have this opportunity? Suddenly I wasn't sure if she was an ally or an enemy.

The music began again and Jeff danced his variation. I wiped sweat off my neck and tried to catch my breath. William nodded as Jeff finished with seven perfect *pirouettes* to the knee.

I ran into the center of the studio for my variation, determined to show William he hadn't make a mistake. The footwork in the choreography came naturally to me. Sweat ran into my eyes and I pushed myself as hard as I could.

At the end of my variation I held the pose for a moment, as if punctuating a sentence. Jeff began the finale section—called the *coda*—as I walked to the side of the room. William looked engaged and watched both of us closely. My image in the mirror said it all: my face was red, I was soaked in sweat, and my hair was a frizzy mess. I looked like someone desperate to please.

Jeff finished his pyrotechnic leaps across the floor and I came back on, nailing the *piqué* turns that traveled in a circle around the room. At the end of the phrase, Jeff ran back towards me for our final steps together. I had never practiced the final sequence with a partner and wished we had tried it once before the full run-thru. I put my arm around his shoulder and he lifted me around backwards in a circle. With the force of the movement, my foot caught on his ankle and we both tripped and fell to the floor.

I landed hard on my rear and Jeff tumbled backward on top of me. He weighed double what I did and it *hurt*. "Ow," I moaned. I saw the angry look on his face. "Sorry," I managed. Lila shut the music off.

"Let's walk through this part," Lila said, waiting for us to recover.

Jeff slowly rose to his feet. I stood up as fast as I could once he was off me. He walked in a circle and shook his legs.

"I can't believe this," he grumbled.

"I'm really sorry."

William stared out the window, disengaging himself. Lila coaxed Jeff into marking the end again, and William stood and left the room.

The next morning, I was surprised to see I had another rehearsal with Jeff for *Spring Season*. After the yesterday, I had thought they might take me out of it.

"Anna," Lila said behind me. I turned around and noticed we were alone in the hallway. "William wants you to dance *Spring Season* on a gig in Park City, Utah next weekend, for his *William Mason and Principal Dancers of Los Angeles Ballet Theatre* group."

"Me?"

"It's quite an honor that William wants to take you," she said, giving me a pointed look.

"Yes, of course. I...wow," I said. "This weekend, you said?"

"Next weekend. You leave next Thursday. Nine days." She turned and hurried down the hall before I could say a word.

I had four private rehearsals for *Spring Season Pas de Deux* the week before we left for the gig. Lila had to rehearse other ballets the company would perform in San Diego the following week, so Jeff and I were supposed to run through things on our own.

To add to my mounting anxiety, Jeff didn't show up to any of our rehearsals. I ended up using the studio time to practice by myself. I wished I had the nerve to say something to him. I could guess why he wouldn't rehearse if he could get away with it. He always danced *Spring Season* when it resurfaced in the repertory, and I knew he saw it as an insult that he had to dance with me. I wasn't even a senior member of the corps. Jeff was also close with Allison, and she hated that I had such a big role.

Once when I was little, my dad had taken me to work with him and introduced me to all his work colleagues. "We've heard so much about you!" they said, looking me over with enthusiasm. "Your dad is very proud." I had blushed, flattered and scared at the same time. Why did they think they knew me so well and what had Dad made me out to be? I felt pressured to live up to whatever their expectations might have been, as murky as they were, and I felt the same way now. William's image of Anna Linado wasn't clear to me, but I knew I had to live up to something big.

Nine

The airport bustled with activity on the day we left for Utah. We stood in the check-in line, William chatting with Natasha in front, Jeff, Adrienne, and Zif discussing the quality of the stage in Park City behind them, Lorenzo listening to his iPod, and Elizabeth filing her nails. When I saw them all at work, they were the most serious and professional people in the company. I was struck by how comfortable they were with William and each other in a different setting.

"Are you excited?" Elizabeth asked me as we boarded the plane, and I nodded, unsure if she meant to be nice or condescending. I sat quietly next to Adrienne and Zif on the flight. When we arrived, a shuttle service took us to the hotel.

"Meet in the lobby at seven," William said before we split up. "The party is at our sponsor's estate."

I was relieved to have some time alone in my hotel room. I had never had my own room on tour because the corps always had to double up. The air was cold in Park City and the snow sparkled crystal clear outside my window.

Five minutes before seven, I walked into the lobby wearing an ankle-length strapless lavender sheath dress and high heels. Everyone had dressed as if we were going to the Academy Awards.

The eight of us climbed into a black stretch limousine outside the hotel and the conversation floated around me as we drove. William looked classy in a black tuxedo. Natasha's cheeks flushed the same deep red as her dress as she laughed at something William said. Lorenzo loosened his tie and thrust his hips forward in the seat like a cologne ad, while Jeff stared straight through me. Adrienne sat up straight in a spaghetti-strap black evening dress and held both of Zif's hands. Zif looked mysterious and handsome, sitting as still as a statue. Elizabeth stared out the window with an excited look on her face. Her champagne-colored dress perfectly highlighted her delicate features.

We drove through a stunning mountain pass. Finally, the limo pulled into a private driveway that wound through enormous trees. Eventually the trees cleared away and an enormous mansion loomed into view.

"Who lives like this?" Lorenzo asked.

"Wow," Adrienne said. She craned her neck to look out the window.

An ice sculpture sparkled in the center of the enormous circular driveway. Through the huge picture window I saw a beautiful grand piano standing in the middle of the living room, where people in gowns and tuxedos circulated holding wine glasses. The scene took my breath away.

The giant front doors opened towards us as we climbed out of the limo, and I heard the faint sound of Frank Sinatra crooning in the background. We walked up the staircase towards an older woman in a blue gown with matching evening gloves. She clasped her hands over the brilliant diamonds around her neck.

"The stars of the evening are here," she said joyously. "William, darling, it's been ages since you brought your kids. Come in…come in." Her gloved hand beckoned to William as if they were old friends.

William joined her in the doorway and she kissed him hard on the mouth. He kissed her back, clearly enjoying himself. We each stopped to greet her. She glanced coolly at Natasha, hugged Adrienne, and looked Elizabeth up and down. Lorenzo, Zif, and Jeff all graciously kissed her hand, much to her delight. As the other dancers walked into the throng of people, the hostess turned her attention to me.

"Who is this tiny young thing?" she asked William, cocking her head to look me over. "You didn't bring her the last time you were in Utah." She ran a gloved hand down his arm. I felt my face flush.

"What's your name, sweetheart?" she said. She looked from me to William and back. "You look like the Lilac Fairy with that snow glowing behind you."

"This is Anna Linado," William said, taking my arm and guiding me into the doorway. "She'll dance *Spring Season Pas de Deux* tomorrow and she's one of my ones to watch."

"William!" she said. "You cast this child in your ballet? Well…isn't she just *ripe*? I don't think she even looks eighteen."

"I'm almost twenty," I said. They chuckled.

"Well, that's old enough for a glass of wine," William said, taking my arm.

"Yes, come on in," said the woman, and we followed her into the main room.

Natasha and Elizabeth were already deep in conversation with some male guests. Elizabeth looked surprisingly animated and Natasha laughed flirtatiously at something a man in a tuxedo whispered to her. The men seemed to be madly in love with them. Natasha looked over when William walked in with me on his arm and a noticeable flicker of jealousy crossed her face. I wondered if I'd imagined it.

A waiter in a tuxedo walked over with a tray of white wine. "Chardonnay?" he asked.

"Thank you," William said, taking two glasses and handing one to me.

"Thanks."

"Let's toast," he said. "To your career. I have big plans for you."

I stared at him, dumbfounded. We clinked glasses.

He winked and rubbed my bare arm. "Now, hold it by the stem. You don't want to warm the wine with your hand." He adjusted my glass accordingly.

A group of donors encircled us and William introduced me around. Small talk dominated the evening and by the time we left, my ears were full of which ballets the patrons liked and how excited they were that we were there. I wasn't the only one anticipating my performance and that was a heady realization. William looked across the room at me with great pride. His expression was one I would always remember, long after that night and even years after I left the company.

William gave class at the theater the next morning. I felt intensely self-aware and glad that

William couldn't possibly overlook me. In a class of seven there was nowhere to hide.

The partnering with Jeff still felt awkward during the dress rehearsal. At least I didn't trip him. He remained disconnected from me when we danced, and I felt relieved that we made it through the *pas de deux* without any major mistakes. That was all I could realistically hope for without having rehearsed together.

We found food laid out for us in the green room between the rehearsal and performance. Lorenzo and Zif put salami over their eyes and broccoli in their teeth and imitated the donors at last night's party. Adrienne and Natasha and I laughed hysterically and Jeff and Elizabeth look on with more reserved amusement.

An hour before curtain, I started my makeup in the dressing room. I wanted a lot of time because I had never felt this nervous about a performance before. It was also new for me to share a dressing room right next to the stage with Natasha, Adrienne, and Elizabeth. Usually I dressed down in the basement of the theaters with the corps and there were always people talking and goofing around. The principals' dressing room was silent, and I wondered if it was always that way or if they just weren't talking because of me. Natasha cracked a few jokes but Elizabeth and Adrienne gave her very little response. Elizabeth put on her iPod and went to work on her face. As I pinned in my headpiece, Adrienne stared at herself in the mirror and Natasha sewed a pair of shoes.

Much as I dreamed of being at the top of my profession, I was painfully aware how young and inexperienced I was in comparison to the seasoned principals. At the moment, there was nothing I could do about it, so I pushed away my fear and pretended I was one of them.

The show began, and I dressed in my long blue romantic-style tutu and went to stage right to warm up. Zif danced *Muses* with Adrienne, Elizabeth, and Natasha. Their performance was perfectly polished, and every movement looked studied and infused with thought. I hoped by the time I was that experienced I would be just as sure of every move I made.

When *Muses* ended, I pulled my leg warmers off and jumped up and down to keep warm. Jeff walked into the back wing and I followed him. There was only a pause in the program before *Spring Season Pas de Deux*.

"*Merde*," I said. It was an important moment in my life and I wanted to share it.

"*Merde*," Jeff replied coldly. Our eyes met for the briefest second.

The curtain went up and the music to *Spring Season* began. Jeff led me on to the stage and under the bright lights. I heard scattered applause.

We began to dance. The smile on my face felt mechanical but at least the steps ran smoothly. My confidence grew when I noticed that William wasn't scrutinizing me in the front wing, which meant he was sitting in the audience. I looked out at the dark house and let myself relax.

We reached the halfway point in the *adagio* and out of nowhere, Jeff broke away from me and ran downstage right. I was shocked. His action wasn't in the choreography. He pantomimed a love gesture completely off the music, turning and kneeling to reach towards me. When he faced away from the audience, I saw a look of panic cross his face as he realized he had made a major mistake. Jeff had jumped ahead and blanked out sixteen counts in the choreography.

His mistake set in motion a tectonic shift. My familiar insecurities floated away in a sea of jumbled emotions. He should have come to rehearsal. If he hadn't been so full of himself and determined to undermine me this would never have happened.

Where did Jeff get off thinking he was so great? He was human just like the rest of us. I was tired of feeling inadequate. His eyes pleaded with me to go along. I would have to invent sixteen counts on the spot. My first performance of a principal role was not supposed to go this way. There was no choice. My next steps felt natural and inevitable.

I smiled at the audience and with a surprising burst of creativity, I improvised some *arabesques* and *piqué* turns. The look on Jeff's face as I danced towards him gave me confidence because he finally looked grateful, and impressed. When I performed a brisk *soutenu* turn on the counts fifteen and sixteen, I was precisely on the music. Jeff looked at me with so much respect I hardly believed he was the same person who had looked right through me five minutes before. We picked up exactly as we should have within the original choreography. William was probably the only audience member who would know anything had gone wrong.

We finished the *adagio* and I ran off so Jeff could begin his solo. I huffed and puffed, trying to catch my breath. Adrienne and Zif gave me the enthusiastic thumbs up from the wing on the other side of the stage.

166 | Miriam Wenger-Landis

I ran on for my variation feeling confident and happy. The studied angles of head and arms, painfully thought out rehearsals I had worked through alone, and anger at Jeff were all forgotten. I performed on a new level. Each movement had resonance rooted in hard work. I didn't have to stay in line anymore and all at once I could just be myself, dancing to my heart's content.

"Bravo!" someone yelled after my variation and I grinned. There was nothing better than unbiased approval.

Jeff started the *coda*. I ran back onstage and whipped out my final sequence of turns. We danced the ending together with no trip and no mistakes.

The stage went black and Jeff lifted me out of the final pose. When the lights came back on he led me forward to bow. No one unhooked my costume before the curtain fell because I wasn't even close to the back row of the corps anymore. All eyes were on me.

I extended my right arm over my head and slowly pointed my right foot behind me. My right hand came to my heart as I kneeled, bowing my head in a *grande révérance*. The applause was earsplitting. When the curtain finally fell, I felt dizzy. I walked to the wing and sat down.

"Good job," Jeff said quietly. I raised my head and he looked me right in the eye and smiled.

A warm hand rested on my shoulder. "How do you feel?" William asked, crouching down to look at my face. We grinned at each other.

"I feel great."

William nodded. "So, Jeff," William said as he stood back up. "Good thing your partner can improvise." Jeff cringed as William winked at me. With the sensation of a runner who has crossed the finish line, I closed my eyes and savored the victory.

A van dropped us back at the hotel after the show. Everyone was starving and tired.

"There's a brew pub across the street," William said as we climbed out of the van. "Let's celebrate."

After a casual meal filled with jokes and camaraderie, we walked back to the hotel. Adrienne, Zif, Jeff, and Elizabeth got off the elevator a floor below Natasha, William, Lorenzo and me. My room was the closest to the elevator, and I stopped to fumble for my key. Lorenzo paused two doors down on the other side as William and Natasha continued walking. Before I went into my room, I glanced down the hall and saw William take Natasha's hand and lead her into his hotel room. My jaw fell open in surprise.

Lorenzo was still there too, and he turned to look back at me. I snapped my mouth shut when our eyes met.

"You didn't know?" he mouthed soundlessly.

"Uh, I do now," I mouthed back.

"I thought everyone knew," he whispered. "They're not very discreet. It's not always Natasha. Sometimes it's Elizabeth." He paused. "Goodnight, Anna." He shook his head before he walked into his room.

My happiness over the performance evaporated, and as I walked in my room I slammed the door. The echo reverberated ominously down the hall. I sat on the bed. How could it be true? I fell backwards and stared at the ceiling.

I thought about a lot of things that night. It started to snow and the flakes fell like a curtain outside my window. I thought of Ethan, and how he was the only thing in my life that had been even better in reality than in my imagination. I thought of Karina's diary, which I hadn't picked up in so long and had only hinted at the truth about William. I thought of my parents, who had supported me my whole life to help me realize this dream, not knowing what it would really be like. I thought of William and Natasha in a passionate embrace just a few rooms away.

I called Ethan and he let me talk it out, but I was still too disturbed to sleep. My respect for William and devotion to the company went so deep that I felt personally betrayed. William wasn't married, but somehow it seemed terribly unethical of him to sleep with his dancers. I saw it as an abuse of power and wished desperately I could forget what I'd seen.

"I missed you," Ethan whispered when he picked me up at the airport. We kissed frantically in the car.

"I missed you too."

He put the car in gear and headed towards my apartment. "Let's drop off your stuff," he said, "and then I was hoping I could take you out to meet some people. We need to feed you anyway. My brother, his girlfriend, and a couple of my buddies from college are meeting up at that new Mexican restaurant near your apartment." He put his hand on my knee.

"You're going to introduce me to your brother and your friends? I can rally. I'd love to meet them and I need to get away from dancers."

He laughed. "I don't blame you."

"So what else have you been up to while I was gone?"

"Well, I've been stripping the wallpaper off the main floor," he said. "You won't believe the difference."

"I can't wait to see it," I said. I liked watching him drive. When he concentrated his face took on a serious expression that was almost childlike.

At the restaurant I met Ethan's older brother, Dave, his girlfriend Lana, and Ethan's college roommates, Tim and Steve. It felt good to be there for someone else and for once, I didn't have to be anyone other than myself.

The easy banter of the guys brought out my sarcastic side and we hit it off right away. Lana was loud and opinionated and fun; a good foil to Dave who initially seemed even more impenetrable than Ethan. Tim and Steve were like rowdy frat boys. They worked together at a start-up and finished each other's sentences. Ethan seemed so comfortable with all of them.

By dessert, they had all drawn me into an animated argument about whether fortune-tellers had any merit. Ethan put his hand over mine and squeezed my fingers. I could tell he was happy, and that made me happy too.

Natasha and Elizabeth huddled in front of the bulletin board before class on our first day back in LA.

"What is this?" Elizabeth snapped, pointing at the schedule. "I get one performance? She's only in the corps."

I walked up behind them to look and Elizabeth glanced over her shoulder. "Oh!" she said sweetly. "Hi, Anna." Natasha turned around sharply.

Spring Season Pas de Deux had been added to the next program. Natasha and Jeff were the opening night cast, and Adrienne and Zif and Elizabeth and Lorenzo each had one scheduled performance. I was cast with Jeff to dance *Spring Season* six times, in Los Angeles, Palm Springs, and San Diego. Even though I wasn't the first cast, I had received far more performances than any of the others.

"Hi," I said awkwardly. Why did I have to feel ashamed of my good fortune?

Hilary and Allison shot dirty looks at me throughout class. Once my big opportunity became more than a one-shot deal, I had clearly become a much more serious threat.

My parents flew in the day before I danced *Spring Season* in Los Angeles. Mom had come for one weekend the year before to see me in *Violins*, but Dad had never seen the company perform. They took a cab from the airport and settled in at my apartment before I came home from work.

I straggled in the door at the end of the day and collapsed on the couch. The smell of dinner cooking filled the room. Mom walked out of the kitchen and regarded me.

"Sweetie," she said. "You look terrible." She turned to look at Dad as he appeared behind her. "Look at the bags under her eyes. Anna, are you eating? There was no food in your fridge."

I didn't bother to tell her I'd been out of town and ate most of my meals at Ethan's. She didn't understand how hard it was to dance eight hours a day, every day. "Working hard, Mom. I've had no time to go the grocery."

"You have to take care of yourself," Dad said.

They were right, of course. I had noticed the bags under my eyes. Despite Ethan's efforts to take care of me, I wasn't with him all the time and my meals weren't consistently healthy, mainly because either I was on the road or didn't have the energy to shop and cook. I took my body for granted.

I barely had the energy to eat with them before I hit the bathtub and bed. It was hard for me to do everything myself. The company took everything I had and I was trying to make energy for a relationship too. The only thing we were supposed to need was dance, but it wasn't true. I needed other things, like love.

Ethan came to opening night with my parents and we all went out to dinner after the show. As I expected, they got along well. He graciously navigated their not-so-subtle interrogation and impressed them by holding the door for my mother and pulling out our chairs. My mother's habit of asking a lot of questions didn't seem to faze him and neither did my dad's intimidating stare. I almost wanted to tease him for trying so hard. His efforts were endearing.

"Anna," said my mom, "guess what I heard the man next to me say when he saw your name in the program?"

"Oh no. What?"

"He turned to his wife and said, 'That girl was just an apprentice last year. How did she get this big role? She must be sleeping with William.'"

I flinched. "Are you serious?" I felt shamed. I'd been dancing so diligently, making myself at home in front of an audience who I imagined found me charming and competent, when in fact, what they saw was a girl too inexperienced to be a star and must have done something shady to earn the role.

Ethan put his arm around the back of my chair protectively. I glanced up at him and could tell he'd heard the incident too.

"I almost leaned over and gave him a piece of my mind," Mom said, "but then I figured if he was going to say something else entertaining I didn't want to stop him."

"Please tell me he made that comment before I danced," I said, looking at Ethan pleadingly.

"He did," said Mom, her face turning sober.

"Don't worry," Ethan said. "He stood up and clapped enthusiastically with the rest of us."

I was unnerved by the image in my head of a random stranger reacting to my performance. I had never thought I might be perceived that way before, and the scenario hovered in my mind the rest of the evening. I would never compromise myself for a role. I hoped Ethan knew that.

Ten

On my birthday, I danced my sixth and last performance of *Afternoon Symphony*. That night, Ethan and I met his brother and a bunch of our friends at a neighborhood restaurant to celebrate. Our group took over a large table in the back.

"Let me buy the birthday girl a drink," Ian announced. He ordered up shots for the table. "Happy Birthday, Golden Ticket."

I had been onstage every night both in the corps and as a principal for the last three months, as long as Ethan and I had been together. The stretch of nonstop performances had been the best time of my life, especially when I was onstage or home alone with Ethan, and the frequency of being in the spotlight made me more and more comfortable and confident with my job.

"Twenty must be your lucky age," Ethan's brother Dave said, smiling at me. He had quickly become one of my biggest supporters and I had developed a major soft spot for him.

"Just be careful, my friend," Ryan said, leaning across the table. "The problem with William's golden ticket is that it expires."

I flinched. "I've heard."

"That sounds pretty cynical, Ryan," Ethan said. "Anna's worked hard for everything she has."

"They'll work her into the ground at a corps salary," Ryan said. "All I'm saying is don't take it for granted. Someone else could be the new favorite next year."

"Thanks, Ryan," I said sarcastically.

"Anna," Stephanie said, crouching down next to my chair and thankfully interrupting the conversation. "I have something to tell you."

"Okay." I turned my back on Ryan to face her, leaving Ethan and Dave to handle Ryan's drunken ramblings.

"Miami offered me a contract," Stephanie whispered. "I'm leaving."

We had talked about other companies beforehand, of course we had, but I had thought they were abstract conversations. I had no idea Stephanie had been serious about leaving anytime soon. She'd just been promoted — there were plenty of other people I saw as more likely candidates to jump ship. "You're leaving us?" If she had a contract lined up, Stephanie had been planning her departure for months and never told any of us. She must have gone down to Miami to audition on a day off.

"I've done the roles I want to do in our repertory," Stephanie said. I smelled her jasmine perfume when she draped her arm over my shoulder. Ethan rested his hand on my knee, not joining our conversation, just making me aware he'd overheard. "Miami is a great company," she went on, "and I'm ready for a change. I'll be closer to my family in North Carolina too. I can't throw the opportunity away."

"I hear you," I said, sighing. "Well, it's a great opportunity. I'm going to miss you." I almost cried then, both because I'd miss her and because she seemed on the edge of a precipice, about to jump into a wider and more exciting universe than the narrow world of LABT. I felt like I was going to be left behind.

"Thanks," Stephanie said, looking happier than I've ever seen her. It occurred to me how lonely her life was in LA. She had lots of casual friends but wasn't particularly close to anyone. I'd never known her family to visit and she didn't really date. All the promotions in the world wouldn't change those aspects of her life.

I noticed Rebecca had returned from the ladies' and given Hilary a dirty look for taking her seat next to Ryan. Rebecca moved over and sat down next to Ian and Faye at the far end of the table. Stephanie, Ethan, and I discussed her plans for the move, and as the evening progressed, I watched Hilary snake her arm around Ryan's shoulder and down his back. He flirted with her and avoided Rebecca's glare across the table. Eventually Rebecca gathered her purse and walked over to Ryan. She tapped him on the shoulder.

"I'm leaving," Rebecca said. "Are you coming?"

"Oh," he said dismissively. "I'm not ready yet. You go on."

She stared at him. Hilary had turned away to chat with Carolyn. We were trying not to stare but the drama was hard to ignore.

"Are you sure?" Rebecca pressed.

"Yeah," Ryan said. "I'm still finishing my drink."

"Fine," she said quietly, and I felt terrible for her. She'd made a few comments about them having problems recently, but I hadn't seen any evidence of it before. "I'm going. Bye. Happy birthday, Anna."

"Thanks."

"Bye," Ryan said, raising his glass to her. He seemed unfazed when she left alone.

"I'm tired of her," Ryan said. "She's so needy."

It had been a strange couple of weeks, full of little things that at the time seemed insignificant, facial expressions, comments whispered in the hallway, all blurred together. It was only in hindsight that the moments rearranged themselves in my mind to form a pattern that had been there for months. Hilary standing quietly behind Rebecca in the dressing room while Rebecca complained about Ryan's inattentiveness. Ryan and Hilary laughing and kicking the vending machine together to free a loose snack. Rebecca's forlorn expression while she watched Ryan dance.

"What does that mean, Ryan?" asked Stephanie. "Are you and Rebecca okay?"

His eyes glazed over, and I would have been willing to bet he was privately weighing how much he could blurt out. "Oh you know, the usual relationship trials and tribulations."

The conversation moved on and shifted to lighter topics, but the question was still on everyone's mind. After a few minutes, Hilary slipped her hand on Ryan's knee, disregarding the stares Stephanie and I gave her.

By then I was ready to go. We said our goodnights and most of us headed out, leaving Hilary and Ryan alone at the table.

"I hope that isn't going where I think it's going," Stephanie said as we parted ways. "I'm going to give Rebecca a call."

"I hope she's okay," I said.

The guys I used to dream about falling in love with were the self-centered and charming ones, like Ryan, who bored easily and took their attractiveness for granted. But someone who appreciated you and had your back was a different thing, a thing that I couldn't have imagined before Ethan. Those qualities made a guy like Ryan pale in comparison. Even that rush of feeling when someone you liked kissed you, or that crackle of electricity in your fingertips when he merely touched your hand, was absolutely nothing compared to the power of being truly loved.

My contract came in the mail a few days later. I had been trying not to admit it to myself, but secretly I had hoped for a promotion. True it was early—I had only technically been in the corps for one year—but with Stephanie leaving, there was an opening for a new soloist.

The letter invited me back as a second-year corps member with a raise of twenty dollars a week. I rationalized the reasons. The company had financial problems. I was too young. It made sense. Next year. Next year.

I called Faye. "Second-year corps," she said. "No one got promoted even though Stephanie quit. The finance people said we're broke. William spent all the company's money on next year's premiere of *America*."

America was a Roizman classic and a huge production for a company of our size. We were not

Ballet New York with ninety dancers. We had forty-five and that meant every single dancer in the company would be in the ballet, without a second cast.

"He's trying to hire some Canadian superstar next year," Faye said. "Grant something-or-other. Supposedly *America* is the lure." That made sense. The *pas de deux* in *America* was a showstopper.

"Things are always changing."

"Speaking of," Faye said, her tone of voice changing from business-like to gossipy, "did you hear that Hilary and Ryan are hooking up? Rebecca is beside herself."

My stomach flipped over. "I didn't think he'd really do it."

"Well, he did and he's still doing it. Rebecca apparently dropped by his apartment a few days ago and Ryan tried to keep her outside. She pushed her way in and there's Hilary wearing only a towel. Apparently Hilary left and Rebecca had a total meltdown. Ryan was all comforting and apologetic and then a few days later she saw him out at dinner with Hilary again."

"I can't believe it. Poor Rebecca. The drama is going to make work extremely tense."

"No kidding," Faye agreed. "I'm heading over to Rebecca's now to check on her. I can't believe Hilary. I just can't believe that girl. When I talked to Rebecca this morning she was still in bed crying."

I didn't blame her. "Can I come?" I asked.

"Sure. I'll meet you on the corner in ten minutes." We hung up. I put on my shoes, texted Rebecca that I was coming over whether she liked it or not, and walked over to pick up some cupcakes from the bakery around the corner. It was the least I could do to cheer her up.

I jogged around the stage in Palm Springs at the ten-minute call for the last show of the season. I knew I should have been thinking about the choreography. Ethan was the only thing on my mind. We had spent every night together for weeks and we hadn't said it yet, but I knew we were in love. After everything Rebecca had been through, I felt scared of losing him. Could love slip away that easily? I was looking forward to spending our few weeks of impending unemployment working on Ethan's house with him and taking a road trip to San Francisco together.

That night I was in the corps of *Pathways*, one of the most difficult ballets in the repertory because there were no exits and the steps required a tremendous amount of stamina. I had only danced it twice. Marcus was my partner and I dreaded dancing with him. Every time we ran the ballet I came away with bruises because he manhandled me. The worst part was his attitude. I had asked him repeatedly not to dig his fingers into my ribs and he had rolled his eyes and pinched harder to punish me for the complaint.

I wondered what it would it be like to work in a situation where I wore normal clothes and didn't have to be touched. Sexual harassment was all over the ballet workplace. It just passed as dancer behavior. We were overly familiar with each other. Making a scene over the way Marcus touched me would be humiliating and might make people think I was difficult to work with. He was doing his job, after all. I just hated the way he touched me.

"Five minutes," said the new stage manager. "Five minutes, please." I glanced over at him as I walked to my starting spot on the stage. Greg had recently left the company for a new job. I missed his consistent and reassuring presence.

"I want Greg back," Marcus said, echoing my thoughts. "I don't think this new guy knows what he's doing."

We relied heavily on the stage manager because *Pathways* didn't have an overture, which meant backstage the only warning that the ballet was about to start was when the stage manager called "places." The audience applauded the silence when the curtain went up. It was exciting to stand there and feel the audience's anticipation. The silent opening gave the illusion that the applause made the ballet start.

Marcus got down on the floor to do some push-ups and I faced the curtain and practiced some *relevés*. Ryan boxed air in front of me, Allison tried a *pirouette*, and Mikey jumped up and down. Rebecca was down on the floor in the splits, glaring at Ryan's back.

"I can't believe this is the last performance of the season," Rebecca said to Mikey. "I'm so ready for vacation." She had been a shadow of herself. A week ago, Rebecca and Hilary had gotten into a screaming match in the dressing room and since then they had kept their distance. It seemed like Ryan had been trying to break it off with Hilary since. People had given him a lot of grief over his fling and he no longer seemed to think it was worth it. I didn't know why he thought the incident would be a private event. The company members always knew everyone else's business.

Lorenzo carried Elizabeth across the stage in a practice lift from their *pas de deux*, and while she was mid-air the curtain unexpectedly started to rise. Although we saw the curtain lift, deep down, I don't think any of us truly believed it was happening. For all the time we spent worrying about messing up onstage, we never contemplated the possibility of a problem so completely out of our control. Only the luckiest of dancers makes it through an entire career without at least one major embarrassment onstage, and while I expected mine would happen eventually, I never thought it would be something as random as the curtain rising at the wrong time. I assumed when the time came, my public humiliation would be my own fault.

"Oh crap," Rebecca said sharply. She jumped up off the floor.

"Why didn't he call places?" Mikey said, his voice rising.

Elizabeth and Lorenzo ran off stage, mumbling obscenities. I hopped to my opening pose, sheer fury rising up inside of me. It was too late. The audience laughed. Our new stage manager had ruined the entire ballet.

I performed the first combination of steps as the music began. I was so shaken up I could hardly remember the choreography. My body knew exactly what to do from muscle memory and that's what saved me, since my mind was somewhere else. I stepped on something and stumbled.

"Watch it, Anna," I heard Marcus say from down on the floor. He hadn't noticed the rising curtain and was still on the floor, mid-push-up. Out of the corner of my eye, I saw him slowly turn his head to the side and look where he thought the curtain should be.

"What the…?" he whispered. The audience roared at the look of utter bewilderment on his face. He lost his temper fast. "I'm going to kill someone," he sputtered.

I fought the urge to laugh. Marcus sprung to his feet, grabbed my hands, and picked up the choreography. The ballet continued and every time he touched me I could feel the explosiveness of his anger. I steeled myself against the abuse.

At the end, the audience applauded and we took our bows. When the curtain fell, I looked down at my wrists and noticed the purple and yellow bruises already forming where Marcus had grabbed me so violently. My ribs throbbed.

"Look what you did," I accused. I pushed my arm in front of his face.

He looked at me, wide-eyed and innocent like a little kid. "Did I do that?" he asked.

"Yes," I said, exasperated. I didn't have the energy to take it any further. I let out a long sigh.

"Sorry," he said dismissively, not looking sorry at all.

The new stage manager walked towards us. "Sorry, guys," he said sheepishly. "I forgot to call places." Didn't he know that our professional reputation was at stake every time the curtain rose?

"You really screwed us," Marcus said bitterly. "If you don't get fired…I'll get you for this. Do you realize that you sank the performance before it even started?"

The stage manager stared dumbly at Marcus. Disgusted, I turned away and followed Allison and Rebecca offstage.

"I've never felt so humiliated," Rebecca muttered. "This goes down in history as one of our most unprofessional moments ever."

Elizabeth sobbed by the prop table. She was the principal, and more than any of us in the corps, the audience would remember her in conjunction with the incident.

"I can't believe this," Lorenzo snapped behind me. I glanced back in time to see him kick the wall as hard as he could. He howled, gritting his teeth in pain and grabbing his foot.

William shoved his way past us as we headed to the dressing room. "Where's that idiot?" he roared. "That was unbelievable. He's dead. He's dead!" William marched over to the stage manager and started shouting at him. I turned away and hurried to the dressing room, eager to leave the mess behind. With that, my second season was over. I spent the next two months recovering from mononucleosis.

Eleven

We started back to work with four new apprentices, three girls and one boy. They seemed so young. Across the room, I noticed the only other new dancer. He looked way too confident to be an apprentice, and had a handsome face, dark hair, soulful brown eyes, and a compact, muscular body. His nose was sunburned and his eyebrows sparkled mischievously. Something about his manner irritated me. He seemed impatient, implying that he had somewhere more interesting to be.

Mikey, standing across from me at his usual *barre* spot, followed my gaze.

"That's Grant," Mikey whispered. "The new guy from Canada. He's only twenty-four. Do we really need a new principal? He doesn't look that great." Mikey sucked in his gut and studied himself in the mirror. I glanced at him and noticed he had put on weight. If Mikey stopped drinking so much he might get somewhere. His hair didn't even look washed.

"I think he's cute," I ventured. "He's short though. I wonder which principal they'll pair him with? Natasha?"

"Or Elizabeth," he said absently. "He's really too short to partner any of the principal girls. Anyway, do you think I look fat?"

I pretended not to hear.

Grant quickly established his position amid company politics. He remained reserved with the dancers and overly ingratiating with the staff. We all knew he was William's pet and watched jealously as William joked around with him during class. The guys hated Grant even more because the girls appreciated his good looks. He whipped off eight beautiful *pirouettes* and sliced through air, inspiring both awe and resentment. One thing was for sure—Grant could dance.

I worked diligently during the rehearsal period. In addition to all the new corps roles in Roizman ballets, I learned one of the principals in *Afternoon in the Park* and a soloist role in *Tidal Moods*. The big focus of the rehearsal season was *America*, which would premiere six months later in January. One of the official people from the Roizman Foundation came in from New York to set *America* for us and William hired several local ballet students to understudy the corps. *America* was the only ballet in our repertory that used every single dancer in the company at the same time. The casting was a logistics nightmare.

The premiere of *America* would be an enormous achievement for a company of our size. Both the dance community and the city of Los Angeles would have to regard us with new respect.

"William and Lila took Grant to dinner?" Allison asked Sasha in the dressing room. "What's up with that?"

"They're in love with him," Sasha said. She studied herself in the mirror. "They'll do anything to make sure he stays. Maybe they're worried he's lonely."

"He's out of place here," Allison said. "He's never danced a Roizman ballet in his life."

"I know, but he seems happy enough," Sasha said. "He's William's baby."

I peeled off my tights. "He doesn't have any friends though, especially if he's spending his free time with the artistic staff."

"What a climber," Allison said. She popped her gum. "He's so conceited. Elizabeth is supposed to dance the premiere of *America* with him and she says he blames everything on her in all their rehearsals. She's really too tall for him to begin with. They're not a good pair."

The season opened in Los Angeles and I danced more than almost anyone else in the corps, every single night. It was an honor to be cast so frequently and reassured me my career was going well. The downside was, I was tired all the time and had very little left to give Ethan.

"Anna, want to go out for dinner before the performance tonight?" Hilary asked unexpectedly in the dressing room.

"No thanks," I said. "Ethan is taking me out."

Hilary sat down on the bench next to me and lowered her voice to a whisper.

"Please, Anna," she said. "The Ryan thing was over months ago. When are people going to get over it? I didn't do anything wrong. He was the jerk. I'm seeing someone else now anyway. Do you know that cute guy that works in the tattoo parlor down the block?"

"No," I said. "But I have to go. Talk to you later, Hilary." I ran for the door. She wasn't fooling anyone.

In early November, I started to rehearse lead Marzipan in the *Nutcracker*. It was my third year performing the ballet and I had officially worked my way out of the lowliest corps roles. I hoped I would finally graduate from Grandma.

At the end of a run of shows in Palm Springs, I drove home late after dancing all three ballets on the program. Faye caught a ride back with me and I was so tired I worried I might drive off the road.

"Talk to me so I stay awake," I said as I pressed down on the gas. All I wanted was to get home and go to bed.

"I don't have much to say," Faye said sadly. She hadn't been cast much. There just hadn't seemed to be much life to her since Ari died. I don't think she cared about ballet for a long time after, but the lack of casting had started to bother her. I took her frustration as a good sign if it meant she was showing interest in her career again.

"I just wish I was dancing more," she continued. "I talked to Lila last week and she said to keep working hard and not get injured. That was it. She didn't say anything."

"She didn't give you any reason for how little they're using you?"

"If they don't say anything specific, they don't have to make promises they won't keep," Faye said sadly.

"*Merde,* Anna," said Kirsten, one of the new apprentices, before we went on for my first performance of lead Marzipan in *The Nutcracker*.

"Is this your first Marzipan?"

She smoothed down her tutu. "Yes," she said. "I'm nervous." She bit her lip.

"*Merde* to you too." I squeezed her hands.

The music began and I led the four corps girls onstage. I noticed Grant in the front wing right behind William. I smiled at them, feeling confident. The orchestra sounded inspired and I put extra emphasis on my musicality. At the end of the variation, I hit a perfect quadruple step-up turn and even hung in the air, perfectly on balance, kneeling precisely on the last note. The audience applauded enthusiastically along with everyone backstage.

"Great job," Faye said, giving me a high-five when I hit the wing before she ran on for *Waltz of the Flowers*. I grabbed some water from the cooler and watched Natasha as the Dewdrop.

Faye finished and came to sit next to me backstage. While we waited for the finale, we both sat transfixed, watching Adrienne and Zif dance the Sugar Plum Fairy's *pas de deux*. They were as stunning as ever.

Nutcracker season raced by and in no time it was January. The holidays were over and we were back in company class. I put my bag down in the studio at my usual *barre* spot next to Carolyn and across from Mikey.

"Welcome back, Golden Ticket," Ryan said sarcastically as he walked past me. "It looks like you hit the jackpot."

"What does that mean?" I had so little patience for him now.

Carolyn looked up from tying her pointe shoes. "Congratulations."

I cocked my head at her inquisitively. "Did you look at the board, Anna?"

"No. I don't even know today's schedule."

Mikey snorted. "You should take a look," he said.

"Uh...okay." I walked out into the hall. Allison, Natasha, and Jeff stood clustered around the board.

"What the hell?" Allison said, pointing at today's schedule, her back to me. I had a strong feeling of *déjà vu*.

"Grant told William a long time ago that he wanted to dance with her," Jeff said to Natasha.

"This is bullshit," Allison said, and it felt just like when the *Spring Season* casting went up. "Why is he replacing Elizabeth?" she continued. "Has she seen this yet?"

"Elizabeth isn't here today," Natasha said. "But I assume she'll be back soon. The premiere is next week."

"Excuse me," I said. "What's going on?"

Allison, Elizabeth, and Jeff turned around. They all seemed to jump at the sound of my voice.

"See for yourself," Allison said. Natasha backed away and Jeff gestured towards the board. I stepped closer and saw that my first rehearsal of the year was for the *America pas de deux* with Grant.

I sat down on a bench and tried to process the news. "What's going on with Elizabeth?"

"Does it matter to you?" Allison snapped. I looked up at her, taken aback. She turned away and stomped into the studio.

William could have let me rehearse the *America* principal last summer if he saw me in the role. This kind of thing never happened. All the principals received plenty of time to prepare and yet if they were actually going to put me onstage, I would only have a week?

Class began and I went through the motions, my mind elsewhere. I wondered if William would say something but he hardly looked at me. I doubted that a twenty-year-old corps girl should be thrown into the *America pas de deux* with minimal preparation. This was not *Spring Season Pas de Deux*. The entire company would dance behind me in *America*. Why would William cast an unknown as Grant's partner? The reputation of Los Angeles Ballet Theatre would rest on my shoulders. It had to be just a rehearsal, not a casting decision. They must have decided I should understudy the role.

Once I settled on a more reasonable explanation I found it easier to concentrate on class. People were jumping to too many conclusions. What was wrong with Elizabeth, anyway?

After class, I met Grant in the small studio. We exchanged a friendly smile and went about our business stretching and examining ourselves in the mirror.

"Do you know what's wrong with Elizabeth?" I asked him.

"Adrienne says she has some sort of virus."

Lila arrived, looking like she spent the vacation at the tanning salon. "Let's get started," she said. "We don't have a lot of time."

I wondered how much she had to do with the rehearsal. Lila seemed like less of ally when I received better roles, and this was just too important to come from anyone but William.

She talked us through the choreography and Grant took my hand so we could mark together. I had watched the *America pas de deux* a few times. I always danced in the *corps de ballet* in rehearsals. The cast used up the entire company, so there was no logistical way I could dance the lead. They would have to hire someone from the school to do my corps part.

Lila indicated the final lift and said, "Okay, Anna. That's the *adagio*. We'll work on your variation, the coda, and the opening and finale later. William should be here in a minute."

Ten minutes to learn it before I danced in front of William? "Okay." I doubted I remembered anything. I frantically reviewed the sequence and Grant marked behind me, resting his warm hands on my back. I found his confidence and professionalism reassuring.

William strode into the studio and leaned on the *barre*, looking handsome in a crisp pink button-down shirt and black pants. "How's it going?" he asked casually.

"Good," Lila said. Grant and I nodded in his direction and continued to mark the steps.

"Let's see what we have," William said. He walked over to stand by Lila in the front of the room.

Lila hit play and Grant and I danced the first thirty-two counts of the *adagio*. Grant was a strong and gentle partner and I did my best to match his competence. My arms shook when he walked me in a circle on pointe in *arabesque*. The partnering was complicated and I felt self-conscious about my lack of experience. Elizabeth could have done the choreography in her sleep.

"Stop," William said. "Let me show you." Lila switched off the music. I wiped sweat off my forehead. Grant stepped to the side so William could take my hand. His palm felt coarse.

"Hold your back," William commanded. He gently brushed my scapula with his free hand to indicate which muscles he wanted me to engage.

"Lock your arm in place," he whispered in my ear. We danced the first few steps. His touch was gentle and expert. "You try," William said to Grant. He took a step away from me but his hands seemed to take forever to let go. Lila watched us from the front and remained removed.

I took Grant's hand and we began again, still shaky and tentative at certain parts. We made it through the beginning.

"Stop," William said. He walked back and took hold of me to show Grant some tricks. I examined my reflection in the mirror. A tiny girl, only five-foot three and ninety-eight pounds, looked back. I seemed so young and vulnerable. On my right, I studied William, a living legend, and on my left, Grant, a younger and handsomer version of him. What was I doing there?

Grant and I danced the adagio several times and I liked dancing with him. He made me feel safe. By the end of the rehearsal we were exhausted. I could do the steps, but could I make them look as good as Elizabeth or Adrienne?

William walked over and put his hand on my shoulder. "You have a lot of work to do," William said. "Your back is too weak. Do push-ups every morning. Grant can't partner you if you can't hold yourself up."

"Yes," I said, nodding emphatically. "I will." He nodded, satisfied, and walked out of the studio. Grant leaned over, slowly, and took my hand. I laughed awkwardly. He squeezed my fingers reassuringly.

I hobbled home every day that week during my lunch hour and sat in the bathtub. My muscles burned. I felt out of shape and the choreography in the *pas de deux* was different than anything I had ever danced. I rehearsed with Grant for two hours every day after morning class, and in the afternoon, I rehearsed my corps part since the artistic staff's casting intentions still weren't clear. Elizabeth remained absent. Teddy had been sick on Monday, and since then I hadn't had a chance to ask him if he knew how she was doing.

My cellphone rang just as I walked in the door after work. I pulled it out of my purse and flopped on the couch.

"Hello?"

"Hi sweetie, it's me," Ethan said. "I'm cooking tonight, how about coming over for dinner? I haven't seen you in three days."

I sighed, happy to hear his voice and at the same time, pressured, because I had no energy left for him. "Oh, that sounds nice. I'm jut so tired I don't think I can go anywhere. I'm sorry. I just want to go to bed. You don't understand how much stress I'm under right now."

"I know," he said. We were silent for a minute and then he added, "I just want to see you. I miss you."

"Me too." My eyes welled up with tears. "I'm just overwhelmed right now. Please try to understand."

"I get it," he said, sounding irritated.

"I'm sorry, Ethan."

"I thought we had something good going here."

"We do," I whispered. "But you know how important it is for me to focus on my career right now."

"I know how important dance is to you," he said, "and I admire you for it. Sometimes I just wonder if you'll ever care about me as much as you seem to care about ballet. I think you love William and the company more than anyone or anything. We both know he likes you. What happens if he decides he wants something more? While the company has such a tight hold on you it's hard to imagine where else this relationship can go."

I sighed. "That's so unfair. I give you everything I have left to offer." I felt my whole body tighten and lost my patience. "I have to go. You don't understand."

"Fine," he said angrily and hung up the phone. I can't explain why I didn't call him back, even though I desperately wanted to change what I had said. After all, he hadn't done anything wrong except let me know how much he cared. Which, ultimately, might have been the thing that scared me the most. Ethan was right, of course. I couldn't possibly muster up what it would take to love him back the way he deserved, not when my career demanded so much.

At work the next day, I was still bleary-eyed and dazed from a night of restless sleep. For all my insistence that I needed to focus on myself, all I could think about was Ethan. I picked up the phone to call him a million times but couldn't bring myself to do it. My pride was in the way. I knew he had some meetings about buying the house and a big project to present at work. I wondered how everything was going. I hoped he would call or stop by.

A day went by and I heard nothing from him. What if he something went wrong with the house sale? I hated to admit it, but more and more I had envisioned moving in with him and eventually getting engaged.

On Friday, on my way to the afternoon rehearsal, I looked at the board and saw the casting for opening weekend had been posted. My name was next to Grant's for opening night. I would dance the principal role in the premiere the following Thursday. That meant I had six days to become a star. How could I do that without the most important person in my life by my side?

We had all been convinced that I was learning *America* just for rehearsal and that Elizabeth would dance the performances. It seemed impossible William would actually put me onstage in such a prominent role. My life had become the kind of story that only happened in ballet movies like *The Turning Point* and *Center Stage*. No matter how hard I worked or how talented I was, there was no reason for this kind of casting drama. We had enough principals who could dance *America* on opening night with Grant, even if Elizabeth was still sick. What about Natasha? Couldn't Adrienne dance with Grant? Or even a soloist or senior corps member who has been in the company much longer than me?

Traditionally, the younger corps members who were on a promotion track spent years dancing their leading roles at the Sunday matinee. It took years before someone to become the marquee star of the company. So why was this happening to me, and why this way? Everyone would be jealous, and the sad part was, I was having a hard time being happy for myself. The pressure felt like a noose around my neck. What if I let everyone down?

The entire company assembled in the big studio. Lila looked stressed out. The rehearsal was a big deal because it was the first time all the sections would come together since we worked on the ballet last summer. William arrived and the dancers cleared out of his way as he cut across the floor to join Lila.

"Let's face away from the mirror," Lila said. She put her chair in the middle of the window in front of the Third Street Promenade and gave us a real audience: the pedestrians. Opening night was only a day away.

A ballet about to premiere was like a meal about to be eaten: the hard work and dirty dishes abandoned in the kitchen, the food about to disappear fast, but the moment when the people sat down to feast made it all worth it. William looked like he was about to eat at the finest restaurant in LA. Pedestrians gathered outside the window at the sight of all the activity.

Mikey noticeably flinched and I followed his eyes to the doorway. Elizabeth stood there dressed in street clothes. She walked in and took a seat in a plastic chair in the corner. Allison hurried over to her and they started whispering. Elizabeth looked pale and tired but otherwise fine. Her first appearance since all of this began unnerved me. I didn't understand how she could let a virus keep her from dancing this important of a role. Elizabeth was never sick.

"Places," Lila called. Fifteen girls formed a triangle in the center of the floor and the music began. I stretched on the side of the room and watched the girl they had hired from the school rehearse my part in the corps. She had been understudying several corps spots since last summer and this was a big opportunity for her. I tried to put Ethan and Elizabeth out of my mind.

A different group of fifteen girls danced the second movement, and while they twirled, I stood up and practiced a few little jumps. Adrienne walked over to me carrying a practice tutu.

"Wear this," Adrienne whispered kindly. She helped me put the tutu on.

Fifteen boys danced the third movement, showing off their high jumps and turns. William watched intently and Lila wrote down corrections to save for the end. Grant winked at me across the room and I smiled back. For all the stress I felt, we had enjoyed working together.

My opinion of him had changed since we'd been rehearsing *America*. The more I knew him the nicer and less conceited he seemed, at least when we were alone together. In company class, he still paraded around like he was king of the world. I wanted to believe it was out of insecurity rather than egotism.

The music to the *pas de deux* began and Grant stepped on to the floor. I walked on four counts later, he offered me his hand, and I placed mine in his. We made eye contact and then I looked out, took in my audience, and realized I had never been so terrified in my life.

Dozens of my peers and closest friends stood or sat on the floor next to Lila and William. Behind them, through the window, a crowd of strangers eyed me expectantly. I stepped on to pointe and took Grant's hand for the *promenade,* but I felt emotionally flooded. Something inside me lurched. Right when I should have danced better than I ever had in my life, I fell flat on my face.

I lay there for a moment in shock while Lila stopped the music. The room went dead silent. Grant helped me stand back up. Tears pooled in my eyes and I bit my lip to stop them from coming. In my own defense, it had been an extremely stressful couple of days. That said, an audience doesn't pay a hundred bucks a ticket to hear excuses. William walked over and took my arm gently, pulling me away from Grant. I felt Elizabeth's eyes boring into my back. They were all staring at me.

"If you're not ready, you don't have to do this," William whispered in my ear. Our eyes met and even if he intended to be kind, all I saw in his expression was a challenge. I looked away and Grant stared at me pleadingly.

"No. I can do it," I insisted, locking eyes with William again. This was what my entire life had been leading up to. It would be absurd not to be ready.

People began to whisper and after a moment of consideration, William nodded. Grant's face broke out in a wide grin.

"Let's try that again," William said. He went back to his seat. I rolled my shoulders a few times, took a deep breath, and walked over to the side of the room. I refused to fall down again.

The music to the *pas de deux* began and Grant stepped on to the floor. I walked on four counts later, he offered me his hand, and I placed mine in his. When I felt his grip, strong and sure, our bodies connected in a way they hadn't before. I could feel the heat coming off him and our shared determination felt like a new kind of power. The renewed energy made the fall seem less important, like a dream, and our connection became the reality. We smiled at each other and I stepped on pointe.

We danced the entire *adagio* and Grant flew through his variation. I made it through my solo without any major hiccups. The coda sped by and while we were finishing, the other dancers walked to the side to get in place for the finale. Forty people posed around us in formation when Grant and I ran back on the floor. We danced alone again briefly before the whole company joined in behind us. As the finale came to an end, Grant lifted me up on his shoulder and I saluted on the last note.

Lila stopped the music. "Good. Let's talk about the first movement," she said. The girls crowded around her and Grant and I moved over to the side of the room. We were both out of breath and exchanged a sympathetic look.

"Not bad, Anna," he said, squeezing my shoulder.

"Thanks," I whispered. "Sorry I was so nervous."

"Don't worry," he said. "I know you can do this, and do it well. I wanted you as my partner since the first time I saw you perform. I've been pushing

William for it ever since. We dance well together. I see so much potential in you."

"Thanks Grant," I said, caught completely by surprise. I realized I was standing close to him, our faces only inches away. We were the perfect height for each other. I felt warm and comfortable, like we were two puppies, finished rumbling and catching our breath together.

William gestured to Jeff, who danced the soloist role in the boys' section, and took some time to coach him on his turns. While we waited for feedback, I turned to face the mirror and practiced some *pirouettes*. Ethan suddenly seemed so far removed from my life. Maybe we weren't going to work out after all.

"Let's talk about your variation," William said to Grant, beckoning to him. I stopped practicing to watch as they walked through a few steps. I leaned on the *barre* and admired Grant mirroring William's *port de bras*. Dancers began to filter out of the room. William indicated that Grant should dance the step full out. Grant launched into the air and bent his knees up above his waist, executing a spectacular jump.

"Good," William said emphatically. "We'll keep working on it, guys. Keep building your arm strength, Anna." He turned to me and nodded approvingly.

"I will." The three of us smiled at each other and I felt a glimmer of excitement.

I walked over to Elizabeth on my way out. She was whispering with Ryan by the door and they wrapped up their conversation quickly.

"Nice job, Anna," Elizabeth said awkwardly. "Congratulations." She didn't seem sick, just sad.

"Thanks. How are you feeling? I really thought you'd be back in time for the premiere."

"I thought I'd be back too," she said wistfully. "I can't even take class for another week though, doctor's orders. It might take awhile to get my stamina back up. The timing couldn't have been worse. Well, don't mind me. I'm happy it worked out well for you." Her painfully forced enthusiasm was kind. She must have felt awful.

"I'm sorry, Elizabeth. Thank you though. It's a great opportunity."

She flinched and I realized the last thing she would want was my pity. "Oh, well, don't worry about it," she said. "Good luck! I have to run, see you later." She gave me an uncomfortable hug and hurried out the door.

I wondered what was actually wrong with her. Any of us would have danced through a virus under the circumstances, no matter what the doctor said. Her illness must have been something serious.

Twelve

At four in the afternoon on the day of the premiere, I tied my sneakers in the dressing room. The tech rehearsal was over and I had to be back by seven-thirty for the half-hour call. The *America pas de deux* was at the end of the program and wouldn't start until ten. Everyone else had already left and I was starving. The door to the dressing room opened and I couldn't believe my eyes when I saw who walked in.

"Jen?"

My old roommate from SBNY threw her arms around me and shouted, "Surprise!"

Jen was so busy with her own career in New York that I couldn't imagine how she was able to get away. My eyes filled with tears.

Back in high school, she was the one who I cried with after terrible classes, laughed with after seeing a good Broadway show, and turned to for help after I fainted in my workshop performance. Jen was there for every big moment I had in New York, so it was fitting she would be there to see the most important performance of my professional career.

"You didn't think I would miss this milestone, did you?" she asked.

We hugged and jumped up and down like little kids. I packed up quickly so we could go out to eat, renewed by the reassurance that our friendship had stood the test of time and distance.

After dinner, I made sure Jen had a ticket. She sat backstage with me while I did my hair and makeup, and then I sent her out front to enjoy the show. I watched the opening ballet from the wings while I warmed up.

At intermission, I returned to the dressing room to put on my costume and found two bouquets on my chair. My parents had sent sunflowers and Grant sent roses. There was a card on top of my makeup case from all the girls in the corps, but there was nothing from Ethan and my heart sank. I had left him his usual ticket at the box office even though I had no idea if he was coming. We hadn't talked in over a week. Jen was the only one who knew about our fight.

A dresser fastened me into my blue and gold costume. I tied my pointe shoes, applied red lipstick, and headed for the stage. I was ready to live out every little girl's dream.

Grant met me onstage at the five-minute call and kissed my cheek. I could tell he was excited.

"Thank you for the flowers," I said as he took both of my hands in his own.

"Of course," he said enthusiastically. "We're going to be great." He led me to the front of the stage so we could practice the lifts that gave us trouble in rehearsal.

"Places," the new stage manager called a few minutes later. Grant caught me off-guard by pecking me on the lips. I was too dumbfounded to say anything. We separated and walked to opposite sides of the stage. I didn't see William, so I assumed he was out in the audience. The fifteen corps girls took their places and everything went black.

There was applause as the overture began and I could feel the energy in the theater. More applause poured out of the house as the curtain rose. The girls grinned as they moved through their formations. I wondered if Elizabeth was in the audience. Something told me she wasn't.

The second group of girls took the stage, kicking their legs all the way to their ears. Time flew by. When the boys went on, I started to jog in place.

"*Merde,*" people whispered as they passed me. I stepped into the back wing and the music to the *pas de deux* began.

Grant stepped onstage and I followed four counts later. He offered me his hand and I put mine in his, feeling his energy like a jolt of electricity. We smiled and danced together in a concentrated effort. My whole body grew warm underneath the spotlight as we performed the *adagio*. Our performance was flawless, except for one small fumble during the partnered turns right at the end. It was a small error I could live with.

"Perfect," Grant whispered. We walked forward to bow. I exited the stage and he launched into his variation. I tried to regain my breath. The audience applauded when I ran on for my solo. I jumped, whirled, and became the music. It was fun.

"Yes!" I said to myself as I whipped out a series of double turns, perfectly on. At the end, I was so physically tired that I couldn't feel my legs. Somehow I managed to bow and run off.

Grant ripped through the air as the coda began. I ran on for the series of consecutive turns on one leg and he saluted while I was already in motion. After a double *pirouette* at the end of the *fouettés*, I marched around on *pointe*, hit the wing, and posed with one leg out behind me in *arabesque*, holding my balance far into the next musical phrase. The audience clapped and whistled. While Grant flew around the stage, I ran around to the back wing.

"Go, Anna!" Faye cheered.

I re-entered, spinning across the stage as Grant stepped in to partner me. He tossed me high into the air and sweat flew off of us like a sprinkler. The music to the *pas de deux* ended with a joyous crescendo as we ran into the wings.

"We're almost done," Grant whispered, pumping his fist victoriously. "We nailed it."

I squeezed his shoulder, too tired and out of breathe to manage anything but a grin.

The corps danced the opening to the finale and then posed as Grant and I ran back under the lights. The entire company danced together as the ballet came to an end. Grant lifted me up on his shoulder and I saluted on the very last note. The curtain fell.

Grant lowered me to the ground. I squeezed his hand. We bowed as the curtain flew up and then back down. Everyone raced for the wings except the first fifteen girls, who hurried to line up. My face glowed with happiness and pride as I watched the rest of the company take their bows.

Grant stepped onstage and offered me his hand. He led me to the center in front of the entire cast and we walked forward to the apron of the stage. I extended my right arm over my head and pointed my right foot behind me. My right hand came to my heart as I kneeled, and I bowed my head in a *grande révérance*.

The audience stood up to applaud. I ran to the front wing and led the conductor out onstage. "You were beautiful," the *maestro* said. I squeezed his hand.

A patron in a tuxedo presented me with a huge bouquet of red, white, and blue flowers, and I pulled out a red rose and presented it to Grant.

"Bravo!" the audience shouted.

Our fingers touched as Grant accepted the rose. He dropped to his knee to kiss my hand as the curtain fell.

"You were amazing," he said, looking up into my eyes. We were both happy.

Dancers exited into the wings, pulling pins out of their hair and tugging at their costumes. I stood at the front of the stage, my arms filled with flowers, inhaling the sweat mixed with roses and rosin.

Lila walked past, her short hair whipping her in the face as she turned to look back at me. "It went well except for the end of the *adagio*," she said curtly. "Good job."

William walked over to kiss my cheek and shake Grant's hand. He rested his hand on my shoulder and his rare smile told me he was pleased.

People patted me on the back and congratulated me as I walked off the stage, eager to go collapse, remove my makeup, and take a long hot shower.

"Wait," Grant said behind me. He took my arm and steered me into a dark corner behind the stage.

"Is everything okay?" I asked. Before the words were out Grant kissed me. Maybe it was the excitement of the evening, or the sheer physicality of our dance connection, but for a split-second, I couldn't help myself and kissed him back. He grabbed my shoulders and pulled me closer.

"Anna?"

I pulled away from Grant and turned to see Ethan standing there, a huge bouquet of dahlias in his hand. The look on his face broke my heart.

"Ethan! It's not...I..." His appearance at just that moment was disastrous.

Ethan dropped the flowers on the ground and stormed off. I ran after him, panic rising in my chest. "Ethan wait! Let me explain."

"There's nothing to explain, Anna," he snapped, stopping to glare at me. "Now I know why you've been pulling away. Hilary was right."

"Hilary? What does she have to do with anything? I haven't been pulling away. I've just been so busy. There's nothing between Grant and me. I wasn't expecting that. The kiss came out of nowhere! This is the worst timing. I miss you! I've been trying to get up my courage to call you all week. It means so much to me that you came."

"I saw you dancing with him and how you kissed him back. I'm an idiot to have come."

"That's not true. I love you, Ethan. I love you!" We were making a scene but I couldn't help it, I was desperate not to lose him. Without Ethan, all of the professional success was meaningless. "What do you mean that Hilary was right?"

"Let me go for now. I need some time to think straight," he said, pulling away. I grabbed his arm and he shook me off. Helplessly, I watched him walk out the stage door while tears streamed down my face.

As always, my professional life interrupted my personal one. "Congratulations, Anna!" said one of the prominent board members, coming up beside me. She gave me a kiss on the cheek and introduced me to her group of friends. I had no choice but to give her a hug and put on my best stage smile. When she let me go, I headed straight for the dressing room. Hilary was at her spot wiping makeup off her face.

"What did you say to him Hilary? Tell me. What did you tell Ethan?"

"What are you talking about, Anna?" Hilary asked innocently.

"Ethan said you told him something about Grant."

"About Grant? Oh. Well, I ran into Ethan the other day and he asked how *America* was going, so I told him it was great and you and Grant have noticeable chemistry together. That's the truth, isn't it?"

"How dare you!"

"Excuse me?" she said calmly. "Look, don't get mad at me if you're having relationship troubles. It's not my problem."

"Next time, mind your own business, Hilary, and leave my boyfriend alone."

"Whatever." She shrugged nonchalantly.

I was so angry with her I couldn't stop shaking. There was nothing to do but walk away. All the joy I gained from the performance had disappeared into thin air. It should have been the most triumphant night of my life, and instead of celebrating, I went home inconsolable.

Jen read me the reviews over breakfast the next morning. "The premiere of *America* is a stunning achievement for William Mason and the Los Angeles Ballet Theatre, and Mason's choice to cast a young corps dancer in the ballerina role was a pleasant surprise. Anna Linado faced the technical demands of the *pas de deux* with charm and ease. It's a role Linado can certainly grow into…"

"That's nice," I said, sipping hot coffee. My eyes were still a puffy mess. "What a relief that the reviews are okay. At least something in my life is working out. It's hard to appreciate when I'm so worried about Ethan. What am I going to do?"

"Who cares?" Jen said. "This is going to make your whole career."

"Oh Jen," I said, "It's pretty crazy. But what should I say to Grant? How can I explain this to Ethan? I'm so confused."

"Anyone would have been caught up considering the situation," Jen said.

"It's no excuse," I said, miserable. "I'm so mad at Hilary. She's a snake."

"She always was," Jen agreed. "But you can't blame everything on her."

All I could do was sigh. "I know."

After I dropped Jen at the airport, I called Ethan on my way to work. He didn't pick up and I was too embarrassed to leave a message. Grant caught my eye and winked in morning class, and much to my chagrin, I realized I kept looking at him. Afterwards, he caught up to me in the hallway as I was on my way to the dressing room.

"Want to get some lunch after the next rehearsal? I'm done at one," he said.

"Oh, I can't, I'm too busy," I said awkwardly.

"We need to talk."

"I know," I said with a sigh. "I need to talk to Ethan first."

"Is it serious with him, Anna? I want to get to know you better. We have a good thing going here." It wasn't what I had expected. I had thought Grant was just playing around.

"Grant, Ethan and I have been together for a long time. I love dancing with you, but I love *him*."

"Do you?" he asked. "I'm sure you think you love him. But I know how passionately you kissed me, and what do you have in common with a non-dancer anyway? Work it out for yourself. You'll come around." He planted a firm kiss on my lips and headed back in to rehearsal, leaving me more confused than ever. Grant was confident he wouldn't have to wait long for me, and he was right about one thing: I had kissed him back and enjoyed it. But in my heart I knew I loved Ethan. He was the one person who made me feel like more than just a dancer. Ethan made me whole.

I walked over to Ethan's house as soon as I left rehearsal. As I expected, he was out in the yard furiously pruning hedges.

"Hi," I said, coming up behind him. "Can we talk?"

He froze and his whole body tensed up. I felt a rush of love for him. He had been my rock through so many things. Why did I mess up everything? Any woman my age would have been prioritizing him. There was a line of single girls who would snatch

Ethan up in a second, and I knew what we had was was rare and special.

"I'm so sorry about yesterday, and about everything," I said, tentatively putting my hand on his shoulder. "I love you, Ethan. You're the most important person in my life and I don't want to lose you. Will you at least look at me?"

He turned his head and let out a long and painful sigh. I breathed a sigh of relief when I saw the look on his face. He still loved me. We could work this out. Then I was in his arms and everything was okay again.

"Anna!" Mikey called down the produce aisle at the grocery store.

"Mikey, how are you?" I called, walking over. He had been out with tendonitis. Between injuries and the drinking problem, his life was a mess.

"I got fired," he said.

"What?"

"Yep. Eight years for nothing. I joined this company when I was seventeen. William got the best years of my life. I can't help that I was injured all year, and I know he blames me about Elizabeth even though he very well could have been the one who got her pregnant. She always told me she was on the pill. " His lower lip trembled.

"What?" I thought maybe I'd heard him wrong.

He covered his mouth with his hand. "You didn't know?"

"Elizabeth is *pregnant*?"

"Well, not anymore," he said matter-of-factly. "She had a miscarriage right before the premiere. You don't think she seriously would have given up that role for a virus, do you?"

"Oh wow." Things started to fall into place. "I knew something was odd but I had no idea. Was it…?"

"She doesn't know for sure who the father was," he said. "I was pretty sure it wasn't mine because of the timing."

"Did William know?"

"He found out when she miscarried. Why do you think he fired me?"

Everyone knew William told Mikey to clean up back in December, before Elizabeth got pregnant, but there was no use in saying that now. "I'm so sorry. How far along was she?"

"About six weeks," he said. "She was still deciding if she was going to keep the baby and trying to get up the nerve to tell William. Then she woke up bleeding and called me in the middle of the night to drive her to the emergency room. She had to tell William after that."

"How did he react?"

"He was nice to her. I think he's just relieved she miscarried. Personally, I feel like such a jerk. I was never there for her and I never loved her when she wanted to be with me so much. She seems so alone and she doesn't even want me to be there for her. It's like she finally realized she didn't have a commitment from William or from me. I just feel so bad. I care about her and would never have wanted this to happen. It could have been my kid too, you know? It probably wasn't, but it could have been."

I put my arms around him and held on tight. "I'm so sorry, Mikey."

He sniffed and pulled away, shutting down his vulnerability. "What are you going to do now?" I asked. He seemed so lost.

"I'm moving home to Minnesota," he said. "I feel totally defeated. My résumé is a joke. I never graduated high school. All I ever wanted to do was dance. Things weren't supposed to turn out this way."

"No, they weren't."

He opened his mouth as if to speak and I felt all the potential of what might come out: self-loathing; anger; frustration. It was painful to see. "You don't have to say anything else, Mikey. I understand."

He looked at me as if he wanted me to do something, but I was helpless and all I could think to offer was sympathy. "I'll see you later," he said finally. His shoulders drooped as he walked away.

The season ended quietly. Things weren't great with Ethan, but they weren't terrible either. We continued to work on things and it felt like a new era for our relationship. We both had realized we couldn't take each other for granted.

After the *America* run, I went back to dancing in the corps. There were no casting surprises and as much as I was hoping I'd get more solos, *America* seemed to be my big moment of the year. I could live with it.

When our contracts came in the mail, I didn't get promoted. I had expected to become a soloist, even though I knew I was young and hadn't been in the company as long as many of the other corps girls. After *America*, I felt I deserved it.

I tried to convince myself that William had a plan for me, as he had promised. I swallowed my pride and jumped right back into work, convinced I would just have to work harder than ever and hope I'd receive more opportunities next year. Eventually William had to promote me. I didn't see how he couldn't if he continued to use me as a principal.

At the end of a long week, I walked over to Ethan's for dinner. The door was open and when I walked in I saw the table had been set and candles were already lit. He came banging through the kitchen door.

"Guess what?" Ethan said.

"What's the occasion?"

"I closed on the house."

"You mean it's officially all yours?"

He lifts my chin up and passionately presses his lips to mine. "We're going to be so happy here," he said. "I love you. I'm sorry things have been strained the last few months."

"'We,' you say?"

"Yes," he said. "We. Will you move in?"

"I love you too," I said, filled with happiness. The ballet stuff melted away when I was with him. Being with Ethan was the most real thing in my life, and the prospect of a future with him, in the house we had worked on together for so long, was an even better reward than a promotion. "But I can't move in unless there's a ring on my finger."

I had been thinking about it long before he asked, and decided that if we moved forward, I wanted to be deliberate. When I danced, I never liked to do things halfway. It didn't make sense to be with Ethan that way either. I wanted it all.

Ethan raised an eyebrow. "Okay then," he said. "I'll make a note of that. We can revisit this discussion later. I was thinking we might go to Hawaii for a week during your layoff."

He looked so handsome and sincere, standing there in the candlelight. I hoped I could be as good to him as he was to me. My biggest fear used to be failing at ballet, but at that moment, I realized that losing him would be the worst thing imaginable.

Thirteen

While my personal life blossomed, my career took a downward turn. On the first day of my fourth season, I looked at the rehearsal schedule and saw that Hilary had been called to learn the lead in *Fire*. I was only called to rehearsals for the corps.

"What is going on?" Faye whispered to me in the back of the studio while the first group executed the *pirouette* combination. "Why is Hilary of all people learning *Fire*? Why not you? You were great in *America*."

"Thanks," I said. "It's not so much that I'm not learning it, although I wonder now if I did something wrong. I just can't believe they picked *her*. This is ballet school all over again! Don't even tell me her parents donated a ton of money to the company. They already pulled that trick in New York. Or is she seriously William's new favorite?"

"I have no idea," said Faye. "But this makes me sick."

Hilary danced front and center in class and looked more full of her self than ever. She wore layers of blue eye shadow and made odd faces at her reflection in the mirror, as if she was trying out her stage smile. Allison, Rebecca, and Sasha glared openly at her from the side of the room.

It rarely seemed possible for us to be completely happy for each other's good fortune, but it was even harder to be pleased for Hilary. Even though we put up with her because we had to, and she worked as hard as any of us and was just as deserving on that count, no one could stand her personality. I found it difficult to see someone ugly on the inside have more success than someone I respected. There was something about it that felt unjust. I knew life wasn't fair, but that didn't stop me from wishing things would work out as I felt they should.

William looked right through me in class. I felt invisible at work and as the rehearsal week continued, I found myself growing angrier. Why were they treating me this way? What did I do?

I picked up Karina's diary that night. I'd forgotten about it for a long time.

William has a new favorite, Teresa. She's only been in the company two years and is all of twenty. I wish we knew what he saw in her. Sure she's thin and has a pretty face, but her feet and extension aren't that great and her technique is sloppy. I hate watching her get the opportunities so many older girls in the corps deserve instead. Allison has been here five years already and she's furious. When I talked to her she didn't even come up for air. She was dying to vent.

Allison: *"I'd like to ask William what he sees in Teresa, and why he plays favorites depending on who he wants to sleep with. William is a father figure to most of us and this company is one big dysfunctional family. Where does he get off treating us like children? We're grown adults. It feels like an insult when he calls us boys and girls instead of women or men.*

Sometimes his attitude towards us is so derogatory, which is amazing because he was a dancer himself! We all work so hard and these are our real careers, just like any other grown-up. Yet he doesn't see us as adults, we're just like his little toys that he takes out to play with and discard.

All I've ever wanted is to be a dancer, so when he casts these fresh-faced kids right out of ballet school into the big roles I've been passed over for, it feels like a big screw-you. I take his decisions very personally.

Honestly, our lives are an illusion. People think we're so glamorous and in reality, we're not treated well or fairly and we never earn enough money. I've been frustrated throughout my career. It's really an internal struggle, because I feel so lucky to have had the career I do and dance with such a great company. So many kids never realize this dream. I just hate that the man who gave me this opportunity is the same one who breaks my heart."

I read Allison's passage in Karina's diary several times. If that was how Allison felt back when the diary was written, I can only imagine what she thought of me when I was dancing *America,* and what she must think of Hilary now. It must be so hard to spend ten years in the corps, watching the cycle of newcomers have their moment in the sun over and over. How many of the favorites actually made it to principal anyway? Not many, apparently. I had never even heard of Teresa. What happened to her?

At the first full company rehearsal of *Fire,* Elizabeth was still out. Lila told Hilary to dance the lead. After my corps part was over, I sat on the side and watched Hilary and Grant dance the *pas de deux.*

I was jealous that she was dancing with him. I had been careful to avoid him since the new season started and I'd heard he was dating someone. It wasn't that I missed Grant; it was the feeling of being special enough to be his partner. Dancing with him, once I had found my confidence, was *fun*.

Grant didn't seem to be having fun with Hilary. She didn't allow him to partner her the way he wanted. Instead, she tried to control and lead every step they executed. They seemed terribly mismatched. His touch was light and relaxed and she tried to power through everything, so together, he made her look frantic and she made him look lazy. She also repeatedly made that horrible face at herself in the mirror, where she fake-smiled for the audience. Their rehearsal made me cringe.

Lila didn't seem to think they looked bad and peppered them with compliments. I wondered if she noticed how much I was glaring at her. The more I watched them the more I wanted to do something crazy, like throw a rock at the mirror. Eventually, I couldn't take it anymore and walked out into the hallway to get some air.

"Hey Ian," I said, sitting down next to him on the bench. He seemed bored. I watched him chug a soda in one gulp.

"Hi princess," he said. "How's it going?"

"Oh, fine, I guess."

"I thought you'd be the one learning *Fire*," he said. "I guess Hilary is the new golden girl."

"Don't get me started."

"Sorry, Linado."

"Ian," I said, "do you know anything about a former dancer in the company named Teresa?"

Adrienne and Zif, who were on the floor stretching, immediately looked up.

"Teresa?" Adrienne echoed.

"Where did you hear about her?" Zif asked.

"Oh geez," Ian said. He sighed deeply.

"I don't know," I said, "I just heard she was William's favorite a few years back and wondered what happened to her. Did she get promoted? Did she go to another company?"

"No, and no," Adrienne said.

"No? Did she quit?"

"No," Ian said quietly. "She overdosed."

"What?"

"She committed suicide," Adrienne said, her voice cracking.

I was speechless. Why would a young beautiful girl who had everything going for her do something like that? "I had *no* idea."

"We don't really talk about it," Zif said, rising to his feet. He gave Adrienne an arm up and they walked back into the studio. I could tell I'd upset them.

"It was a real tragedy," Ian whispered. "The company did their best to sweep it under the rug."

"She really died?" The story was starting to sink in.

He nodded. "She was one of William's favorites, like you were and Hilary is now. I don't know exactly what happened, but apparently she wanted a promotion and he didn't want to give it to her.

She did principal roles for two years and at the end of the first year she was upset she didn't get promoted. The second year she complained to him and even though he was initially polite, he started casting her less and less, even in the corps. He was trying to make a point that he could cast whomever he wanted, when he wanted, and no one could tell him what to do.

That was also the year Natasha joined the company and William started sleeping with her. They're more discreet about it now, but that first year they were flagrant and the whole company was furious about it. Everyone knew and saw things.

Teresa was particularly troubled by the politics of the company and after the contracts came out again and she wasn't promoted, she took a bunch of pills. Her whole life was ballet. I guess she'd started on antidepressants shortly before, and she just took a whole bottle of them. She lived alone and they didn't even find her for several days."

That was the girl Allison was talking about in Karina's journal? They both thought she had everything. We all would have thought she had everything.

"That's the saddest thing I've ever heard," I said. "What did William do?"

"Not much," Ian said, shrugging. "He went to the funeral. Might have made a speech or something about how much we all loved her and blah blah blah. I'm sure he never assumed any responsibility. She was just a little ballet kid, after all. We're all disposable, remember?"

"I'm sorry I asked," I said. "I feel horrible now."

"Don't," Ian said. "You didn't know. We all felt terrible about it because she was so alone and none of us noticed. Everyone was just jealous of her and we all missed that she was seriously depressed. The world shouldn't end if William overlooks any of us. He's not worth it, despite how much we put into this."

"I know," I said. "I just can't believe he's still doing the same stuff he did to her. He must have known he didn't treat her fairly. That frightens me. What if I'm on the same career downward spiral? It sure seems that way."

"Maybe you are," Ian said. "It isn't the end of the world. At least you have Ethan. At the end of the day, that's the stuff that really matters."

I stared at him blankly. What went through Teresa's mind? I can only imagine. I was still crushed I hadn't been promoted at the end of last season. What was going to happen if I didn't get promoted this year either? I might not even get to dance soloist roles at all anymore. How would I feel then?

For the first time it occurred to me that I should find Karina. It had only been about five years since she left the company. I had so many questions. Maybe she had wondered where her diary was all this time. Once I finished reading it, I was going to track her down. I wanted to know how her story turned out.

Fourteen

After I read the last entry, I finally told Ethan about the journal. I couldn't keep it in anymore and thinking about Teresa's story made me crazy.

"We should find Karina," he agreed. "What you need is some good sound advice from someone who has been in the trenches and moved beyond it. I know things are tough now and I hate to see you this distraught over work. William is such a jerk. He's just not worth it. You're the one who matters. These mind games aren't good for you. William can't be counted on to take care of anyone except himself."

I knew he was right. "I'm thinking about auditioning for other companies. I don't think my career is going in the right direction anymore."

"It's not a bad idea. Let's think about it. But that would mean leaving LA, wouldn't it?" My heart sank as I realized he was right, and I couldn't ask him to leave his job and his house.

After dinner, Ethan took the journal and sat down in his favorite easy chair. He read while I sewed a pair of pointe shoes.

"I thought I knew a lot about the company, but this is really eye-opening, isn't it?" he said, without looking up.

"Yes."

He sat there for hours, reading, and after awhile I grew tired and went to bed. I fell sound asleep in minutes. I didn't even stir when he crawled in next to me at three in the morning.

The next day, I walked to work with renewed resolve. I wasn't ready to give up.

When I arrived, I noticed a couple kissing in front of the entrance. The guy pushed against the girl as she drew her arms tighter around his neck. I recognized Hilary's bun.

They came up for air and I saw it was Hilary and Grant. I felt like I was falling from the sky in slow motion. Was this why Hillary was the new favorite? Was it because I rejected Grant and Hilary moved in on him? Grant had requested me as a partner. Of course he could change his mind and tell William he wanted someone else instead.

"Excuse me." I shoved past them. Hilary turned and our eyes met, her expression triumphant. I turned away, determined to not give her the satisfaction of seeing my reaction.

Allison and Faye were in the dressing room when I stumbled through the door. Faye noticed my distress immediately. "Are you okay?" she asked. I nodded and walked over to hide in the corner. It wasn't the time or place to be upset, but I couldn't stop myself. I started crying as I changed my clothes. Faye watched me, concerned.

Hilary appeared a minute later and marched right over. "Are you upset?" Hilary asked. "I can't imagine why. You have a boyfriend. Nothing happened between you and Grant. You were too naïve to seize the opportunity when you had it." Faye and

Allison stared. The dressing room continued to fill up and others glanced over.

"Do you always have to do something underhanded to get your parts?" I snapped. "You're a good enough dancer, Hilary. Why can't you let your talent speak for itself? Why do you have to be such a witch?" My hands were shaking and I dropped my ballet slippers. Faye bent down to pick them up. She held out my shoes and I took them without looking at her.

"What's going on?" Faye asked.

"Hilary and Grant were just making out outside the studio," I said, still glaring at Hilary.

"Ah," Faye said. She let out a deep sigh, processing the news. "Of *course* they were. Well, I guess we should have known."

"You didn't want him, Anna," Hilary snapped. "If you actually knew what was good for your career you would have taken that opportunity when you had the chance. It's not my fault you're so stupid. Besides, he's crazy about me. He said he made a big mistake about you anyway and that you're too insecure."

The comment stung. "Do you actually care about him?" I couldn't stop myself. "Or is it all about climbing the ladder for your career?"

"Shut up," she hissed. "Not every relationship has to be about love. Not all of us can have what you found with Ethan, okay? Besides, who said you deserved *America* any more than I did? You just got lucky. Well I'm William's favorite now, how do you like that? You're just jealous."

I was about to explode at her when I caught a glimpse of Allison's face, which put the whole scene in perspective. Who did Hilary and I think we were? We hadn't even been in the company more than a few years. I dug my nails into my arms and took a deep breath.

"Stay away from me, Hilary. I would never have done something like this. You make me sick." I walked away and let the door slam as I left the dressing room.

It was like the last two years never happened. William and Lila seemed to forget, but I could not. The weeks went by and going to work became more and more difficult. I cried a lot of the mornings on my walk in. It was just so hard. I felt humiliated to have fallen so out of favor and resented how bitter and jealous I had become.

When I saw Hilary rehearse the lead in *Tidal Moods* I wanted to scream. Roizman's choreography looked terrible on her. Her style wasn't fluid enough for the role and her movements were much too jerky. She acted in a ballet that had no story and violated everything we were ever taught at SBNY. Grant must have been coaching her in a more classical style. When Lila scheduled rehearsals for Grant and Hilary to work on the *America pas de deux,* I started to wonder if I was losing my mind.

I didn't understand how they could all act as if nothing was wrong.

Work was a constant exercise in rage. I began to wish I had never danced any plum roles because now the corps parts felt like a let down. Ballet wasn't a passion anymore: it was my job. I constantly felt angry and self-righteous.

In September, my parents went to Italy for three months on sabbatical. "It's our second honeymoon," Mom said over the phone. "Don't expect us to call much."

I was so miserable I couldn't be happy for anyone else. Ethan noticed my depression and grew increasingly impatient with me. He wanted me to quit and asked persistently why I hadn't tried to find Karina. I just didn't have the energy. I wasn't even sure I wanted to hear what she had to say.

My family and friends had lives of their own, and as Ethan pulled away from me in frustration, I felt like I was no one's priority. During my off-hours, I daydreamed about auditioning for other companies, pretending that Ethan would agree to move with me. Companies didn't hire until January and February, and even though it was early, I sent preliminary letters to San Francisco, Miami, and several companies in Europe. I was scared to go into a new company as an older professional. Despite all that had happened, I didn't want to leave William and LA. I used to have such high hopes for how things would turn out. The reality was difficult to accept. There was nothing I wanted to grow into at LABT anymore.

At five-thirty the night before LABT left on an east coast tour, I sat in the back of the studio after I danced my corps role in *Fire*. Grant and Hilary rehearsed the *pas de deux*. They were cast to make their debut on tour. Sasha, who had also been given the opportunity to learn the role, marked behind them. She was angry that she had been cast behind Hilary. The whole scene killed me to watch.

William sat in the front of the studio, his arms crossed, while Hilary danced her solo confidently right in front of him. I wondered if he noticed that she sickled her feet and danced off the music.

"She's so full of herself," Faye whispered. It was all I could do not to walk out of the room.

I stood up and followed Allison on for the finale. I had danced the corps in *Fire* so many times I didn't even have to think about it. As I danced, a million thoughts ran through my head. William: "I have big plans for you." Sally Mitchell, my favorite teacher in New York: "Talent means nothing without desire." Jen: "The mirror has a million faces." My mom: "You feel passionate about things in a way others can't."

All eight *Fire* corps girls jumped with the right leg extended high in the air. When I landed, my foot slid out from under me and I fell on my left arm. Karina had broken her leg executing the exact same step. My scream was so loud I didn't recognize my own voice.

Faye, who was in the second cast and wasn't dancing when I fell, drove me to the company doctor while they finished the *Fire* rehearsal. I held an ice bag over my elbow and sobbed in the car. "It's broken—I can tell. There's no way I'm going on the tour. This is horrible. I'm left-handed and couldn't even manage to break my right arm. I won't even be able to wash my hair."

"Everything will be okay," Faye said quietly. She glanced over at me. "I must say you're pretty pathetic." She cracked a smile.

I had lost my sense of humor. "Was I that bad in *America*?"

"Bad?" she asked, tightening her grip on the wheel. "Of course not. I thought you were great."

"Why does William hate me now?"

"He doesn't hate you," she said. "I don't think it's personal at all. There are other dancers that deserve a chance too. Maybe not Hilary, but one person shouldn't get every role."

"How can I not take it personally?"

"You just can't," she said. "Look. If we want to last here, we have to shut our eyes to what we don't want to see. You know ballet isn't just satin slippers and curtain calls."

"I think this is self-torture."

"Anna. You love ballet." I wished she would get angry once—just once.

"If I love ballet so much, why am I this miserable?"

Faye sighed and gave up.

The doctor x-rayed my left arm and told me what I already knew. The broken arm would take six weeks to heal. I begged him not to put me in a hard cast but he said that if I didn't wear it, my arm might heal dislocated. That meant I'd probably have arthritis when I got older. Either way I lost. If I let the doctor put the hard cast on, my arm would atrophy and it would take twice as long to get back to dancing.

My priority was the present, not the future, because I couldn't see beyond the current crisis. In ballet there wasn't later, there was only now. I decided against the hard cast. I was determined to be back in five weeks.

The company left on tour without me. My dominant arm was useless. My parents were in Italy and they didn't even know what had happened. I had never had to depend so much on Ethan. In addition to his full-time job, he cooked, cleaned, and even gently washed my hair. I loved him more than ever and wished I could be the person I was when we first fell in love. Where was that girl?

We didn't talk about an engagement anymore. Everything seemed so up in the air.

A week after my accident, Ethan woke me up and handed me a vanilla latte, my favorite. "We're going on a little day trip today," he announced. "There's somewhere I need to take you."

"We are? I don't think I feel like going out."

"Too bad," he said. "Let's get you dressed."

"Where are we going?"

"Santa Cruz. We've got a big drive so let's get going."

"What's in Santa Cruz?" I had never been there.

"You'll see."

We had a good time on the drive up. The rolling hills looked open and free and the farther we drove from LA the more hopeful and alive I started to feel. We stopped for lunch along the way and as I looked at Ethan across the table I realize I hadn't really *looked* at him in weeks. He seemed excited too and it made me happy to see him smile.

After lunch we drove into Santa Cruz. The air was foggy from the coast and the sleepy feel of the town wrapped around me, comforting and safe. We drove through downtown and headed north, eventually pulling onto a small side street.

"This is it," Ethan said, parking in front of a small gray house with a white picket fence.

It dawned on me at last. "We're going to meet Karina."

"Yes," he said.

"How did you find her?"

"The internet is a magical place," he said. "I sent a lot of emails to the wrong people and got lucky with one."

"Wow. So she knows we're coming?"

"She knows." He looked pleased with himself.

"I didn't bring the journal. Does she know about it?"

"Yes, and I have it here." He pulled it out of his pocket. "She was thrilled to learn we had it."

"Oh. Good," I said, suddenly sad at the idea of returning it. "Do we have to give it back?"

"Yes. It's not ours. You have your own story to tell, anyway."

"I guess I do."

The woman who opened the door took my breath away. "Karina?" She was younger-looking than I expected and shockingly beautiful. Tall with long pitch-black hair, her striking features, big eyes, long neck, and narrow head make her the picture-perfect prima ballerina.

She nodded. "Hi Anna. Ethan. Come on in."

We followed her into the living room. Her house felt warm, decorated with plush brown sofas, cozy blankets, black and white artwork, and a big stone fireplace.

"Sit," she commanded. "Would you like something to drink?"

"That sounds great," Ethan said.

"Sweetheart," she called, "will you bring in the coffee?"

"Coming," a man hollered from the other room.

"It's so good to meet you," I said.

"Thank you. So, you really found my old journal?" she asked eagerly. "I've been looking for it for ages."

"Yes," I said, my heart beating loudly in my ears. Ethan held her diary out to her and she stared at it in disbelief.

"Wow," she said, taking the book gingerly as if it might break. We watched quietly while she opened the cover. Tears filled her eyes almost immediately.

A tall handsome man with silver hair walked into the room carrying a tray with a teapot and mugs. He set everything down on the coffee table.

"I'm Matt," he said, reaching out his hand so we could shake it. I was happy to see she had someone like him.

"Nice to meet you," Ethan said, "and sorry to drop in out of the clear blue like this."

"Oh no," Matt said. "You should have seen her when she found out you had the diary. You can't imagine what this means to her."

"I can imagine," I said. Karina continued leafing through the book, clearly trying to collect herself. Tears ran down her cheeks. Matt poured the coffee and handed each of us a cup. I took mine awkwardly with my right hand and set it down right away.

"I'm sorry about your arm," Matt said. "What happened?"

"Oh," I said, "I fell rehearsing *Fire*."

Karina looked up and closed her journal. "You fell in *Fire*?"

I nodded, staring at her. "Karina, we read the diary."

Much to my relief, she didn't even blink. "I assumed. Why else would you have found me?"

I breathed a sigh of relief. She was right. I had worried she would be angry. "I'm sorry if we invaded your privacy. But yes, I fell in *Fire*. The exact same step you fell when you broke your leg."

She sucked in her breath. "I can't believe it. That's so strange," she said.

"I have so many questions for you," I blurted out, and as soon as I said it tears welled up in my eyes.

"Oh dear. It's that bad," Karina said.

"I've been so worried," Ethan said. "The company is killing her. William gave her all these big roles. She performed them and did a great job. Then he just took them all away with no explanation."

"I heard the story about Teresa," I said. "Your journal ends when she was getting the big roles, and I started wondering what had happened to her. I asked Ian, and Adrienne and Zif were there and they looked like they'd seen a ghost. Ian told me the story. I haven't been able to get it out of my head. In the meantime, my rival started dating my former partner and now she's the favorite and getting all the big parts."

"Nothing changes," Karina said. "Is William still sleeping with both Natasha and Elizabeth?"

"I don't think Elizabeth anymore," I said. "She had a miscarriage and no one knows if it was William's or Mikey's."

"Geez," Matt said, letting out a low whistle. "That place is such a soap opera. I hate that guy."

"Karina, why did you finally leave?" I asked.

She glanced at Matt. "Go on," he prompted. "Tell her."

Karina sat for a minute, collecting herself. "I was the one who found Teresa," she finally said.

"Oh my God," I gasped. Ethan put his hand on my knee. I stared at Karina's beautiful face, trying to imagine. I couldn't.

"We lived on the same block," she said matter-of-factly. "So after she didn't show up at work for a few days I stopped by. I had a spare key because I'd water her plants and stuff when she went home to see her parents in Iowa. I went back to work the following week. I'd almost finished my physical therapy and had been starting to take class. But it was just too hard to take, seeing William every day. We were all so angry with him and he didn't even seem to understand his role in what happened to Teresa. A lot of people left after that season. I think there were fourteen dancers who quit. I made it back for a few performances and realized I just didn't care anymore. I spent that whole year working towards getting back onstage, and when I finally did it felt horrible. I just couldn't look at William anymore."

"I don't blame you," Ethan murmured.

"So what did you do?" I asked. "After you left, I mean."

"What most of us do," she said. "I moved back home with my parents for awhile. They live in Los Altos. I taught some ballet classes at my old studio and started school at Santa Clara. It was the best year of my life. Teaching reminded me why I liked to dance in the first place, and even though college was intimidating, it made me feel hopeful, like there was a future beyond my ballet career. I felt so liberated."

"Did you tell William why you left?"

"I sure did," she said. "He didn't get it. He just said something about how an injury is very difficult and I would never dance the same anyway. When I brought up Teresa, he dismissed it and said she had mental problems and it wasn't the company's fault."

"I can't believe how blind he is," said Ethan.

"I can," I said. Somehow William's lack of insight didn't surprise me at all.

Ethan deftly changed the subject. "So how did you and Matt meet?"

"We met in college," Matt said. "She was an undergrad and I was doing a master's degree. I was her history professor's assistant." He winked at us.

"Nice," Ethan said, grinning back at Matt.

"What do you do now?" I asked.

"I'm applying to grad school in psychology and teaching ballet," Karina said. "Matt's a history professor."

"Wow."

"And," Karina says, putting her hand on her belly and smiling at Matt, "We're going to be parents in about six months."

"Congratulations," Ethan said.

"That's so exciting," I chimed in, amazed, and even more surprised to realize I was jealous. Her life seemed so *full*.

"Thanks," Karina and Matt said at the same time.

"Anna," Karina said, her voice changing to a more serious tone, "if you're unhappy, you don't have to stay. There are so many ways to have ballet in your life, and so much life beyond the company. It's a dysfunctional place, as you know. College opens a lot of doors. When you're in a company, you're around dancers all the time, and that gives you only one limited view of the world. My years there were the hardest of my life, and now I couldn't be happier."

I nodded. It was hard to digest her words. They made sense logically, but it was so hard to imagine changing my life so completely.

"We should probably get going," Ethan said, checking his watch. "We still have to drive back."

"Okay," Karina said. "Will you stay in touch? I'd love to hear how you're doing."

"Of course." We all walked to the door and exchanged hugs. Ethan took my hand and led me down the front walk. Halfway to the car, I stopped and walked back to Karina. She was standing in the door watching us.

"Karina," I said. "I hope you publish your journal. Just write the end first, okay? You have an amazing story."

"I'll think about it," she said. "I'm glad you got something out of it. That means a lot to me." We hugged one last time.

As Ethan pulled the car away from the curb, I looked back and watched her gently close her front door. I wondered if I could have a life like hers, with a wonderful husband, an education, a beautiful house, and a baby on the way. There was no glamour in it; no stage lights and admiring fans and beautiful costumes. A younger me would have thought her life sounded dull and ordinary, but now it sounded perfect.

"What happens now?" Ethan asked.

"Nothing," I said. "I go back to work when they get back. I hold my head up. I don't want to leave the way Teresa or Karina did. When I quit, I'm leaving on my own terms with my head held high." He nodded. I knew he understood.

When the company returned from tour, I took as much of class as possible with my arm in a sling. I was surprised how much I wanted to dance. I missed it. This was what I had always done best, even if my body was completely out of shape. I felt desperate to move my arm and frustrated at my limitations. The worst part of going back was that everyone felt sorry for me. I felt offended by the pity. What I needed is respect.

William watched me closely throughout the class. "How are you?" he asked in the back of the room during *grand allegro*.

"Fine. Thank you." I wasn't in the mood to talk to him.

He looked thoughtful for a second, and then he said, "I want you to take your dancing to the next level."

Surprised, I nodded, unsure where he was coming from. What did he mean by "the next level?" To my dismay, he moved on without elaborating.

I had no idea what he was talking about and the ambiguity made me mad. How did he expect me to take my dancing to another level? He and Lila didn't give me any specific guidance. Nothing I had rehearsed in the last seven months had challenged me. The last thing I needed was to be left alone and expected to improve.

After a few days back in the studio, my desire to dance again faded in the presence of all the workplace negativity.

By the time *Nutcracker* arrived, I had physically healed. They gave me one show of lead Marzipan, but the casting felt like pity over my broken arm. William stood impassively in the front wing while I danced Marzipan with renewed thought. The other dancers applauded for me in the wings. The worst part was that I couldn't get excited to perform. My stage smile had become the ultimate lie.

After *Nutcracker*, I drove up to San Francisco during the week off. Jen was in the Bay Area visiting her grandparents and we decided I would pick her up and bring her to LA for New Year's. Ethan had to stay in town for work and I figured the alone time with Jen would be nice.

Jen greeted me at the door with a huge hug. "Anna! I've missed you so much." We held on to each other for dear life. It always felt like no time had passed when we reunited.

That night, we crawled into the twin beds at her grandparent's house and caught up on the last year.

"I can't believe everything that's happened," she said when I finish the long saga about Karina and the diary and William and Teresa and everything else.

"I can't really either."

"I wish you could come back to New York," she said. "Maybe you should audition for NBT. Things have been pretty good for me this last year. I've been doing some solos and my weight has been fine. I'm starting some college classes at Fordham in January. They have a pretty flexible program and a lot of the dancers go there."

"That sounds great, Jen. I'm so glad things are going well."

"Really," she urged. "You should audition!"

"I can't," I said. "I can't leave Ethan and there's no way I could ask him to leave his job and his mother's house. I love him and we're going to get married eventually."

"I think you're going to marry him too," Jen said. "That makes sense. Maybe things will get better at LABT?"

"Maybe," I said skeptically.

We drove down to LA the next morning. My car flew down the freeway at sixty-five miles an hour as we sung along with the radio. Jen whipped her ponytail as she danced in her seat.

"I'm sad the holidays are over," Jen said. "We'll be back at work way too soon."

"Tell me about it."

As we pulled off at the next exit to refill the gas tank, the car behind me wasn't slowing down. My foot eased off the gas. I braked as slowly as I could without hitting the car in front of me, hoping the driver behind would notice and follow my lead.

He didn't. There was just enough time to glance in the rear-view mirror before the sedan loomed in the reflection, bearing down much too fast. His grill hit us from behind and pushed us into the back of the sports coupe in front of us. Jen screamed. The seat belt jerked me back from my reflection in the windshield. Smoke started to rise from my crumpled hood.

My hands shook as I yanked on the seatbelt. "We better get out," I said, worried the car would explode. I threw the door open and scrambled out. Jen hopped out on her side and ran around towards me. The other two drivers climbed out of their cars and started yelling at each other. There was minimal damage to the other two vehicles, from what I could tell. My car looked the worst, with a bashed-up bumper, broken headlights and taillights, and a misshapen front hood.

"Are you okay?" I asked.

"I think so," Jen said. "You?"

"I think so too."

The police arrived and an officer took our statement. Both of our cellphones were in the glove compartment and smashed beyond repair. The policeman wouldn't let me use his cell phone for a civilian call and said I should ask someone else. I didn't know whom to approach because the other two drivers had been herded into the ambulance, one complaining about his neck and the other about a cut on his forehead. Jen and I insisted we were fine, but the officer instructed us not to leave until we were officially dismissed. Stuck, we sat on the side of the road for two hours and watched the police assess the scene. Another ambulance arrived, followed by a fire truck.

Two female EMTs came over to us. "We should really check you both out," one insisted. We stood and let them take our vitals and ask a bunch of questions. Besides a little bit of chest soreness where the seatbelt pulled us back, we felt fine.

"Are you sure you don't want to go to the hospital?" they asked.

"No, we're okay." I didn't even let myself think about what could have happened. I had to be ready to go back to work.

An older man pulled over when they started to let traffic trickle back through. "Do you need anything?" he asked.

"Can I use your phone?"

"Of course," he said, handing it to me.

Ethan didn't pick up. I didn't want to scare him so I didn't leave a message. Disappointed, I gave the man his phone back. "Thanks." He wished us luck and drove away.

"My chest still hurts," Jen confessed.

"Mine too."

An hour later, a car pulled up next to us. I looked up and realized it was Ethan. How did he know? "Ethan!" I stood and ran into his arms as he climbed out of the car.

Jen walked over to the officer. "Can we go?" she asked.

"Okay, we'll contact you if we need more information," the officer said briskly.

"What happened?" Ethan asked.

"We got rear-ended. How did you know to come?"

"I saw a strange number on my caller ID," he said. "So I called it. The man told me there was an accident and where to go."

"Thank you," I said, hugging him tightly.

He pushed me away to arm distance. "Are you really all right?" he asked. "Your car looks totaled. I don't understand."

"We're fine. Can we please go home?"

"Yes, okay, of course," he says, furrowing his brow. He gave me a concerned look and I smiled back weakly to prove I had it together.

At home, I went into overdrive. Jen lay down on the couch and called her parents while I did laundry, cooked dinner, and paid bills. I tried to call my parents in Italy and all I reached was an answering machine I didn't understand. Ethan followed me around and tried to get me to stop, with no luck. I couldn't bring myself to talk about anything and it felt right to keep moving to shut off my brain. By the time I crawled in bed, I had almost convinced myself nothing had happened.

The phone woke me out of a deep sleep and it took me a minute to realize it wasn't a dream.

"Anna?" Mom said. "It's us."

It was the first time I'd heard my mother's voice since before I broke my arm. I started to cry.

"What's wrong, sweetie? We just got your message. Is everything okay?"

A strange gurgle was all that came out of my mouth. Ethan sat up and looked at me. I held the phone out for him and he took it.

"Anna? Anna?" Dad said through the receiver. Ethan touched my arm and I couldn't help it, I started to cry uncontrollably.

"Susan? Michael?" Ethan said into the phone. He gave me a concerned look. "This is Ethan. Anna and Jen were in a car accident today. They were rear-ended but they're not hurt. Don't panic."

"Yes," he said after a moment. "The car needs repairs. Anna was driving. No. They were examined at the scene but didn't go to the hospital. There was some pain in their chests from the seatbelt. That's it." He rubbed my shoulder gently.

"We don't know exactly what happened to the other people, but their injuries were minor," Ethan continued. "The police didn't pay much attention to the girls once they knew they were fine. Okay. Okay, Susan, I will. Here she is." Ethan held the phone up against my ear.

"Anna?" Mom said. "Make sure you go see your regular doctor. You have to get looked at again. Please don't pretend this didn't happen. I know how you cope with things. Trauma doesn't go away. It has invisible effects."

I nodded miserably. Ethan took the phone back and said goodbye.

Two days later, Ethan and I dropped Jen at the airport. I was shattered to see her go. She was the only one who knew how it felt to be in that car. It hardly seemed real. I knew how lucky I was that I had no physical injuries and struggled with how little that mattered to me. I couldn't stop thinking that I almost killed my best friend.

That night, I called Lila's cellphone for the first time. "Hi Lila, this is Anna Linado."

"Anna!" she said, surprised.

"I'm sorry to bother you outside of work."

"No that's fine, what's going on?" she asked.

"Well, I was in a car accident. A dump truck rear-ended me on the freeway. I'm okay as far as we know. I just wanted to let you know because it was pretty serious and three other people went to the hospital. I'm not sure if there will be any legal issues."

"Oh, I'm sure that's not a concern," she said. "We can provide a letter if you need anything documenting your job. My main concern is that you'll still be able to be back at work and ready to dance next week. If you're out, I'll need to take that into consideration for rehearsals and casting."

"No, no, I'm fine and I'll be there ready to dance, Lila, really. I'm sorry. I didn't mean to worry you. There's no need to adjust casting or anything."

"Okay then," she said. "That's good. Have a good weekend and I'll see you soon."

After we hung up, I wondered why I had bothered her. She didn't care about me. All that mattered was what I could do for the company. I walked over to the mirror and stared at myself. The girl in the reflection looked like a skeleton.

The night before we started back to work, Ethan and I went to a party at Faye's new condo. Her parents helped her buy her own place and I took it as a sign she planned to be in the company for the long haul.

Faye greeted me at the door wearing a tight blue dress. Her face glowed with happiness. "Let's party!" she said.

"Hi Faye, how was Christmas?" Ethan said, giving her a hug.

"Good," Faye said. She smiled at him. "I spent it with Dave, that screenwriter I met at the art gallery. He's here and you both have to tell me what you think. He's great so far. So what about you? I heard you were in some sort of accident."

"How did you hear?" I asked, surprised.

"Oh, I saw Lila at the grocery yesterday," she said.

"Wow, that didn't take long."

"You were in an accident?" Sasha asked, walking up behind Faye. Her long black evening dress hugged every curve. She looked gorgeous, as always.

"I'm okay. My car is toast."

"Oh, no," Sasha said. "I'm so sorry. I'm glad you're all right."

"Me too," said Faye.

"Thanks," I said, biting back tears. I was embarrassed to have yet another problem. Bad casting, broken arm, car accident...as much as they cared, none of them could really understand.

"Come on," Ethan said. "Enough on this subject." He took my hand and led me into the living room. I found it hard to be at a party, and after an hour I was already whispering to him that I wanted to go.

"We've got to be on the beach at midnight," Ryan said, jabbing Ethan's shoulder. Ryan was drunk and had been hitting on Rebecca all night. "Grab your champagne," he continued, patting my cheek.

"We'll just go for a minute on our way out," Ethan whispered.

Faye put her arm through mine as we all headed outside. "Are you sure you're okay, Anna? You seem awfully quiet tonight."

"I'm fine. Thanks." I squeezed her hand.

When we reached the sand, I pulled my heels off and let my toes sink into the sand. My friends ran towards the water. I picked up the bottom of my dress so it didn't get dirty and tried to chug my glass of champagne, choking on it. Faye kissed her new boyfriend and Ian stripped off all his clothes and dove naked into the surf. Sasha, Rebecca, and Ryan followed Ian's lead.

"Ballet sucks!" Ryan shouted, his arms waving wildly over his head as he ran into the ocean. Rebecca threw her arms around his neck and they kissed. Apparently, she was done being angry with him.

Ethan put a hand on my arm. "Well, then," he chuckled. "The moon is out tonight. Ready to go, sweetie?"

I nodded. Ethan cradled my chin in his hands and kissed me. His mouth was warm. I let the champagne glass fall to the sand.

At work, I became a dancing machine. I found myself cast in the back row of the corps. Every ballet. Every night. I was the only corps girl that didn't even have a second cast for any of my parts. The company worked me harder than I thought possible.

Hilary danced all her new leading roles. I was too tired to get worked up over it anymore. I hid in the dressing room as much as possible and tried not to watch.

At the beginning of March, my fifth-year corps contract arrived in the mail. I signed it without a thought, since I had no idea what else I should do and no energy to make any major changes. I realized that my plans to audition elsewhere had evaporated. William promoted Hilary to soloist.

During performances, I could only go through the motions. My sternum bothered me when I danced and I continued to have nonspecific pain where the seatbelt stopped me from flying through the windshield.

My spark was gone. I couldn't even find pleasure in listening to music. I had regular nightmares that Jen died in the car accident and I had been left paralyzed. At mealtimes, I forced myself to eat strictly for the sake of energy to do my job. I bordered on hysterics every time I climbed in a car. Ethan laughed when I told him I would never drive again. He thought I was kidding.

Trauma did seem to have consequences, no matter how much I pretended I was fine. No one understood what was happening to me—least of all me. Ethan felt further and further away and I blamed myself. I was the one who had chosen to become a ballerina. I had been so naïve.

The last thing I wanted was to be a burden. I went out for long walks at night to stay away from Ethan and avoided phone calls from my family and friends. If I didn't talk to them, maybe they wouldn't worry.

The sun poured in the window of the studio one morning near the end of the season. William cracked a joke and all the usual people gave him the obligatory laugh. I stood in the back of class near the piano, lost in thought. I felt like screaming but, as always, I remained silent. Dancers were always mute. All I could do was clap with the others when class was over.

Fifteen

Our final performance of the season was in Palm Springs. I almost felt happy when I went to class on the last day. There were two months of freedom ahead. All I wanted was to get away from those people.

I walked to the side of the stage after the *adagio* combination. "Anna," Adrienne whispered behind me.

The second group began the exercise. Adrienne's famous dark eyes met my puzzled expression and she gave a small indication with her head. William was walking towards me. Others turned to look. It had been a year since I was his favorite. No one expected him to take any notice of me anymore.

He reached me and the curious faces of the other dancers seemed to melt away. I smelled his familiar musky cologne when he leaned over. "What are your plans for layoff?" he asked.

I was surprised, to say the least. "I'm not sure. Take class. Visit my parents, maybe?"

Our eyes met briefly and then he turned his head to watch the class. His gaze seemed intentional and my eyes followed his to Hilary, who was falling out of a pirouette at the front of the stage. She stomped off the floor in frustration.

"You need to work on partnering during the layoff," he said. He paused and I struggled for a response. Nothing came out. He turned away, already finished with the conversation.

"Partnering?" I realized he was going to leave me without any answers, again. "Where am I supposed to go to work on partnering?"

William glanced back, annoyed. "That's not my problem, honey."

His words hit me like a blast of cold water in the face. My hands were shaking and my voice quivered with the injustice of it all. "Excuse me, William, but my name is *not honey*."

He slowly turned all the way around to stare at me, his jaw open in surprise.

"I can't believe this," he snapped. When our eyes met I didn't drop my gaze, and he was the one who turned away, shaking his head. He marched to the front of the stage and demonstrated the next combination, as if nothing had happened.

I walked into the wing and picked up my bag. When I glanced back, people were dancing. Sasha, Ryan, and Allison whirled across the floor. Adrienne and Elizabeth whispered in the back. Lorenzo and Grant stood next to each other with their arms crossed and watched. Faye sat, icing her knee in the opposite wing.

No one looked at me anymore. I knew a lot of them had heard what happened. They were pretending not to notice, just like always. Pretending was the only way to go on, and I couldn't do it anymore.

I ran downstairs to the corps dressing room and locked myself in a bathroom stall. My sobs grew louder as I realized I was completely alone. Over the loudspeaker, I could still hear the piano music from class.

While the company danced above me, I cried so hard my whole body began to ache. I trembled as if something inside me needed to explode. I had never felt so much anger and sorrow. William knew everything about the way I danced, but he didn't know *me* at all.

I worried all the way through the tech rehearsal that afternoon. Faye asked me what happened with William and when I told her, she looked at me as if I had committed high treason. "No one talks back to William," she said, her eyes opened wide. "What were you thinking?"

My anger from the morning melted under a mountain of fear. I had probably committed professional suicide, even though I thought I had asked a valid question. Where *was* I supposed to go to work on partnering? I hadn't rehearsed anything with partnering since *America*. Unlike many of the other girls, I didn't have a boyfriend in the company I could ask to practice with me outside of work hours. There was no school for professional dancers to practice partnering. I knew I should have just nodded and agreed. But I didn't have it in me anymore. Not for him.

And, as William well knew, I had a name.

That evening, when I walked offstage after the first ballet, William seized my arm the moment I came past the wing. I jumped. He pulled me right up to his face. In the darkness backstage, all I could see were his eyes.

"We're going to have words—right now," he said threateningly. Somehow I managed to nod and he let me go. I followed him into the hall and he gestured to a small room he used as his office in the theater. When I walked inside, he slammed the door.

I was still in the middle of a performance and wasn't yet done for the night. Sweat trickled down my forehead into my eyes and I started to pull pins out of my hair. There was less than an hour before I had to be ready to go back onstage to dance *Frontiers*. I needed to change my hairdo and fix my makeup. William was the last person I wanted to talk to in the middle of the show.

When William turned around, he looked surprised to see me frantically pulling out my hairdo. I took a step back. "I'm in *Frontiers*."

"Screw *Frontiers*!" The last thing he cared about at that moment was the performance. I had never seen him like this, and it was shocking to see his anger fully directed at me.

"You listen here," he said. "If you ever speak to me again the way you did this morning, I'll ask you to leave." He stepped closer to me. My hand fell away from my hair and the pins tumbled to the floor. The meeting had nothing to do with my professional conduct. My relationship with William had finally becomes personal.

He moved right up in my face, waiting for my response, staring me down.

"I'm sorry, I didn't mean to be rude," I managed, tears starting to trickle down my cheeks. My voice came out more desperate than I intended. "Please try to understand how I feel. You almost never speak to me any more. I was in a car accident three months ago. I have nightmares. I don't eat. I don't sleep."

"Stop crying," he said. He paced across the room. "I don't want to hear pathetic excuses. Your behavior is inexcusable." He turned back to me, leaned against the far wall and crossed his arms. We stared at each other.

"I don't mean to make excuses." I stood up tall, gathering my courage. The whole scene was absurd. The legendary William Mason, worked into a state of total agitation over a twenty-three-year-old corps girl who didn't want to be called 'honey?' Something about my relationship with him made me sick.

"All I've ever wanted is to dance well for you. I'm trying to explain myself. You've barely said a sentence to me this whole year. Last year you threw me onstage in a principal role in one week. Then you bury me in the corps with no explanation? What am I supposed to think?"

He paused and gave me a long look I couldn't read. Then he dropped his arms and laughed in a breathless burst. My heart was pounding. He walked over to me, reaching his arm out to touch my shoulder. Instinctively, I stepped back out of his reach.

"Your opinion means everything to me, to all of us," I said. I knew I sounded juvenile and melodramatic, which only made me feel more desperate. "You gave me enough opportunities for several lifetimes. I did the best I could. What more can you ask? Can't you see me as more than just a body? I'm a person too."

It took him a fraction of a section to process my words. "Okay, Anna," he said. He took a step back. "Maybe I misunderstood."

I let out a sigh. "I have to get ready for *Frontiers*."

"Okay. Right. Go."

I left the room and ran down the stairs, my blood pounding in my ears. As I redid my hair in the dressing room, I decided I didn't want to be looked at on a stage anymore. I needed to be touched. Maybe Ethan was just waiting for me to leave before he was willing to propose.

When I danced *Frontiers* twenty minutes later, William stood in his usual spot in the front wing. I felt his eyes on me and could tell the storm had passed, for him at least. For me, I didn't think I'd ever feel the same way about him again. It was the first time I hated ballet so much that I wanted to walk offstage in the middle of my own performance.

The season came to an end. Ethan and I went to see the new ballet movie and I recognized the people in it. When we walked out, I wanted to rip the movie poster off the wall. It killed me to see my real life turned into a series of clichés. What happened to those girls after ballet school? No one cared about the consequences.

Ballet New York came to LA on tour for the first time in ten years and Faye joined me at the performance. Ethan had an important dinner meeting for work, so both of us went out separately for the night. I didn't mind, because I had a special reason to go to the performance. It had been six years since I saw Tyler, my old boyfriend from high school, and he would be there with the company. He was my first love. It had been years since we last spoke. A lifetime.

To my surprise, Tyler was in the lobby of the theater when we arrived. He looked older, but so familiar that I felt like I had just seen him. Tyler was as tall and handsome as always.

He spotted us immediately. "Anna! Faye!" he called. We walked over to him. "Did you get my message?" he asked me as we hugged. I shook my head.

"Hey Tyler, good to see you," Faye said. They squeezed hands.

"I didn't get your message," I said. "You called me? How did you get my number? Aren't you dancing tonight?"

"Yes," he said. "I'm in the last ballet so I thought I'd sneak out and see if you were here before I warm up. I tried to leave you a message at the LABT office."

"Oh shoot, I didn't get it." I loved that he had tried. "How are you? You look great."

"Thanks, you too," he said. "I'm good. I'm a soloist now. I heard you danced the lead in *America*?"

"Yes, last year," I said, suddenly embarrassed that I wasn't a soloist, and in fact had been relegated to the last row. Tyler had such high hopes for me when I left New York.

"Will you come backstage after?" Tyler asked. "Maybe we could get something to eat."

"Sure. I'll find you." I didn't feel anything romantically towards him anymore so it felt natural, like reconnecting with an old best friend.

"He's still hot," Faye whispered. She raised her eyebrows twice. "I think I'll let you have dinner alone with him. I hope Ethan doesn't mind."

"I don't think I'm into the dancer thing at all anymore." Tyler didn't look like the man of my dreams the way he used to when I was seventeen. "Ethan won't care. He knows all about Tyler and I think he was just as relieved not to have to meet him. Besides, Ethan knows I love him."

"Yeah, I agree," said Faye. "Let's go watch the show."

I waited eagerly through the first two ballets to watch Tyler in the last piece. He danced a romantic *pas de deux* with one of the principal women and was even better than I remembered. Everyone had known he was going to be a big star back in ballet school, and there was no doubt we had all been right. He commanded the stage with a confidence that shined all the way up to the last row in the balcony.

Over pizza after the performance, Tyler and I talked non-stop for two hours about the only thing we ever had in common: ballet. He told me all about the roles he had danced and how much the company loved him. His life was filled with rave reviews, standing ovations, exciting tours, and a string of casual girlfriends. He listened as I told him about Ethan and my rollercoaster ballet career.

"I knew you'd make it," Tyler said. "You need to dance more than anyone I've ever met."

The gulf between us widened after that. Maybe he couldn't tell, but I was different than the girl he had loved years ago. I didn't think he knew everything anymore.

After we split the check, I walked him back to his hotel. "It was great to see you," he said. He shoved his hands in his pockets and stared at the ground.

"Yeah. You too."

"I wish you were single," Tyler blurted out. "You're so much more confident now than when you left New York. You've always been different. I can tell you've grown up a lot. Ethan is a lucky guy."

"Thank you," I said, both flattered and embarrassed. "I—it was great to see you too." I held my arms open and hugged him for a long time. When we pulled away, we looked at each other. His vulnerability was almost painful. I was certain he was letting me see a side of him he hid from the rest of the world, a little boy lost underneath all that success. After a moment, he leaned in to kiss my lips and I turned my cheek. He recovered quickly and said a hasty goodnight.

I realized that while I had changed, Tyler had stayed much the same. I waved at him one last time before I hurried home to Ethan.

Work was over for several months and I had a lot of time to think. I floated in the ocean every morning and pondered how I was a speck in the midst of infinite. The car accident still lurked in my dreams, and every day I wished more and more that I hadn't signed my contract for the upcoming season.

During the second week of layoff, I read an article in *Dance Magazine* about how dancers in San Francisco took classes through a special program to earn college credit. I knew Jen was doing that in New York. I started to think more about a college degree. The professor who ran the program for professional dancers in San Francisco was very receptive when I called and asked her for more information.

"If you want to get this going in LA, you should talk to someone at one of the local colleges,"

260 | *Miriam Wenger-Landis*

she said over the phone. "You can't run this program long distance with us. Maybe UCLA would be open to something similar? I'd be happy to help you in whatever way I can. The first step would be to talk to the artistic staff at LABT. You're going to need their endorsement and full support."

"Oh," I said, my heart sinking. "I hadn't thought about that. I don't know if that's realistic." I couldn't imagine approaching the artistic staff with something I knew they would view as subversive.

A few days later, I ran into Lila on the Third Street Promenade. I was window-shopping by myself when I walked smack into her. She looked like she hadn't left the beach since we finished work. Her skin was five shades darker than it had been three weeks before.

"Hey, did you see the article in *Dance Magazine* about San Francisco's college program?" I asked casually after we'd been chatting awhile.

"Yes," she said. "I saw it."

"What do you think about starting something like that here?"

"Oh," she said. "Anna, college classes? We don't have the time or money."

"This is important. I know a lot of the dancers would love a program like this. Won't an education make us better artists?"

"You have a ballet education," she said. "That's all you need to be a dancer. It isn't our priority to help you get a college degree. This is a business. We make ballerinas, not college students. You know that. William can't have everyone distracted by schoolwork.

Your focus should be on your job." She ruffled her short hair and looked away, clearly uncomfortable.

"I'm focused," I insisted.

"Look, no one pays sixty-five dollars a ticket to see you after the curtain comes down," she said. "Let me give you some advice. Knock this notion right out of your head. You've stirred up enough trouble."

I could tell the subject was closed. It had been a mistake to even try. "You're right, it's a stupid idea."

She brightened up. "Okay then. Have a nice layoff. Don't come back out of shape."

As she walked away, I muttered, "Screw you."

During the following weeks, I fell apart. I cried for an hour before I went to class at the ballet school, and eventually I quit trying to stay in shape and stopped going out at all. My voicemail filled up with messages I couldn't bring myself to return. Ethan tried his best to coax me out of my depression. All I could manage to do was sit on the couch and stare at the television. I told myself I was nothing if I wasn't a dancer. The irony was that when I *was* a dancer, I was less than nothing.

Ethan came by my apartment after work one day and found me on the couch, still in my pajamas at four in the afternoon. His eyes filled with concern.

"Anna," he said as he wrapped me in his arms. "I am so worried about you." He brought his hand up to touch my cheek.

"I'm worried about me too." The words caught in my throat. I grabbed his hand. "Please, Ethan. Help me."

He brushed the hair from my face. "Everything will be okay," he said. "I promise."

I looked up into his eyes. "Will you help me quit?"

"Quit?" he asked. "Hold up. You know I'll support you in whatever you do, but you can't quit like this. You're depressed. We need to get you to a doctor first. You don't want to leave this way. Remember?"

I hated hearing my own words thrown back at me. "I don't need a doctor. I need to quit ballet." Saying it made me more certain.

"You've loved ballet since you could walk. It's your whole life. Quit when you're too depressed to leave the house? It doesn't make sense."

The honesty hurt. I sank down into the couch. He watched me with deep concern as I started crying so hard I forgot he was even there. At some point, I was so exhausted I fell asleep.

Ethan convinced me to see the company-recommended psychiatrist and came with me to the appointment. Dr. Fuller couldn't have been more than ten years older than me. He had dark hair and spectacles, two Ivy League degrees, and expensive clothes. I sat in a chair in his office and felt small and humiliated. Ethan held my hand protectively.

I found it impossible to articulate my problems in a way that made sense to an outsider. When I told him my story, it sounded romantic instead of heartbreaking.

"I go to the ballet all the time," Dr. Fuller said when I finished. He crossed his arms, displaying authoritative biceps. "I saw you dance those star-

making roles. You were superb in *America*. Don't
worry. I know all about the ballet and what it takes.
William is actually one of my patients." He
straightened his designer tie.

"Can you actually say that to us?" Ethan asked,
echoing my own thoughts.

"Well, that'll just stay between us," Dr. Fuller
said nonchalantly. Ethan and I exchanged a startled
look. "Back to you," he continued. "It sounds like
you're suffering from post-traumatic stress disorder
related to your car accident. We'll get you on some
medication and you'll be back dancing in no time."

"No. I don't want medication. I want to quit."

"Anna," Dr. Fuller said as if he were speaking
to a small child. "You can't make any decisions until
you're not depressed. You have a huge career ahead of
you. I don't think you realize how depressed you are.
You're living every little girl's dream. William's favor
is not something you walk away from. You can't quit."

Of course he won't listen to me, I said to myself.
I was so good at hiding the extent of my suffering that I
had made a career out of it. I forced myself to nod
anyway. I nodded, but he was wrong. Ballet wasn't my
dream anymore.

"Ethan," I said when we were back in the car.
"How can he just drop that he's William's doctor? Isn't
that against the doctor-patient privilege? If he's telling
us that information, what will he tell William about
me?"

"That was off, I agree," said Ethan. "I don't
know."

"I'm scared."

"Let's just get you feeling better first." Ethan
drove us to the pharmacy. He ran in to fill my

prescription while I sat in the car, staring blankly out the window.

The anti-depressants and anti-anxiety medication made me want to sleep all the time. Ethan hovered over me. My friends called a few times and Ethan told them I was sick. He didn't explain what was wrong and they didn't press him.

I felt myself pulling away from my dance friends and worried what they would think if they knew I was serious about quitting. No one quit. It was like leaving a cult. No matter how many times it happened, when you were as committed as we were to ballet, it came as a shock if someone actually followed through. As bad as it was on the inside, when you were as sheltered as we were from the outside world, the unknown was far more frightening than the pain and suffering we knew so well.

Dr. Fuller told me over the phone that it took a few weeks for the medication to take effect, and even though I wasn't quite as prone to crying, I still felt hopeless. Even when I stopped being depressed, I knew I would still be in the same situation.

"Fine," Ethan said. "Why don't we drive over and look at the options at UCLA? Your high school GPA and your test scores are impeccable. With that and your life experience, I bet you could get in. Maybe you could take a few classes while you apply for full matriculation. We'll talk to the dean. You could start college in the fall."

"I signed a contract."

"People break contracts all the time," he said. "I'm sure that's happened before."

"I don't want to leave by breaking my contract. I'm scared of William. I'm so scared of letting him down."

"Don't worry about that now," he said. "Let's go to for a ride and explore the campus. You can start over." I allowed myself a glimmer of hope, but life without ballet seemed impossible. It's all I had ever known.

Ethan and I met with the Dean of Admissions and took a tour of the school. Students passed us on their way to class and all I could think was that they looked nothing like LABT dancers. The hunched shoulders, casual clothing, and academic self-importance made me feel completely out of place. I was older than all of them.

Ethan and I sat in on an American history class. The professor's lecture flew over my head. When the students joined in the class discussion, I was intimidated. How did they know all this stuff? What gave them the right to ask questions and speak out? I had never had that right.

After the class, Ethan took my hand and we walked for a while.

"Did you like it?" he asked. His expression was hopeful. He only wanted me to be happy, and I knew I had let him down. How could he consider marrying me when I was this lost? I didn't expect him to be the solution to my problems, and I knew at that moment that I needed to take responsibility for myself. He'd done more than he should have already.

A few days later we went to follow up with Dr. Fuller. He looked even more handsome than I remembered.

"You look better, Anna," he said. "How are things?"

"Okay," I said. "I think I may have turned a corner."

"Excellent."

"I still want to leave the company."

"Don't be silly. William told me you have a very bright future," he said. He sounded like he was repeating a line when he added, "You need to be ready to dance next season."

"You talked to William about me?" I was horrified. "Dr. Fuller. You had no right to do that. How can I face him?"

"This is unbelievable," Ethan said.

"Don't get carried away," said Dr. Fuller. "He doesn't know anything specific. I just asked him how he felt about different dancers in the company and he said some nice things about Anna. You wouldn't give your whole life to ballet only to walk away now."

"I think I might," I said with more conviction.

"Come on," he said. He leaned back in his chair and crossed his arms. "What will you do with yourself?"

"I have no idea. Start over?"

He looked at me as if I was the craziest patient he'd ever had.

"Thanks for all your help, Dr. Fuller," Ethan said, standing up. "We won't be coming back." He took my arm and guided me out of the office.

"Thanks, Ethan," I said in the elevator. "Thank you for always being on my side."

He smiled. "I'm proud of you."

Ethan took me on a weekend river-rafting trip. "Come on." He climbed in the raft. I looked at his floppy hat and cargo shorts and admired how cute he looked. "Let's have fun," he said.

Did he think it was that easy? I felt angry that even being here didn't wash away the past.

He noticed my hesitation. "Don't you want to have fun, sweetie?" he asked.

"I don't know how to have fun anymore." I tightened my life preserver and climbed in the raft. When I looked over I saw Ethan had started to cry.

"Ethan. Stop it. Please."

He wouldn't look at me—instead he stared into the water. "I don't care if you never dance again. It doesn't matter to me if you spend your life bagging groceries. You can be ugly, get arrested, or join the circus. Just, please. Please don't tell me you don't know how to have fun anymore."

His words hit hard and I didn't know what to say. We moved on from the conversation, but I stewed over it in my head the whole weekend.

On the drive home I managed to put my hand on his shoulder and say, "I'm ready."

Ethan could see how at peace I was after I started verbalizing which direction I wanted to go, and my parents gave me their unconditional support. Then it was just a matter of finding the courage to follow my heart.

I started to see a new doctor. Dr. Silver's office was in the back of her house. Her white hair and honest eyes put me at ease. We sipped tea. The room smelled like lemon and the fresh roses on the table. Her windows looked out onto the garden. I spoke. She listened.

When I wasn't at therapy, I slept. The new medication she prescribed worked better and didn't make me tremble. Sleep was where I was safe. The nightmares were finally gone.

Ethan was the one who coaxed me out of bed. We watched a lot of reality television. A month went by. The first day of the season was a week away.

"Anna," Dr. Silver said, after endless sessions piecing together my journey and figuring out what was next. "Let's cut to the chase. Time is running out. What do you really want to do?"

"I can't talk to William. I'm still too scared." Her calico cat looked at me through the window, turned up her nose, and leaped gently into the garden.

"Forget about William," Dr. Silver said. She chewed on a pen. "What do you want to do with your life?"

"I want to be more than just a dancer. And it's pretty clear that the shelf-life of a professional ballerina is fairly limited."

She nodded. "I know."

Even if I could know ahead that I would achieve everything the ballet world could possibly offer, I didn't want it anymore. My dreams had changed, my goals had changed, and I knew I had to find the courage within myself to move on with my life. There was no way I could go back.

At the beginning of September, I called the studios and waited while the secretary directed my call.

William came on the line after several minutes. "Yes?"

"Hi, William. This is Anna Linado."

"Anna," he said. He sounded pleased. "How are you?"

"I'm good. Thank you for asking."

"Glad to hear," he said, "I haven't seen you in class over the layoff. Have you been staying in shape? We leave on tour at the end of next month."

Ethan put his hands on my shoulders and I took a deep breath. "I'm calling to tell you that I'm not coming back."

There was a long pause. "What?" William said. "What was that?"

"I'm starting classes at UCLA. I'm sorry. I just can't dance for someone else anymore."

He started to say something, then stopped and let out a long sigh. "Are you sure about this?" he asked. "This is a big decision."

"I know how lucky I was to dance for you, but this is the right thing. If I don't want to be there, you don't want me. I can't be what you want."

"I see," he said. "I suppose there's nothing I can say. I wish you would reconsider. Well. We'll miss you."

"Thanks." It hurt to end everything this way.

"Goodbye. Best of luck," he said. The line went dead. After a moment, I hung up the phone.

Ethan held me for a long time, and when I said I was ready, he collected his keys to take me out for a celebratory dinner. He seemed almost more relieved than me that the link had been broken.

I walked to the mirror. My performance was over. I'd never seen anything more beautiful than the ballet. Maybe ballet was too beautiful. Not enough people appreciate it and maybe they're right. I was learning to like human flaws, specifically, my own. My life didn't belong in a work of art anymore, and I had come to the realization that I was the only person who should choreograph how I lived.

The beautiful girl I saw in the reflection made my heart ache. Her life was about to fill up with new possibilities. I saw a girl who didn't want applause anymore. She wanted to be happy.

I extended my right arm over my head and pointed my right foot behind my back. My hand came to my heart as I kneeled, bowing my head in a *grande révérance*.

Epilogue

A year after I left Los Angeles Ballet Theatre and started college, I found my way back into a ballet studio for the first time. It was a revelation to discover that I could dance only for myself. My body remembered how much I needed to dance, even if my mind and heart wanted to forget.

To help pay for school, I started teaching fifteen- to eighteen-year-olds at a local ballet school. When I watched them, I remembered what I loved about ballet—how the discipline fed our dreams. But these girls frightened me, with their youthful determination and desire to learn, and their almost mystical devotion to the art. How could they really know what they were getting into?

I didn't think that the ballet world was a terrible place—how could it be when I had so many incredible memories of it? There were times when I never felt happier to have a calling, a talent, and the ability to give myself joy at the same time that I spread it to so many others. But the competitiveness, stress, lack of affirmation, and constant feeling of inadequacy took its toll.

I have no doubt that leaving was one of the best decisions I ever made.

Shortly after I started college classes, Ethan asked me to marry him. I said yes. Finally, I felt like it was okay to grow up.

My old ballet friends remained an important part of my life. We had been through something critical that bonded us forever. Jen left NBT a year after I quit and started classes at Columbia. We debated majors in the same way we used to debate ballet companies. New dancers had filled our places.

Nothing inside me actually died when my ballet career did. I simply changed.

One rainy Saturday over a Thanksgiving break, I caught my reflection in the mirror and realized what I should do.

I sat down at the kitchen table and opened my laptop. My thoughts began to focus as my hands flew over the keys.

"Fifteen minutes. Fifteen minutes, please." The stage manager's voice on the loudspeaker rose over the backstage noise, bringing with it the sounds of the orchestra tuning up and the hum of the audience..."

When illusions shatter, someone should tell the story. This time I will not be silent. I think of young girls, placing their soft hands on the *barre* for the very first time, and know that something has to change.

About the Author

Miriam Wenger-Landis was a student at the School of American Ballet and a professional ballerina with the Miami City Ballet. She graduated from Stanford University and lives in Seattle.

CPSIA information can be obtained at www.ICGtesting.com
Printed in the USA
LVOW052045290812

296548LV00001B/275/P